"Any anthology containing a story by Harold Adams
must live with the encomium 'distinguished,'
and this book has two count 'em *two* Adamses."
—HARLAN ELLISON

"(This is) an amazing collection and belongs on every
serious mystery reader's bookshelf."
—ED GORMAN

"An awesome anthology from my all time favorite bookstore EVER"
—JON JORDAN, *Crimespree Magazine*

"*Writes of Spring* is a top-notch anthology that celebrates a top-notch
independent bookstore. The contributors are among the best the crime-
fiction field has to offer. Which means the best anywhere. The anthology would be worth the cover price just for the two Carl Wilcox stories
by Harold Adams, to whom the book is dedicated, but it's loaded with
great stuff. On top of all that, the royalties are going to a fine charity. Buy
the book. You can't go wrong."
—BILL CRIDER, *Mystery Scene Magazine*

"A dandy of a short story anthology"
—GEORGE EASTER, *Deadly Pleasures*

"What a great idea the *Writes of Spring* is as an event, and what a great
idea this celebratory book is. Damn! I wish I had thought of it first."
—OTTO PENZLER, The Mysterious Bookshop

"*Writes of Spring* serves up a delicio
and mayhem. Savor the hai
flavored by the seasons, ai
—CARA I

Writes of Spring

Edited by
Gary Shulze and Pat Frovarp

With introductions by
Reed Farrel Coleman and Barbara Mayor
and an afterword by Jon Jordan

*Celebrating the 10th annual Write of Spring
and the 25th anniversary of Once Upon A Crime*

NODIN PRESS

COPYRIGHT © 2012 by Once Upon A Crime
COVER AND BOOK DESIGN by Linda Koutsky

LIBRARY OF CONGRESS CIP INFORMATION
Writes of spring : stories and prose celebrating the tenth annual
Write of Spring and the 25th anniversary of Once upon a Crime /
edited by Gary Shulze, Pat Frovarp.
pages cm
Includes bibliographical references and index.
ISBN 978-1-935666-37-0
1. American literature—21st century.
I. Shulze, Gary, editor of compilation.
II. Frovarp, Pat, editor of compilation.
PS536.3.W75 2012
810.8'006—DC23
2011048178

PRINTED IN THE UNITED STATES
1 3 5 7 9 8 6 4 2
FIRST EDITION | FIRST PRINTING

Nodin Press
530 North Third Street, Suite 120
Minneapolis, Minnesota 55401
(612) 333-6300 www.nodinpress.com

Once Upon A Crime
604 West 26th Street
Minneapolis, Minnesota 55405
(612) 870-3785 www.onceuponacrimebooks.com

To Harold Adams

"I consider Harold Adams to be one of the major voices of his generation of crime fiction writers. His unique voice, his strong sense of story and structure, and his rich, wry depictions of the Depression era Midwest have stayed with me long after the works of flashier writers have faded. There's music in his books, a melancholy prairie song that you carry with you for life. I studied his books because I consider him to be a master. And of course I stole everything I could."

—Ed Gorman
Cedar Rapids Iowa
January 14, 2012

A Note from the Editors

THERE'S SOMETHING ABOUT ROUND NUMBERS. When we were approaching preparations for the ninth annual Write of Spring (and how optimistic it was of us to name the original Write of Spring "the first annual"), it struck us that the tenth annual Write of Spring would coincide with Once Upon a Crime's 25th anniversary. This seemed to us too big of a coincidence to pass up. As is said with history, one thing led to another, and now you are holding, and we hope purchasing and reading, the result.

We went through past years of programs, made of list of all 92 authors who have attended the Write of Spring at one time or another and asked them nicely if they could contribute stories. The response was overwhelming; our only regret is that we couldn't print all of them without making this a multi-volume set.

Despite the title for this collection, there is something here for every season and taste. We gave the authors free rein, with only the merest suggestion to use springtime as a setting, and to make "crime" an important element. A number of writers stretched their legs and wrote something completely different than what you might expect from them. Some chose to abandon reality a bit and delve into other genres; a few chose nonfiction. Others offered up a chapter or two from novels in progress.

It's hard to believe that what at first was a modest open house with 22 authors in attendance has blossomed in ten years into a nationally recognized festival bringing in over 60 authors for a four hour event. The first Write of Spring, in 2003, doubled as a release party for *The Fourth of July Wake* by Harold Adams, who was also our featured Guest of Honor. Harold is no longer writing, but contained herein are two previously unpublished Carl Wilcox stories. This collection is fondly and respectfully dedicated to him.

—Gary Shulze
Pat Frovarp
Once Upon a Crime
Minneapolis, Minnesota

Contents

Introduction

Home Away From Home
REED FARREL COLEMAN

I'VE OFTEN SAID THAT I STUMBLED INTO Once Upon A Crime while in search of another bookstore, but of course I'm joking . . . sort of. You see, as an author on tour and visiting an indie bookstore for the first time, you don't actually know what you're in for. *What will the owners be like? Will they even be there? What publicity have they done, if any? How big a crowd will* . . . You get the picture. Touring, even under the best of circumstances, can be a risky proposition. I, like many of my colleagues, have had my share of nightmare tour and signing experiences. Yes, I've been seated at a table by the register and been asked, "Excuse me, are you the gift-wrapping person?"

Many of us who spend parts of our year on the road touring our books have what I guess we consider our home stores. Stores where we might launch our new titles and where we're pretty sure they handsell our work or, at the very least, won't use our books for doorstops or kindling. For me, the great revelations are those stores that catch you by surprise, the stores you take a chance on that in turn take a chance on you. I knew the first time I walked down the stairs and through the door of Once Upon A Crime that, although I'd never met Pat and Gary, they were chance takers and true believers: believers in the value of good books, believers in the value of independence, believers in the value of hard work and passion. Mostly, they believe in writers and readers, and their faith has been rewarded.

A few years ago, it was my dubious fortune to have timed my signing at Once Upon A Crime to coincide with Brett Favre's first game in Minneapolis as a Minnesota Viking versus his former team, the Green Bay Packers. If that wasn't enough, it was also timed with a Minnesota Twins playoff game against the Detroit Tigers. I figured to have a pleasant chat with rows of empty folding chairs and a nice visit with Pat and Gary. I should have known better, because there was a very nice crowd waiting for me that night when I walked through the door. Pat and Gary had worked their magic and that faith of theirs had once again paid off. It was as if the two of them had willed me an audience. The thing about Once Upon A Crime is that it is like a home away from home for me. Each time I travel to the store, Pat and Gary are as welcoming and as enthusiastic about my arrival as they were the first time I signed there, but Once Upon A Crime is a business, not just a safe haven for authors on the road. And as a business, Once Upon A Crime is no less successful than as a safe port. Regardless of how many times I sign at the store, I am always caught off guard by the huge numbers of my books—old and new—that Pat and Gary have ordered. These books are not for show, either. When Pat and Gary order books, they mean to sell them, every one of them. Again, regardless of the personal affinity I have for them and they for me, it is, in the end, about the books. When they love a book or a series, their commitment is abiding and deep. How else could a mid-list author from New York—writing a PI series set in Brooklyn about a broken-down Jewish ex-cop more interested in the metaphysics of crime than the crimes themselves—become the fourth-largest seller in an indie bookstore in the middle of Minneapolis?

This is not to say that Once Upon A Crime doesn't support local authors. On the contrary, Pat and Gary are huge supporters of local talent, nurturing new talent and keeping the fires burning for more established authors. I had the honor of presenting the Mystery Writers of America Raven Award to Pat and Gary at the Edgar Award Banquet this past April. To add to my speech, I sought comment from Minnesota authors, and to a person they couldn't have been more enthusiastic in their love for Pat and Gary. Jess Lourey, Julie Kramer, David Housewright, and

William Kent Krueger jumped at the chance to give a little something back to Pat and Gary, the people who had been so generous to them.

Pat and Gary have overcome some huge obstacles in their lives to make their partnership and the store work. They are good and charitable people who are committed to their local community, to the mystery community, and to the continuing existence of independent bookstores. So please, give your support to them and the charities they support by purchasing this book and enjoying the stories within.

Introduction

The Man Who Loved to Write
BARBARA MAYOR

ALTHOUGH HE WAS BORN IN CLARK, SOUTH DAKOTA, known in his books as Corden, Harold Adams spent only summers there. He and his brother Dick, five years older, were put to work in his grandparents' hotel as soon as they were able to lift a suitcase or swat flies. His Uncle Sid, named Carl Wilcox in the books, lived at the hotel those first years, and his reputation lived ever after. Except for solving murders, the rest was pretty authentic. Sid, like Carl, really did lie, fight, steal, go to prison and chase women, but, somehow, remained smart and likeable. He built a chinning bar for Harold and sent boxes of sea shells from the South Pacific. The grandparents were depicted very true to life and fortunately for Harold, weren't around to read any of his books.

Harold wrote in a journal daily, and if you ever met him, you are somewhere in one of them. This one dates back to a brief encounter with an encyclopedia salesman:

> *Feel like a heel tonight . . . a young salesman from Britannica rang my buzzer and wanted to talk. I said I wasn't interested. Saw him go by in front, a very young pleasant fellow in a sportshirt, carrying his portfolio and looking discouraged. It is very difficult being young and alternately hopeful and crushed.*

Harold began writing stories in college and early mornings before going to work. He worked at the Better Business Bureau for several years where he and my husband John became good friends. Later he became head of the Charities Review Council where he worked until he retired. In all, he wrote 18 novels—16 in the Carl Wilcox series. He was a three-time finalist for the Shamus award, winning for *The Man Who Was Taller Than God* in 1992.

I was fortunate enough to be his first reader. He read his first, serious books aloud to me, which were never published. Then he began the mystery books. He asked my advice on all of them, sometimes taken, sometimes not. If I liked it, he'd ask, *"Well, why?"* If I didn't, same question. Often we argued. Won some, lost some.

> *B. read* The Missing Moon *last night and found only three places she thought needed clarification, and that it was great. That isn't quite what I'm looking for . . . without specifics I feel there is no real input. It's foolish to expect her to solve my problems, but I always hope for more. Of course, my defensiveness when criticized does not encourage candor.*

Such candid introspection is evident throughout his journals:

> *Ever since publishing my first book, I have sensed a tendency on my part to be more easily bored. I find conversations most entertaining when my writing is the subject. God, I hope this passes. It would be ghastly if it grew worse.*

And this during a canoeing and camping trip on the St. Croix River:

> *The moon was full last night, lovely in the dark sky. The air was sweet with spruce and I should be full of hope and anticipation. I think it is bad to have no small desires, to be stuck with only want for fame and acceptance.*

Harold spent weekends with John and me, and moved in with us a few years before retiring. We traveled 18 times to Europe, and as many to the Caribbean and Mexico, always eager to see and try *almost* anything.

> *On the boat going to an island to snorkel, Claudia, a golden-skinned woman with a breezy wise-cracking manner, met us to demonstrate the placement of the mask and its handling. 'The band goes above the ear and one touches only that metal rim, never the delicate inner linings which can tear. Keep the glass vertical, with the water at the upper edge, and grip the tube as*

if you're puckering for a kiss, use the fins properly with a bold
butterfly stroke and keep your hands behind your back to avoid
coral. The tide is low and the sea quite rough, so be careful.'
That's when I decided the hell with it.

For a man who spent years writing mysteries and plotting murders,
he was an extremely kind and gentle man. He was also quite protec-
tive of our garden. Here's his journal entry after a deadly encounter
with a woodchuck:

I was so mad at that damned woodchuck every time I saw what
he had done to the garden. He seemed absolutely malicious. But
when he turned on me desperate and defiant, I felt sorry. I can't
understand hunting for fun or the idea of thrill in killing . . .
.22 cartridges are so small . . . hardly larger than the victim's
teeth . . . it haunts me . . . Well, I was glad the damned thing
was dead and I buried it about as deep as I could dig and said
no prayers and made no apologies, but all the same it left me
depressed and I hope the other critter doesn't hang around until
I kill him—which I will do if I get the chance.

All through these years he had time to spend with his beloved daughter, Wendy. Every week when she was a child and as often as possible as
a grownup.

Last night Wendy and I had another steak bash and a flood
of talk at my apartment. We had a marvelous dialogue, cov-
ering politics, my books, writers, relatives and friends. We
chattered until 11:30 and made a date for next week. She is so
trim and pretty.

I think he never lost a friend, and being head of the Charities Review
Council, he probably had a few enemies. But even now, a few of his fans
still write, and his friends keep in touch.

WRITES OF SPRING

The Outsider

HAROLD ADAMS

BACK IN THE MIDTHIRTIES, I ordinarily went to small towns like Wynot, looking for sign painting jobs. In this case it came from a telephone call made by the founder's son, Junior Whye. A customer at the Whye Hardware passed my name as a guy who'd helped Corden's cop solve a couple murders, and Junior decided they needed me.

He called long distance and explained that a woman named Audrey Azcue had been killed in her home sometime after midnight. There was nothing like a suspect, no notion of a motive. She was in her early thirties and lived alone in a small house on the edge of town. There were no signs of rape or robbery.

"I'm not real sure when she came to Wynot," Junior told me, "just know she's been around a couple years or so. Wasn't much into buying hardware . . ."

"What's your local law going to make of you asking me in?"

"Oh, Sheriff Summers won't mind. I told him I was calling you. He lives right here and isn't too excited about stirring up local folks."

"He'd rather a stranger did the dirty work, huh?"

"Something like that."

"Is there an angle here you're not telling me?"

"Well, yeah, sort of. Look, it's complicated. Why don't you just come on to town? I'll cover your travel and board and if you can get this thing sorted out, we'll see you get paid for your trouble."

"How'd the lady die?" I asked.

"Her throat was cut, just something awful. About took her head off. There was blood all over the bedroom."

"You say she died after midnight?'

"That's as close as Doc can make it."

"Was she a widow?'

"I don't know."

By this time he was getting antsy about his growing telephone bill and suggested I climb in my jalopy and hightail it northwest where we could really get down to cases.

It didn't sound promising, but nothing I had planned looked better, so I packed my bag and took off. The trip took an hour and a half and the sun baked me by the time I reached town.

Wynot's Main Street was a block long, with a grain elevator towering over the east end, and railroad tracks running east to west on the south side of it. The scattered residential area sported several boxelders, a few elms and one cottonwood. It all looked lively as the shrinking slough I'd passed on the road coming in, where the only occupants were two black mudhens floating in the brackish water.

Junior owned the only hardware in town. His round face was boyish despite a receding hairline, and when I walked in and introduced myself he grinned, took off an apron, stuffed it under the counter and told a young man stocking a bin with nails that he'd be back in about an hour or two.

"What'd Audrey do for income?" I asked as we walked west.

"Nobody knows. She rented her house when she first came, didn't take in wash or do anybody's cleaning like most single ladies. Took in a boarder once, Miz Thorley, an old lady from Minnesota who wanted to stay around a while when her nephew, Morris, was working the creamery. He was a college student who came to work that summer and never went back to school."

"Where's she now?"

"Died about six months ago. Real quiet. One of those women never caused a fuss, even dying."

"And the nephew's still working at the creamery?"

"Right. Nice quiet boy."

"What makes poking into this murder a problem for the sheriff?"

"Well, there's the church stuff. About a month after she moved to town, Pastor Skogswell coaxed Audrey into visiting the Lutheran Church and she went back pretty regular. Then all of a sudden she started going to the Methodist Church and there was a little fuss about that. Didn't amount to anything . . ."

"Who made the fuss?"

"Pastor Skogswell's wife, Tilda. She carries a lot of weight, and I don't mean just on her feet, although there's plenty there. Claimed Pastor Wilkes sweet-talked Audrey around —him being a widower and about her age —"

"Tilda have a case?"

"Well, I hear the pastor did go to Audrey's house a time or two and they shared meals a few times at Kinman's Café."

The case began to interest me. I'd never had a preacher for a suspect in a murder, and here was a possibility for two.

Audrey Azcue's house was a white bungalow with a porch across the front and square pillars at each corner framing the two-steps-up approach. The man sitting on a rocker on the porch looked like a cop even from the street, so it was no surprise to learn this was the Sheriff Summers, the county's top lawman. Close up he seemed past too old for any job, and the crevices framing his mouth were deep enough to be hatchet scars.

Nothing in his tone suggested hostility when Junior introduced us, but on the other hand he didn't exactly radiate welcome.

"This is a hell of a thing," he told me in a growly voice. "We went over sixty years since Junior's pa founded this town, and never a killing 'til now. Folks're real upset. You won't find 'em friendly. They're gonna be sore at Junior bringing in an outsider to poke around in their family closets."

"How come you didn't object to him calling me?"

"Cause it might take the heat off me. If I can't figure this thing out, you'll get the blame. And if you do get it settled, I'll be happy it's not me putting the finger on an old neighbor."

I could see he was going to be a big help.

"So you figure it was a citizen that did it?"

"Well, nobody's admitted to seeing any strangers around and there ain't been any gypsies in the territory all summer."

"Who found the body?"

"Neighbor lady, Mrs. Rudolph. She was used to seeing Audrey out in her garden early every morning and when she hadn't showed up by noon she went over and knocked. There was no answer so she went in and pretty soon found that bloody mess in the bedroom."

Sheriff Summers had found Audrey on her back, eyes and mouth open, blood all over. It seemed like the thing that bothered him most was the flies on her. There was a hole in the screen and they'd come in thick.

We went inside and up to the bedroom for a look around. The whole place was a surprise to me. The carpets were like new, the furniture was nothing grand but in good shape, none of your hand-me-downs, or stuff picked up at rummage sales. There were two bedrooms, both small. The one where she'd died had been fixed up as a library and there was a desk with a Remington Rand typewriter, and bookshelves on two walls. Her bloodstains seemed to cover half the center carpet.

I asked Junior if he'd ever been in the house before and he shook his head.

"Looks like she had plenty money," I said.

"Yeah," he admitted. "Somehow it doesn't figure . . ."

Sheriff Summers said he'd gone through the desk drawers and found nothing personal. The bottom right drawer was empty, which made him wonder. The matching drawer on the left had stationery, carbon paper, and yellow copy sheets. There had been no address book or diary.

"What do you make of it?" he asked me.

"I'd guess whoever cut her, took letters and stuff out that might get him in trouble."

"That, or he just went through and took anything he could cash in on. Maybe there was money around."

"She ever travel you know of?" I asked them.

Neither one knew.

We went over to see the neighbor, Mrs. Rudolph. She was young, and held a tiny baby girl when she came to the door. She let us in and we settled on a sagging couch in a cluttered living room. It was obvious she had been very fond of Audrey and the death had terrified and saddened her. No, she'd not been up the night of the murder and had heard nothing.

I asked if Miz Azcue ever had any visitors, day or night. She only remembered Morris, the nephew of the boarder, who came around almost daily but seldom stayed after dark.

"Were you close friends with Audrey?" I asked.

"Not close enough," she said, looking sadder than ever. "I never felt I really got to know her. She was awful nice, always asked about the baby and how I was, but somehow never told anything about herself. When I think back, I realize she knew all about me and I never learned anything about her. It's so sad. I think there was some kind of tragedy in her life. When the baby woke me nights, I'd get up and walk around the house, nursing her, and twice, on moonlit nights, I saw Audrey, out there in the garden, looking lonely and haunted. I wanted to ask her what she thought about those nights, but somehow, you didn't ask her questions like that. It would seem like you were snooping . . ."

"Did you know Mrs. Thorley?"

"Not much. She was nearly blind, and mostly listened to a radio in her room."

"How'd she get along with Audrey?"

"Oh, just fine. Audrey treated her like she was her mother."

"And the nephew, Morris, was he around much?"

"Oh yes. Every day. He read to his aunt every evening until she died. Got into the habit of helping out Audrey, did shopping for her, brought in wood for the stove. This spring he spaded up her garden."

"That was after the aunt died, wasn't it? He still came around to the house then?"

"Yes. He was so grateful for the way Audrey cared for his aunt, you see."

Sheriff Summers, Junior and I walked back downtown and over to the depot, a small red building with a broad, red brick loading area in front. The ticket man, wearing a green visor and sleeve garters, like something out of a western movie, said yes, Miz Azcue had taken the train to the Twin Cities over Christmas the last year, and another time in the summer, she went for nearly a week. She traveled alone and carried one hefty suitcase. No, she'd not said a word about who she was visiting or what her plans were.

We left the depot and I suggested a visit with Pastor Skogswell.

The sheriff suddenly had duties elsewhere. Junior, a bit reluctantly, led me to the rectory.

It was a small, two story house with a closed-in porch, next door to a clapboard church with an enclosed bell tower.

Junior's cautious knock was answered by a stout matron with graying hair, who smiled at us with the measured warmth of a woman who has spent her life making friends for her husband. I got the feeling she avoided looking at me too closely, for fear she might give away what she was thinking of this scruffy man brought in to stir up trouble.

Junior introduced her as Tilda, the parson's wife. She offered the inevitable coffee, apologized for the absences of her husband, who was at a meeting of the elders in the church. We settled in a dimly lit, reasonably cool parlor, with open windows and closed blinds that moved gently in the draft from outside.

Junior introduced me with background I suspected needed no review for our hostess. She listened and nodded wisely.

"How well did you get to know Miz Azcue?" I asked.

"Hardly at all. She came to our church half a dozen times maybe a year and a half ago. She was too uppity to talk with any of us. Dressed in fancy clothes and looked down on us all."

"You think she was coaxed away by Reverend Wilkes?"

She shrugged. "For all I know, she may have seen him in the grocery store or the butchers, and decided he had more promise for her than my husband."

"I understand Reverend Wilkes and Miz Azcue ate together at the café a few times?"

"Three, I believe."

"And he's a widower."

"That's right. Barely three years."

"She show any interest in other men you know of?"

She gave me a disapproving stare. "I never attempted to keep track of her social life, whatever ideas you may have picked up since you arrived."

She carefully avoided looking Junior's way.

"Nobody's told me you were a gossip," I said, "but this is a small town, you're a social leader here, you're bound to know what goes on in your parish. All I'm after is some idea what kind of a woman she was, what kind of people got interested in her—anything that'll give a lead on why she was murdered. I'm not asking for accusations, just leads. Talking with people who know what's going on and are smart enough to figure people out a little, can save a lot of time. That's why we're here."

Her smile wasn't warm. "You're here," she said, "to confront my husband. Since he isn't handy, you're working on me. That's alright, I understand that. But you're not going to soft soap me into showing my prejudices or ideas about this whole sorry affair."

Before I could ask when her husband's meeting would end, we heard the front door open and a second later he was with us.

Pastor Skogswell was a stocky man with dense, graying hair, dark eyebrows and a worried brow that didn't quite match the mouth framed by laugh wrinkles. I had the impression of a man in love with his work, but some weighed down by it. Or maybe the problem was being married to Tilda.

He greeted me warmly enough, accepted his wife's offer of coffee, took his seat in the corner chair Tilda had occupied and told me he was aware of why I was in town and wanted to offer his fullest cooperation.

"Unfortunately," he said, "I never had a private conversation with Miss Azcue, although I suggested she visit me if she were so inclined, the first time she attended our services. She was very pleasant, but vaguely distant. I felt she was deeply reserved, almost shy. She tried to hide it by asking questions."

"About what?"

"My sermons, my beliefs. She realized that would turn attention from her, you know what I mean?"

I wasn't so sure, but said I understood he had persuaded her to attend his church about a month after she moved into town.

"Well, I did speak to her when she was in Kinman's Café shortly after she arrived, that's true. But my persuasion was limited to welcoming her to Wynot and telling her how welcome she would be in our church. She was polite. Frankly I didn't really expect her to come and was pleasantly surprised when she did."

You didn't talk to her after she started going to the Methodists?"

"Never."

"You and Reverend Wilkes ever talk?"

"We've spoken on the rare occasions when we've met downtown. We're not intimates and would certainly never discuss a parishioner."

"You ever hear where Audrey's money came from?"

"Never."

"You ever watch a new person in your church and try to figure reactions to you sermon?"

He smiled for the first time. "Yes, of course. The first time she attended, she slipped in quietly and sat in the rear so I couldn't really tell anything about her reactions. The second time she sat well down front, the second row, and was most attentive. I confess, I felt rather flattered, until her later decision to try the Methodists."

He said he didn't remember where she sat the few times she attended later and didn't recall what his sermons were about. Certainly none had been prepared with her in mind.

Junior and I went over to see Pastor Wilkes. A gray and wrinkled housekeeper answered the bell and led us to a small study where the pastor sat at a desk and rose to meet us.

He was about forty, slim with dark thinning hair, pale blue eyes and a sharp jaw and chiseled mouth. He listened to Junior's introduction of me and the explanation of my mission. His expression was blank all through Junior's brief report on our talk with Pastor Skogswell.

"I'll try to help," he said, "but I'm afraid I've nothing to offer."

"How'd you manage to convert Audrey Azcue?" I asked.

He shook his head. "It was nothing like a conversion; she simply came to my church one Sunday morning, and sat far in the back. After the services, when I was at the door greeting the flock, we spoke briefly, the usual sort of thing: 'welcome, hope you'll come back . . .' She was cordial but very reserved, actually, rather stand-offish."

"You had dinners together, I hear."

"Not that many—no more than three . . ."

"How'd the first one happen?"

"Well, one evening I went to the restaurant and was just seated when she came in. She asked if she could join me. Had a question about my sermon of the Sunday before. Naturally I was responsive. It isn't often anyone cares to discuss a sermon."

"Was that after the first one she heard?"

"No, it was after the second, I think."

"What was her question?"

He shifted uncomfortably, and frowned. "I'm sorry, it's hard for me to talk about her since what happened. It distorts the memory, you understand? It's all so horribly, I don't know, distorting. First impressions seem unreliable somehow . . ."

"What was her question?"

"Well, in my sermon, I said when we see a watch, we think of the maker; when we see a car, we know about Mr. Ford, and when we look at the world around us, we know that, too, had to have a creator, and this is why we believe in God. And her question was, 'who made God?' I never answered that to her satisfaction. I explained there simply has to be an ultimate beginning, but she was incapable of grasping that concept. It was very frustrating."

"How'd she react?"

"She apologized for embarrassing me, said she hoped I wasn't offended. I assured her I was not. If anything, I was embarrassed for her, but of course I didn't tell her that. Then we talked of other things . . ."

"Did she tell you why she came to Wynot and how she supported herself?"

"No, I never asked anything like that, and she never talked of herself except about what she read and observed. We talked of people and differences in religious beliefs. She's done lots of reading alien to me, things I couldn't or wouldn't imagine reading."

"Didn't you ask her any personal questions?"

"Well, I asked if she had been a teacher. She smiled and said not in any school. She didn't invite personal questions, somehow. The evening after dinner, I kept trying to remember things she'd said and somehow it came down to her asking me questions and me talking. It was always like that. She was, I'm afraid, more interested in questioning other people's beliefs. She didn't care to expose herself to questions about her own."

"She ever talk about the old woman who boarded with her a while?"

"Only about her death. That seemed to bother her deeply. She tried to give the impression it was because of her fondness for the old woman, but I suspect it had more to do with making her realize her own mortality. After all, she had nothing else in common with Mrs. Thorley except a love of cooking. They liked working in the kitchen together. I remember Audrey mentioning the problems because Mrs. Thorley was nearly blind, but somehow she managed to be useful until her last month."

"I understand the nephew came around a lot."

"Oh yes, regularly. He did all sorts of chores for her, and hung about evenings there even after his aunt's death. He's a rather bookish boy, very intense, and she encouraged his reading and loaned him things from her library."

"You think he was in love with her?"

He sighed, "I was afraid you'd ask that. Of course he was. I wasn't around enough to really observe anything first hand, but it would hardly be normal for a young man like that to hover about once his aunt had died, if he weren't rather unnaturally attracted to this woman who seemed to know so much and of course, would be very attractive to an impressionable young man without any experience with the opposite sex. I can see why you'd raise the question. Audrey was probably his senior by at least ten years, but that wasn't very obvious in her appearance, although it was in her manner and style. I have a vague impression of her being very kind to him, and perhaps even encouraging his interest. It's a natural thing for a woman like that to do. It gives them a sense of power and importance."

After we left pastor Wilkes, I learned from Junior that the nephew lived in Jenson's boarding house, just half a block from Audrey Azcue's place. After dinner at Kinman's Café, I drifted around to Jenson's and asked for Morris. The landlady said he wasn't in. He regularly went for walks after dinner. No, she had no idea where.

Junior said he had to get back to his store and we parted. I stopped by the post office and learned that Miz Azcue had sent and received mail regularly from Minneapolis and New York. In fact there was an envelope from New York that came the day after her death. He let me see the return address and I took it down, got a pocketful of quarters at the bank and made a telephone call.

After dinner at Kinman's, I walked around the outskirts of town, taking my time, and worked back toward the Azcue house at dusk. A young man was leaning against an elm tree in the back lot, staring at the garden.

He looked up at my approach.

"Morris?" I said.

"Uh-huh."

"Carl Wilcox. Like to talk to you."

"Why?"

"Help me figure out why Audrey Azcue got murdered."

"I can't help you."

"Try. Tell me what she was like. Nobody knows. Not reverend Wilkes, or pastor Skogswell, or any of them. Was she going to marry Wilkes?"

He stared at me. His eyes seemed old for such a young man.

"What gives you that idea?"

"Far as anybody knows, they were both single, near the same age, got together pretty often. Were you in love with her?"

"I don't think that's any of your business."

You care who killed her?"

He took a deep breath, and slowly settled back on his heels, then let himself to the ground and tipped his head back against the tree trunk.

"Of course."

"Then help me."

"It won't help her."

"No. But you want it left in the air?"

"It won't stay there."

An owl hooted in the distance and the wind rustled tree leaves overhead. Crickets were tuning up.

I squatted in front of him.

"Was she going to leave town?"

For a moment he was motionless and silent, then he nodded, almost absentmindedly.

"When did you learn that?"

He looked at me, and his eyes narrowed. For the first time he was really paying attention to what I was trying to do.

"Well, why wouldn't she? There was no reason to stay here."

"Why'd she come in the first place?"

"How'd I know?"

"You were in her house a lot. She gave you books, must have talked with you. I understand that you got on great and kept coming around after your aunt died."

"Well, Audrey had come to depend on my help. Since she'd been so nice to Auntie, I figured I owed her."

"Do you know what she wrote on that typewriter she had?"

"She was writing a book."

"She was an author?"

"That's what they call people that write books, isn't it?"

"You ever see anything of her work?"

"Well, I saw those piles of paper she'd typed, and the carbon copies. But she kept all that in her room up there. Didn't show it to me."

"Did she ask you lots of questions, about what you were doing and planned to do?"

"Yeah. She was at me to go back to school."

"Why didn't you go?"

Morris shrugged.

"Wilkes says she was a very good looking woman, thinks you might have been in love with her. Was that why you didn't go back to college last fall?"

"That's baloney, I was too young for her."

"Then why didn't you go back to college?"

"I was sick of all that stuff, required courses, snooty profs, all the ring-around."

"She must have liked you to let you hang around so much."

He shrugged again. "It was just that she had ideas about how a fellow should make the most of things. She thought I was wasting my time in Wynot. She'd liked Auntie real well and wanted her nephew to make the most of himself"

"Why was she wasting her time here?"

"Said she was researching for her book."

"She ever talk of leaving Wynot?"

"Nah, but she sure as hell didn't figure to die here."

"Where'd she come from?"

"Minneapolis."

"What'd you two talk about the night she died?"

"I didn't see her then."

"That's not what I've been told. A neighbor saw you go inside that night."

He studied me for a moment, then shook his head. "I don't believe that."

"It's a fact." I lied.

"If anyone saw a man go in, it was probably Pastor Wilkes. An old gossip could easily mistake him for me in the dark."

"Did he visit her nights?"

"Not when I was around. Anyway. She wasn't interested in him as a guy. She was interested in religion. That's what her book was about. She couldn't figure why so many people went for all that stuff. She was trying to work it all out."

"How come she didn't talk more with Parson Skogswell?"

"Because he was dumb. She went to hear his sermons about six times or more and gave up. He wasn't even dull enough to be colorful."

And Wilkes was?"

"Well, he was different. She said he was capable of thought. He was a guy had to explain everything, he didn't just insist on faith. It was like he was trying to convince himself of what he said because Christianity simply appealed to his heart but ran into trouble with his brain."

"She ever tell him anything like that?"

"Probably not. Audrey didn't tell people much of anything, just asked."

"She seems to have told you quite a bit."

"Well, I was around a lot and she got to sort of bouncing ideas off me."

"Who do you think killed her?"

His face twisted some and he scowled, and shook his head.

"I just can't figure it. Old Tilda, Skogswell's biddy would sure like to have. Skogswell's too dense to do anything that wild. I suppose it comes down to somebody who's a nut and has kept it hidden somehow. All I can think of is Wilkes. She was too young for him but she had him worked up, you can bet on it. Maybe he made a pass—he was probably dumb enough to even ask her to marry him. If she said no, he might've flipped. It's got to be somebody, for god's sake."

"How about you? If you made a pass and she told you you were just a dumb kid, you might've lost your head there."

"Not a chance. I was never dumb enough to try. Yeah, I was in love with her, but I didn't go crazy. I'd've never hurt her. Now, a guy like Wilkes, who wants to believe he's on the right hand of God, he's got to take himself real seriously. If she told him he was stupid to believe in the Bible and all that stuff, he could've gone nuts I bet. And besides, everybody in town knew he was making a fool of himself over her. If she left him flat, he'd been laughed out of town."

I told him not to leave town, and headed for Wilke's place.

He answered the door himself and took me into his study where the only light was from a small lamp on an old desk.

I told him of my talk with Morris and the accusations made.

Pastor Wilkes' reaction was, as far as I could judge, purely sorrowful. He shook his head, peered at me, and asked if I really believed the boy.

"I'd like to hear your side."

"It's all transparently ridiculous. I would never have been fool enough to propose. Audrey wasn't a woman a man like me could live with. She had no religious belief, no concern for the soul. Certainly she was attractive, and her interest in my sermons was stimulating until I realized she believed in none of the things I did. Very frankly, she was too coldly intellectual for me, we had no basic beliefs in common, however civil and pleasant it was to talk with her, and I confess, I felt obligated to try and persuade her to accept the true Jesus. I actually once asked if there was something in her past, if she had been married, or had an unfortunate love affair. She said she didn't care to discuss her past; she had left it and that was sufficient. I asked her another time, if Morris weren't in love with her, and she said it seemed likely, but she hadn't encouraged him in any way and was sure he'd get over it and turn to girls his own age."

"You ever find out how she supported herself?"

"No. She never told me. I couldn't, somehow, ask.

"You know she was writing a novel that made fun of a preacher?"

His face froze momentarily, then he managed to look thoughtful.

"What makes you think that?"

"She wrote regularly, told Morris something about it."

"Well, I wouldn't rely much on anything she told a boy like him—or that he might tell you. Obviously he was jealous of the time she spent with me."

"What made you think that?"

"For heaven's sake, isn't it obvious? With all due respect for the dead, Audrey was a woman, with all the wiles and vanity; she led him on but granted him none of the liberties he desperately wanted—so there had to be a villain in his way. Who but me? And naturally, he would try to turn suspicions on me when he lost his head and killed her."

"Reverend Wilkes, a couple of hours ago I talked with a publisher in New York. They've got an almost completed manuscript of a book about a town like Wynot, with people plainly living here. One of the main characters is a minister named Wiley. He comes off pretty bad. When did you get around to reading what Audrey's been writing?"

His mouth went slack, he shook his head. "I've no idea what you're talking about. This is a fabrication . . ."

"Didn't she tell you she sent the whole story to her publisher? Isn't that what you learned about that night you killed her after finding out why she'd talked with you so much?"

He drew back, his eyes popping, "Dear God, no, it's not true—it wasn't finished—"

I smiled at him. "You're right. She hadn't done the last chapter. She wanted her editor's opinion about the last chapter before she finished it off. Now, you want to just get this whole business off your conscience by telling me all about it?"

He lowered his head to the table, clasped his bony hands over his balding skull, and wept.

I found his telephone and called the sheriff.

Murder in the Blitz

GERALD ANDERSON

D R. JOHNSON SAID, "He who is tired of London is tired of life."
Detective Inspector Robert Wainwright was tired of neither. He
had just returned from Nottingham where he had been called in on a
missing persons case and now stood outside St. Pancras station soaking in
the April sunshine. There was still time to return to Scotland Yard to put
in a few hours of paperwork, but there was no hurry, and he decided he
would walk and admire the cheery daffodils that brightened every small
park. This was his London, he thought, and she had never looked finer.
He strolled down Euston Road, Tottenham Court Road, and turned onto
the bustling Oxford Street. He recalled his days as a young constable, fascinated by the people who could actually afford Oxford Street prices.

On impulse he turned south and eventually came to Carnaby Street.
The newspapers had been filled with articles on pop culture in this spring
of 1966, but he could not recall, after fifty years of living in London, that he
had ever actually been to the little street. He stared at the short skirts of the
shopgirls, and looked with distain at the hairstyles of the young men. There
was paisley everywhere, and there were wide ties and bell-bottom trousers
and shops that sold bits of curious apparatus designed, there could be no
doubt, to facilitate the smoking of cannabis, or, as they seemed to want to
call it, "pot." And from every store there came the music of The Beatles,
The Rolling Stones, The Animals, and all manner of ill-suited names.

This was not his London—it was the London of spotty-faced, foul-mouthed ingrates who had never faced Hitler. Still, he thought, he would have to adjust to the times. He recalled just last week when he had come into his daughter's room and heard her listening to a pleasant ballad—none of that "can't get no satisfaction" stuff—and he had said, "There, now that's what I call music! None of that Stones or Beatles junk! What's it called, anyway?" His daughter had replied, with rather unseemly sarcasm and infinite patience, "That's 'Yesterday.' By Paul McCartney. You know, The Beatles?" He had been mortified.

As he came to the end of Carnaby Street, he walked on to Piccadilly Circus and turned right. He felt the need to know that "his" London still existed, and so he decided to postpone his hike to the Yard and directed his feet to Fortnum and Mason's tea room.

He was shown to a table with a crisp white tablecloth and a carnation in a lovely vase. A pleasant and respectful lady soon appeared to take his order and, even though he was concerned about the growing length of his belt, he ordered a Bakewell tart to go along with his pot of tea. When she had gone, he settled back and listened to the sounds around him. In point of fact, there was hardly a sound to be heard. There were murmured voices on either side of him, and the occasional "clink" of a cup on a saucer, but other than that—in light of his Carnaby Street experience—there was a most blessed silence. "Ah," he said to himself, "This is the England we fought for."

Except he hadn't, a fact he sometimes regretted. A month before the war broke out, he had tried to break up an argy-bargy in a pub and a wide-boy had unexpectedly pulled a knife on him. He received a severe cut, which badly damaged the nerves of two fingers. At other times he may have been cashiered out of the force, but he could still hold a truncheon, and with the manpower demands of the army and the navy, the Metropolitan Police Force needed every man they could get. All in all, it had worked out rather well for him. He had joined the force at age twenty, at a time when his friends had called him "Bobby the bobby," but in the summer of 1940, with an extraordinary number of departures, he had been promoted to Detective Sergeant, the youngest DS in the whole force. His patch had been the area of his birth, Shoreditch and Bethnal Green, an area that the Luftwaffe seemed to take a perverse delight in destroying.

He began to ruminate on his first murder case. The murder was never solved, and because it continued to gnaw at him, he remembered it as though it were yesterday. It was early September of 1940, and the Nazis were trying to destroy England. The sound of the sirens and the smell of burning buildings crept into his mind. His eyes lost focus as he stared unseeing at the nearby tables. Suddenly, his unconscious mind registered an ocean of pastel flowers, and a blink later his conscious mind focused on a woman's dress. He looked up to see a silver-haired lady, complete with white hat and gloves, who seemed to be staring at him. As he returned her gaze, she said, "I'm sure you don't remember me, but I remember you. May I join you?"

Startled, but not so much as to forget his manners, he rose, pulled back another chair, and said, "Please do."

The lady sat, folded her hands in her lap, and said, "My name is Betty Lyons. We met in September of 1940. Tell me, are you still a policeman, Mr. Wainwright?"

"Yes, er, that's right, Robert Wainwright. And I am still a policeman. May I offer you some tea?"

"That would be lovely, dear."

Wainwright signaled a waitress and another cup was brought to the table. "Would you like a sweet, Mrs., er, Lyons?"

"No, luv, I've 'ad quite enough for today. Now, I'm sure you are curious as to 'ow and when we met before."

"Yes, I'm sorry, but I am unable to place you."

"I'm not surprised. You seemed like a very young bobby, but I seem to remember we called you Sergeant Wainwright back then."

"Yes, but now I'm Detective Chief Inspector Wainwright. Curiously, I was just recollecting those days. I had just been promoted in September of 1940, but, er . . ."

"Yes, well, it was during the Blitz, wasn't it? My three friends and I always went to the same little corner in the Old Street tube station whenever the air raid siren went off. We all brought our knitting and we made it into quite a cozy little nest. At the time, we all lived next door to each other in attached houses in Stepney. We would never 'ave thought of going to the shelter by ourselves."

"Wait a minute. Are you telling me that you were one of the ladies that I interviewed in connection with the Old Street Station Murder?"

"That's right, luv, but I don't remember you doing much talking. It was that older bloke what did all the questioning. Seems to me you mostly just took notes."

"Yes, well, it was my first murder case, and Inspector Carter tended to keep the lower ranks in their place. He is no longer with us, by the way. He passed on about ten years ago."

"Ah, sorry to 'ear it. He was a nice gent. Still, we all 'ave to go some-time, don't we? I'm the last of us girls still above ground. When I saw you sitting 'ere, I just became curious. After you and the inspector left us, we never 'eard any more about the case. Did you ever arrest anyone?"

"No, and I suppose we didn't really try too hard. The victim, a Mr. Goff, had no relatives and apparently no friends, either, if it came to that. Needless to say, there was a lot going on at that time, and after a few days, we just didn't have much time to pursue that case. We always meant to go back to it, but as far as I know, nobody ever did. Did you and your three friends discuss it much?"

"After you and the inspector came to talk to us, I don't think any of us mentioned it for the rest of our lives. But in fact, there 'asn't been a day when I 'aven't thought about it. You know, Chief Inspector, none of us actually told you the whole truth about that night."

"Really? What did you leave out?"

"I'm not really sure I should tell you. Still, Goldy and Annie and 'elen are all gone now, and, well, I 'ave just come from 'arley Street. I don't 'ave much time m'self, if one can believe that young doctor. First of all, you must remember the times. Every night in September Mr. 'itler's bombers gave us all the 'ell they could. We would come out of the tube station wondering if our 'omes would still be there, which of our neighbors would still be alive, what kind of 'elp we could give to the others. That area of Stepney was pretty tight-knit back in them days. The four of us decided that we didn't want to spend time with the police when we 'ad so much else to do. So we made up a story and stuck to it. Well, we didn't make things up—we just didn't tell you everything."

Mrs. Lyons took a demure sip of tea, then smacked her lips loudly. Wainwright leaned forward and said, "As I recall, the four of you told us that you had gone down into the Old Street tube station at about nine thirty that night."

"That's right, the Thirteenth of September. Unlucky day for many, including the man who joined us."

"And you told us that he seemed drunk and that he quietly settled himself next to the wall and went to sleep. He didn't speak to you and you didn't speak to him. After the all-clear signal was given, you assumed he was sound asleep and so you simply left the station, leaving him to sleep it off. We interviewed each of you separately, and each of you expressed surprise when, several hours later, you found out he had been found dead. An autopsy revealed he had been killed by a narrow, sharp object that had pierced his heart. The medical examiner refused to rule out accidental death, saying it was possible he had tripped and sustained a serious wound by falling on something that may have protruded from the rubble, which, as you remember, was all around. Nevertheless, it was his opinion that he had been murdered. Whether he had been stabbed before he came down to the station or had been stabbed after you had left was impossible to determine. So, is there anything you would like to add to this account?"

"Yes, Inspector, I think there is." Mrs. Lyons took another sip of tea and a deep breath and said, "You see, Chief Inspector, we were not quite telling the truth when we told you that we never spoke to that man."

"Ah . . .," said the inspector.

"There we were, 'aving ever so nice a time—those really were lovely nights, Chief Inspector, in spite of what was going on outside. We were knitting away by the dim light of a lantern when this rather nasty man joined us without so much as a 'by your leave.' We tried to ignore 'im, but 'e soon started to rant on and on about 'ow we were fighting the wrong enemy. 'E said that we should be fighting *with* 'err 'itler to clean out the Reds and to take care of the Jews once and for all. In fact, 'e said some pretty wicked things that I'd rather not repeat even now."

"Were any of you Jewish?" the Chief Inspector asked.

"What's that got to do with anything? We were Englishwomen fighting the war with as much courage as our men-folk. As it turns out, two of us were Jewish, but I'm not even going to tell you which ones. We stuck together, we did. 'All for one, one for all'—Four Musketeers! And we'd all given a lot of our families to keep 'itler and his gang away from our shores. Goldy Boyle 'ad a boy who was in the navy and another boy who 'ad been captured by the Krauts before 'e could make it to Dunkirk. Annie Furst's 'usband 'ad been killed in Wipers in 1917, and she raised three lads and a girl all by 'erself. And 'elen, well, whenever those Kraut bombers came over, she was convinced it was 'er Jack that was up there shooting 'em down. You didn't find many pilots from our class back then, but Jack, well, 'e was something else. Jack was shot down over the Channel a week later, and they never did find 'im. And me? Well, a week before that night down in the tube station, my 'usband Ed, who was a fireman, was out during the Blitz and a bomb fell right on 'is 'ead. They said 'is coffin contained most of 'im, and maybe it did. Oh, yeah, Mr. Policeman, we fought the war, too."

"I know you did. I saw scenes of heroism every night. I'll never forget the sacrifices you, and thousands like you, made."

"So, anyways, you might imagine that what 'e said went over with us like a turd in a teacup. I don't know if 'e was one of them British Union of Fascists—one of Mosley's boys—or not. Well, we 'ad been listening to this nonsense for a while when a bomb must 'ave fallen right above us. The lights flickered, our lantern went out, and we just sat there in the dark until we got the all-clear. When the lights came back on, the bloke was laying pretty much as we last saw 'im. I suppose that's all there is to say. None of us wanted to be in a position to speak ill of the dead, 'owever much of a rotter 'e was, so we kept quiet. I won't get into trouble for keeping this a secret for twenty-six years, will I?"

"I don't think you have to worry about that, Mrs. Lyons, but I'm glad you told me about it."

"That's all right, then, is it, Inspector? In that case, I'm glad I got it off my chest and, well, I don't suppose we will ever meet again. If there is a Mrs. Wainwright, tell 'er she is married to a fine copper."

As Mrs. Lyons stood to leave, Wainwright said, "There is a Mrs. Wainwright, and I shall be most proud to tell her what you said."

He watched her leave the tea room, and decided that he was in no hurry to get back to the Yard. He poured out the last dregs of his pot of tea, and put in more sugar than was good for him. He thought about Inspector Carter and his interrogation skills and looked back with nostalgia at his very first murder case, one that would never be solved. Little old ladies! They put the "Great" in Great Britain and always had! He pictured them sitting in the dim light of an underground station, calmly knitting while the future of the nation hung in the balance. Perhaps one of the scarves they knit would one day have made it to Berlin.

Suddenly, all of the patrons of the dainty tea room turned toward Wainwright's table as he clapped his hands together and cried: "Of course! A knitting needle!"

Hole in the Fence

JOEL ARNOLD

"**W**AT HAVE YOU GOTTEN INTO, NOW?**"** I knelt down next to my dachshund, Hilde, steadying her head with one hand while trying to get a hold of whatever it was that was sticking out of her mouth with the other. I pried her jaw open, and pulled out the remains of a dead crow. I grimaced as I realized it was not a fresh kill—it must've been rotting for a while before my only companion for the last four months had found it.

I scolded her. "Dead birds don't make good chew toys." Her furiously wagging tail disagreed.

A few months ago, after getting her from the animal shelter, I would have worried about her getting sick, but this was the third dead creature she'd brought home in the last month—ever since the thaw. The first had been a frog, then a week later a tiny black vole. She didn't have much interest in eating them, just carrying them around for a while until I caught her and pried the poor dead things out from her jaws. And so far, at least, she'd been just fine.

"Hilde!"

She was loose again. I'd let her out in the backyard—the *fenced-in* backyard—but there she was, running around happy as a clam in the street out front. It was my own fault that she wasn't very well trained. I admit to spoiling her with table scraps and her own spot on the bed next to me. But she understood the pain I was going through, the loneliness.

Okay, I guess that's a lie if you get right down to it; there was no way she could know why I was lonely any more than I could understand why she liked to carry old dead things in her mouth. But I believe deep down that she—like all dogs—could sense the different moods of men and women.

It's no use calling after her. She'll let you get within a few feet and then take right off again, like it's a game to her. I worry about a car hitting her, or the Johnson's Rottweiler down the street deciding to use her as a chew toy. Hell, a large enough *bird* could carry her away.

"Hilde!"

She waited at the front door for me an hour later, filthy and reeking. I guess it was time to examine the fence. It was a wooden privacy fence that had come with the house when Linda and I moved here fifteen years earlier; big cedar planks stained ochre. Since Hilde was too small to jump the fence, there had to be a hole somewhere—perhaps a board missing or broken. But with the thaw, our backyard had turned to a mud pit, and I'd avoided the inevitable repairs.

I picked Hilde up and took her to the tub, rinsing off bits of dead leaves and dirt with the detachable showerhead. I shampooed away the awful odor that clung to her fur. "What have you been into?" I asked.

An awful thought crossed my mind, but I swallowed it deep. She was just a little dog after all.

I scooped her shivering body into a towel and rubbed her dry, ran my fingers gently over her sleek body, examining her from head to toe. She turned her head to lick my face, and I let her, but the smell of her breath nearly made me gag.

Just a little dog.

"Better brush your teeth tonight," I told her, looking for the small canine toothbrush the vet had given me.

I figured I'd best start chaining her up when I let her out back—at least until I could mend the fence. But that night she woke me out of a deep sleep with a volley of sharp yips. I'd been dreaming about Linda again, about that night she'd left me for good, and it was hard to let that go. I stumbled to the back door in my boxers and t-shirt and let Hilde out without thinking much about it. I waited for her. And waited. And then I remembered about that damn hole in the fence. "Hilde!"

Hell . . .

I dropped onto the couch, my eyes drifting shut, until I heard scratching at the back door. I stood, yawned, probably scratched some part of myself, and let her in.

Filthy again and she stank to high heaven. "What's that you got in your mouth this time?" I asked.

I knelt down groggily and pried her jaw open as her thin tail whipped back and forth.

A finger dropped to the hardwood floor. A blackened, rotting human finger, the flesh peeling from the bones.

I stared at it, trying to hold back the bile threatening to rise from the depths of my throat.

"Hilde," I whispered, absently petting her sleek fur. "What have you gotten into?"

I found a flashlight. Pulled on jeans, a flannel shirt, black jacket, workman boots and a black woolen cap. Grabbed a spade from the garage. I decided it was best if I left Hilde inside the house for this.

There's no real path through the woods behind our house, but Linda and I used to love traipsing back there when autumn had turned the maple and birch leaves into flaming yellows and reds. But it looked different at night, the trees skeletal in the early spring with their bare branches letting droplets of starlight bleed through. I stepped carefully, shining my flashlight here and there, trying to orient myself. I smelled the stagnant pond close by, ripe with the spring run-off, and I smelled something else, too.

Finally, I found it. Nearly tripped over it in fact, but stopped myself just in time. Linda's hand protruded grotesquely from the earth. The middle finger was, of course, missing.

I barely held back an anguished cry, but a small tear managed to escape, sliding warmly down my cheek and growing cold at the corner of my mouth as I jabbed the business end of the spade into the forest floor. I scooped up dead leaves, twigs and dirt, and piled them on top of her hand. I continued to scoop dirt over the shallow grave until it was no longer so shallow, and Linda, my wife who had "run off to Italy to be with another man" was once again secure beneath the weight of the fecund soil.

When I got back inside the house, Hilde greeted me, tail wagging furiously as she tried to lick the dirt from my hands. I knelt down and let her lick my face. "Hilde," I said, patting the top of her head. "I do believe it's about time we fixed that fence."

Spring Rowing

JUDITH YATES BORGER

THE SPRING WATER RUSHING DOWN the Mississippi River was fast, hard and cold. It's like that every spring. *Cold*. Cold enough that someone caught in the current would know the affects of hypothermia in minutes. Do you know what that feels like? Human tissue becomes useless. Muscles are unmanageable. Gumby has better control of his arms and legs. Then the mind gets weird. Odd thoughts float in and out in time that seems suspended, even though it can be measured in seconds.

I had given this a lot of thought. Even researched the facts, like actual temperatures, and how long it takes for a person to die from a sudden drop in body warmth so low that tissue no longer functions, and never will again. Hypothermia sets in when torso temperature falls below ninety-five degrees Fahrenheit. That's only about four degrees below healthy, but it happens fast, especially in water that is sixty or sixty-five degrees. Even on a warm day, cold water can suck the heat right out of a body.

That's why I chose a sunny, almost balmy day in early April to take my husband, who is, or was, my rowing partner, on the Mississippi. I had decided that this would be the last spring we would be putting the boat in the water together.

It wasn't hard to convince him to go out with me. He loves rowing as much as I do. More, actually. The loamy smell, the sight of a eagle circling overhead or a blue heron perched on a log are all part of the experience on the Mississippi River, which runs smack down the middle of a metro area of more than two million people. When you're on the river you're one with the earth, even if you had to battle traffic to get there.

And we love our boat. It's a Vespoli, hand-made of many layers of carbon fiber with a honeycomb core, then cured under intense heat for stiffness and durability. The riggers are made of aircraft-grade aluminum. Our fathers, who were best friends, won the 1984 summer Olympics in Los Angeles in that beauty. They named her *Both Of Us*.

Considering my husband and I are different genders, it's surprising how similar our bodies are. Because our legs are the same length—give or take an inch—we never have to adjust foot stretchers. Our arms are about the same length, too, so we're easily interchangeable in the bow or the stern. When we're rowing together, our timing in perfect sync, our muscles warm and strong, it's better than sex.

But our sex life these days was as dry and uncomfortable as the beach in the middle of a drought. He wasn't much interested in me, nor I in him. In fact, the only time we shared much of anything was when we were in the boat.

So, on this spring day we took her from the boathouse under the Lake Street Bridge. Safely cradled in our arms, we carried her through the grass to the floating dock before gently lowering her into the water, bow upstream, stern down.

"I'll take the bow today," I said.

"Fine," he said, climbing in.

The sun hadn't been up long and there was no one on the river when we began to row upstream. As we passed a momma duck who was leading her four ducklings along the shore in front of the University of Minnesota docks, I rued that we had never created babies.

"Weigh enough in two," I said, giving the command to stop rowing in two strokes as we neared a spot under the 35W bridge. "That's one. That's two. Weigh enough."

We rested our paddles on the water, taking a second to sniff the sweet smell of the morning spring air.

"We've been married five years," I said to him.

"So?" he asked.

"So, I figure you've been fooling around with that little cox for four of those years," I said.

"More like four and half," he said, turning around to look at me with the cute grin that made me fall in love with him. "I suppose you want a divorce now."

I had thought about that. A divorce would have certainly been simpler. We had each come to the marriage with a little property. A car apiece. The couch was mine. The LED screen television was his. We'd initialed our own books and CDs. Dividing things up and going our separate ways would have been pretty easy, with one exception.

The boat. I knew he would want to keep the boat.

I gave my butt a little wiggle, just enough to jar him a bit.

"What are you doing?" he said.

The number one rule of sculling is keep a hand on oar handles at all times. If you have to scratch your nose or grab a water bottle you hold both handles in one hand and keep the blades flat on the water—that is, if you don't want to tip and fall in the river. It was a rule he violated on occasion.

"Looking at the eagle," I said, nodding east, where I knew the rays of the sun were blinding him.

He let go of his starboard oar for just a second, long enough to raise his left hand to shield his eyes from the rising sun.

I gave my butt a hard jiggle this time, shifting my weight enough to topple him over the gunnel.

Because he was so lean he had little fat to insulate his organs, which made hypothermia set in fairly quickly. Just before his windpipe closed in response to his panic, he managed to squeeze out his last word.

"Why?"

"Because I can always get another husband, and another rowing partner, but I'll never get another *Both Of Us*," I told him as I watched him sink into the icy foam of the rushing spring water.

Firestorm

CARL BROOKINS

SEPTEMBER, 1918

"**W**AL, MR. TEDVEDT. I'm relieved to hear my money's easily available. I've never been real comfortable with banks. No offense, sir."

Banker Byron Tedvedt, a large blond man, nodded as he made the pretense of a friendly gesture to the speaker, a tall man in dirty overalls seated across from him. They were separated by a big, walnut desk. The polished surface reflected soft light from the windows into the lower face of the bank's client. It was all Banker Tedvedt could do to keep from sneering in disgust. Out of sight beneath the desktop, he squeezed the fingers of one hand into a meaty fist. Carl Oleason, the man across from him, smelled of manure and sweat and unwashed clothing. They looked at each other in silence.

"You just give me my due, Mr. Tedvedt, and maybe a little extra for my trouble and we'll call it even . . ." At that, the banker stood up and told Oleason that maybe they should finish their talk outside on the street.

Inwardly, Oleason was exulting. *By God, Mary had been right!* There *was* something peculiar about their account. He'd never noticed it, but Mary had. She'd pushed and pestered him for days after he'd let slip that they were running a little short of cash and might not have enough to buy all the seed he'd planned for spring planting. Seed for crops they desperately needed to keep their farm going.

She'd gone over their records and discovered her accounts didn't square with the bank records. There should have been at least thirty dollars more. She told him he ought to talk to the banker, Mr. Tedvedt about the discrepancy. He'd been reluctant. The squiggly figures in neat columns on those pages that Mary used to keep track of their affairs meant little to him. *Like little black worms,* he thought. But finally, her gentle nagging had sent him into Prairie Center this hot fall day.

And then, when he confronted the banker with it, by golly, he'd seen it. He didn't know what that something was that flickered in the man's face. Oh, he was too slick to admit anything, all right, and he'd covered up pretty good. But there was something there, just for a moment, and Oleason realized that something was going on. That was for sure. It was then, sitting right there across that big, shiny desk, he got the idea. If Banker Tedvedt was fiddling with his, Carl Oleason's, money, mightn't he be doing it with others? Oleason's wasn't a big account in Mr. Tedvedt's bank. There were lots of farmers and tradespeople who had accounts at the bank. They were mostly small and medium-sized accounts. People moved away or died and he'd bet some of the accounts were forgotten. Did the bank keep that money? Was it legal? Oleason didn't think so.

But if Tedvedt was playing games, why couldn't he, Oleason, get in on it? Share the wealth, as it were. Hell, he didn't like Tedvedt much and who would the banker complain to? Oleason had a commonly held kind of contempt for men who didn't work the land, who had soft, well-kept hands. He saw them as people who often took advantage, who profited from the labor and sometimes the misfortunes of farmers and tradespeople. It appealed to Oleason to take advantage of a banker. To get a little back. He wouldn't ask for much, just a few hundred here or there to kind of ease things along . . .maybe get a new horse, or better yet, one of them new tractors. Hell, if he was careful and kept his mouth shut, this arrangement could go on for years.

He had no inkling that he'd turned up just one small corner of a very large carpet, a carpet that covered a surprising amount of dirt.

Shoving aside the gate in the railing, Oleason clomped through the small lobby in his heavy boots onto the boardwalk outside the one-story wooden building. The soles of his work boots left small deposits of sand from his shoes on the recently swept board flooring. The bank's wooden false front cast a long shadow on the dusty street before the two men.

They stopped on the plank walk in front of the bank, feeling the heat of the noon-time sun streaming down. There'd been a lot of that, this summer, and not near enough rain. Most times about now, there was the smell of fall grass and damp fields from overnight rain. But not this year. This year, the fields were parched and some talked about the possibility of serious fire in the big forests north and west of town.

Oleason breathed deeply. Was that a tang on the breeze?

"Look there, Oleason," said Tedvedt. "Is that smoke on the horizon?"

Oleason squinted off to the north through the shimmering heat and shrugged. Sweat started in his armpits. His thoughts were taken with the new money that was now within his grasp. He shrugged again. "Later," was all he said, as he stepped off the walk and went down the dusty, unpaved street, stepping aside for a pair of mules and an iron-wheeled wagon rattling along. Dust raised by the rig hung in the still, hot air.

"Later" turned out to be well after dark that same night behind the bank. It was hours before moonrise would occur and out of sight of any citizens of Prairie Center who happened to be taking a late night stroll. Oleason walked carefully across the empty stubble field behind the bank, careless of the crackling sound of dry crushed stubble, but not wanting to twist his ankle in a prairie dog burrow. When he crossed the railroad track the smell of burned grass stung his nostrils. Passing trains sometimes started small fires in the grass that grew along the right of way. That had been happening since the tracks were laid, and residents of the area had grown used to them, beating them out whenever necessary. Most fires died in the ditches against the wet earth. Pretty dry, Oleason thought, mopping his face. Still damnall hot, too.

There was no one about when Oleason rapped softly at the door in the back of the bank building. The town was dark in the hot night. Residents of small country towns retired with nightfall, preferring not to waste precious kerosene after the sun went down. Electricity was coming, and many towns had electric lights in some stores, but few residents could afford it. Rural electrification was years away.

The door slowly opened and Banker Byron Tedvedt slipped out. He latched the padlock that hung from the shiny hasp and secured the door. Motioning silently he led the other man back the way he'd come, angling north toward a small copse growing beside a bank covered with waist-high prairie grass. In a normal summer a small stream ran between the gentle banks. In the summer of 1918 only dampness remained in occasional low spots along the bottom of the creek bed.

"Where we goin'?" hissed Oleason. He was getting a little nervous. He'd had too much time to think about what he was doing. Oleason hadn't explained to Mary why he was going out late that night. He wasn't in the habit of discussing all his business with his wife. Besides, he knew she'd never approve. But he didn't realize how hard it was to keep silent. How would he explain to his wife when he went and bought a new horse, or something? This was more complicated than he'd first reckoned.

Banker Tedvedt seemed unconcerned, now they were well away from town, as they trudged along the bank of the dry creek. "Down here," he said. "You don't think I keep all my funds in the bank do you? What if the examiners came around without warning?" Tedvedt spoke in low but almost normal tones.

Oleason made no response, bank examiners being something outside his experience. The other man bent over and scrabbled about under a bush. He laid hands on a short-handled spade that had been nested there. If Oleason wondered how the banker came to find the shovel without a light, he made no mention of his wonder. Tedvedt scrambled a few more paces down the bank until he was nearly at the bottom. Then he began to dig, his back to Oleason. After watching for a moment, Oleason's reason began to function better and it occurred to him that the place Tedvedt was digging would be under water or at least real wet most seasons. How could he keep money there? It'd rot in no time.

Oleason scrambled around to stand in front of Tedvedt in order to ask him about that. "Ain't the money gonna be wet, you keep it down there?"

"Sealed. In oiled cloth bags," Tedvedt puffed. He wasn't used to such concentrated exercise in this heat. The shovel thunked into something solid.

Carl Oleason bent over in the dim starlight to get a look. Tedvedt straightened suddenly. Oleason, still hovering over the hole, turned his head and looked up at the banker.

Even if the uneducated farmer had no understanding of the true dimensions of the embezzlements, and even if he kept his demands to small amounts, Tedvedt doubted Oleason would be able to conceal his new prosperity. Moreover, like most greedy men, Banker Tedvedt resented having to part with a single dime of his illegal profits. It simply didn't occur to him to write off the small payoff proposed by Carl Oleason as a minor cost of doing business.

He had resolved to find a permanent solution.

The last thing Oleason saw, in momentary astonishment, was the dirty blade of the shovel whistling toward him as the banker rounded up with all his strength and smashed the shovel full into Carl Oleason's face. The impact sent vibrations through Tedvedt's arms to his elbows.

The farmer went down without another sound. His head split open, brains and blood spilled out and leaked into the thirsty soil. He died instantly.

Banker, embezzler, now murderer, Tedvedt glanced around. A light breeze sighed briefly and nocturnal insects sang in the heat. Sweat ran down Tedvedt's face and dripped onto the ground at his feet. In the distance over the horizon, he saw flickering light and smelled the faint tang of burning grass. He returned to his labor and soon had a hole dug into the side of the bank near his buried cache.

"I'll bury you so deep even the spring thaw won't find you," he puffed to the dead man. There were several good sized rocks about to use as weights. But the ground was no longer soft. The unremitting sun and lack of rain had hardened the earth, even here in the creek. The life Banker Tedvedt had been living hadn't conditioned him for grave digging. Soon exhausted, he gave up after making a shallow trench in the bank.

His arms and legs trembled from the exertion. He threw the shovel to the ground beside the shallow pit, gasping in the hot air. Even now, in the small hours of the morning, the heat had not lessened appreciably. Tedvedt rolled Oleason's body into the shallow grave. He mopped his sweaty face and heaved some rocks on the body. Then he shoveled the loose dirt back in the hole until the body was covered. Finally he threw on handfuls of dead grass and twigs and a few branches off nearby dead bushes. Even so, he knew the freshly turned ground would be obvious in the daylight to anyone walking along the bank, unless . . .

Clambering out of the creek bed, Tedvedt walked a score of yards south, parallel to the railroad tracks that ran behind the town. Overhead, clouds scudded across the horizon from the Dakotas, fitfully lit from the ground by flickering reddish light that seemed to come from somewhere over the horizon.

Squatting, he took out a cigar and lit it, shielding the match flame from the town with his body. His fingers shook and it took a second match before he got the cigar really going. After a last look around, especially at the small cluster of dark buildings called Prairie Center, he took a handful of dry grass and held it against the glowing coal of his cigar. It surprised him, how quickly the grass caught. The fire flared and singed his fingers.

Tedvedt dropped the cigar and the smoldering grass. Flame flickered and caught. In moments a thin red line of fire was running away from him across the stubble field. Here and there brief flares of orange light marked clumps of grass that had escaped the flail of the horse-drawn grain binder. One end of the fire line raced toward town and died against the steel railroad tracks. The rest of it sped in fits and starts into the brush and then among the small trees along the little creek. Before long the entire length of the creek from where Tedvedt had squatted with his cigar to where it disappeared into the forest was ablaze. As it passed it charred the earth over Carl Oleason's body, until only an expert tracker could have found the grave.

At the edge of the forest, the fire settled into rotting logs, smoldered and waited.

The fire set by Banker Tedvedt went away from Prairie Center, racing north toward the horizon. The few residents who'd been awakened by the smoke went back to bed for the final hours of sleep before sunrise.

Three days later, clouds of acrid smoke loomed over the landscape as far as one could see. It stung the eyes and throats of the remaining inhabitants. Trains, passing through the tinder-dry countryside, had started dozens of small fires and with the continued dry conditions, those fires had joined in many places across the northern tier of Minnesota counties.

Suddenly much of northern Minnesota was afire. Towering columns of dirty ash and blue smoke rose into the sky. The sun disappeared behind the huge, billowing clouds. Daylight dimmed and a disturbing midday twilight spread over the communities and farms.

A lot of young able-bodied men who should have been available to fight the fires were in Europe, fighting the Hun. Towns and farms north of Prairie Center had already been burned out, it was said. Clouqet had been destroyed, they said. Multiple blazes were eating into the outskirts of Duluth, it was rumored. Tales of harrowing escapes and worse filtered into Prairie Center from panicked refugees fleeing south, some barely able to stay ahead of the monster. Some wouldn't make it.

Trees exploded, one after another when superheated sap burst the trunks into flaming shreds. They sounded like cannon shots over the constant roar of the fire, each explosion closer to town, marching south through the grove.

Small ponds and drying bogs turned to steam in moments. Earth dried and cracked and small animals were seared to death where they paused.

Inexorable. Unstoppable.

Hot greedy death stalked the land.

"Mandy! Mandy, for God's sake! Forget the damn furniture. Get into the wagon. Go south along the road to Big Lake. If the fire overtakes you, try to get into the lake. Or that swamp."

"Byron, come too. Please. The fire's too close to town." Samantha Tedvedt was a tall patrician woman with long auburn hair she normally wore coiled in an elaborate rope high on her head. Today the coil was loose and untidy. The banker's wife commanded respect in Prairie Center and the surrounding towns where her husband had banking interests. She had few women friends, none close. Samantha Tedvedt could deal with any social situation, face even the hatred from a farmer's wife recently evicted from her home.

Today she was faced with nothing that would be charmed or would listen to reasoned arguments. Today, she was perilously close to complete destruction.

Their hired hand, a young tough from the streets of Chicago, jittered beside the loaded wagon and watched the approaching fire with terror on his face. He'd heard the stories about the great Chicago fire from his parents not that many years before. It was the one thing he knew he couldn't best in a contest of strength or skill or cunning.

"No, Mandy. Looks like everything will burn but there's still enough time." Her husband sawed at the reins of his prancing horse, turned the nervous animal north, toward Prairie Center and the ravening monster. "Go! Go. I'll find you," he called and rode off into the thickening haze toward town half a mile away, toward the fire. *We'll need this money,* he thought, *if the fire destroys everything.* Riding into the thickening smoke he realized that the fire brought one blessing. No one would ever be able to question his handling of bank accounts and records. Hell, there wouldn't be any records. He spurred his reluctant mount north.

As her husband disappeared in the pall of smoke, Samantha said, "Quick, Jerome. Get up there. We'll leave the rest." Samantha Tedvedt scrambled onto the seat of the wagon. With sure fingers, she gathered the reins and flicked the horse's rump with one end of the leather. Jerry Owens reached down and released the brake and they rattled out of the yard, heading south.

Samantha knew all about the stake her husband was after. It had been she, in fact, who goaded her nervous husband to continue and expand his skimming operations, taking a little here and a little there. When it became clear to Byron there was slim chance of being discovered, it was Samantha who reined him in, insisted he keep the amounts small so there'd be even less chance of discovery. Patience, she had counseled. There was plenty of time.

Samantha didn't know her husband had become a murderer.

Tedvedt banged his heels on the reluctant horse's ribs and slashed the animal's rump with his reins. He watched the fire anxiously while he galloped closer, dodging fleeing survivors. Finally he turned off the road to avoid the thickening traffic and raced across a field.

Smoke limited his vision. He had to reach two hiding holes. *Would there be time?* he wondered. The larger stash was west of town in the field behind the bank; a heavy iron box with papers and cash buried deep in a hole along the creek. A creek no longer even damp.

Buried near the body of Carl Oleason.

Tedvedt glanced at the sky. It looked as if the town was doomed. He'd better get to that box along the creek first. Then he'd try for the back room of the bank. If the fire outraced him to that stash, he'd still have plenty of money. They'd start over. He and Samantha. Help rebuild the town. For part ownership, of course.

Somebody's got to pay for this, he thought grimly, flogging the now terrified horse. These fires are the result of somebody's carelessness. *I'll sue somebody.*

When he reached the creek and stopped just above the place he'd hidden the money, Tedvedt was careful to tie his horse securely. It spelled disaster to be left afoot today.

The fire advanced, roaring its choking song, sending sparks in great arcing showers into the sky. Ash and dust fell more thickly around him as Tedvedt shoveled dry earth aside as fast as he could. His concentration was intense.

Near the Great Northern tracks that ran through Prairie Center and on up to Superior, one line of the fire had raced beyond the town and reached the creek bank where it hardly hesitated, then leaped across, catching in the bushes on the south side. The heat was fast becoming intolerable. The wind rose, tearing Tedvedt's hat off and clutching insistently at his coat. Smoke roiled across the field and stung his watering eyes. The heat and smoke brought on a coughing spell and he staggered for a few steps. Sweat poured down his cheeks. The noise of the fire increased.

Tedvedt's horse whinnied suddenly and reared as a glowing spark seared its hide. The tree above the banker burst into flame. Glowing twigs and branches rained down, burned his hands, and charred the fabric of his coat. The branch that held his tethered horse caught fire and burned away the reins.

The horse reared again, screaming, and turned away from the fire, its hooves describing flashing arcs in the smoke. Tedvedt raised his head to see the horse and looked straight into the searing heat of a burning branch as it crashed into his face and drove him to the ground.

No one heard his final screams.

Thick and Thin

GARY R. BUSH

EDDY LEBERT WAS GROSSLY FAT. There was nothing glandular about his condition. Eddy was a glutton. In time his breath became shorter, his heart weakened, and he was beginning to show symptoms of diabetes. His arteries were so clogged with fat, they could be spread like butter.

A stomach bypass was discussed. However, the doctors found an anomaly in his system, making the surgery impossible. No reputable surgeon would attempt it. They assured him that with proper diet and exercise, he could lose the weight. If he didn't, they warned, he would surely die—from either heart failure or stroke. He didn't want to die or diet. *There has to be an easier way.*

Eddy read about a doctor in Brazil who claimed to have a new surefire procedure. In correspondence, the Brazilian assured him it was simple and risk free. There was a drawback however—it was expensive.

Eddy needed money to pay for the trip and the operation. He knew how he could get the money. The way he always got money; he'd steal it.

He studied the obits for wealthy widows, then would gain entry to their homes by claiming he was an insurance man paying off a policy. Then, he'd rob and kill them. In truth, Eddy Lebert was a monster.

He needed just one more robbery to get enough money for the trip. After a little research, he found his mark. Mrs. Hilda Cathcart recently lost her husband, a wealthy entrepreneur.

Eddy cased the Cathcart residence and determined the maid had Thursday evening off. At exactly 7 PM the next Thursday, Eddy put on his suit, filled his briefcase with rope and a silk cord, and drove to the Cathcart house. Once he was inside it was easy enough to force the old lady to open the safe, where he found bearer bonds, cash and jewelry. Then he strangled poor Mrs. Cathcart.

As Eddy was leaving, the maid came home early. He overpowered her, raped her, then killed her. By the time he was through, Eddy's breath came in short gasps and his chest ached something fierce. He really needed that Brazilian operation. Now he had the money he needed. *Next stop, Rio,* he thought.

The next afternoon Eddy went to get new passport pictures taken, but his car wouldn't start. Lucky for him a cab drove up and Eddy hailed it. The driver, a good-looking young man with a body Eddy envied, helped him settle his bulk into the backseat.

That's when he saw the brochure on the seat next to him. He read the headline:

GUARANTEED WEIGHT LOSS!

"What the hell?" he said aloud. Then read the rest of the brochure.

GUARANTEED WEIGHT LOSS!

The Galaxy Institute has developed a new medical breakthrough.

This revolutionary new weight loss program

is guaranteed to work quickly without dieting.

If you are not completely satisfied with your weight loss,

Galaxy will not only refund your money, we will double it!

Visit the Institute at 6070 Nestor Street today!

No appointment necessary.

Damn, Eddy thought. *I could save me a trip to Brazil, and perhaps the danger of an operation. With the money I've got, I could go anywhere. But where the hell is Nestor Street?*

"Hey, cabbie. Do you know where 6070 Nestor Street is?"

"Sure. Nestor is in a new development just west of the city," the driver said.

"Take me there," Eddy demanded. The man nodded and in what seemed like no time, pulled up in front of a round steel and glass building.

"Funny," Eddy said, "I don't remember this building being here or even this part of town."

"It is new," the driver replied.

Eddy paid his fare, tipped the driver and entered the well-lit lobby.

The place was empty except for an attractive, no, beautiful, dark-haired woman sitting behind a reception desk. She smiled and asked, "How may I help you, Sir?"

Clutching the brochure in his hand, Eddy stammered, "A-about this weight-loss program."

"Of course, Sir. Would you like to sign up?"

"Well, how much does it cost and how does it work?"

"The cost, sir, is two-thousand dollars. We put your money in an escrow account. If you are not satisfied with the results, we will give you a double refund. As to how it works—well, that's confidential until you sign up. But it works." She stood up; her tight white uniform clung to every voluptuous curve. "I went through a program here and look at me."

Practically drooling, Eddy, asked, "Can I sign up now? I have the money with me."

The woman bent over her computer screen, giving Eddy an eyeful of firm breasts. "You are in luck. Dr. Xanthe has an open schedule. I need you to fill out the paperwork so we can get you started."

He filled out the forms, and turned them in. "Dr. Xanthe will be out in a few minutes," the woman said. "Please have a seat."

Eddy settled in a large chair and thought if he were thin and handsome, women like the receptionist would want him. And after all, what did he have to lose? If he didn't lose the weight he would get four thousand dollars, a bonus to what he had, more than enough for South America and the surgery.

In a moment, the most beautiful blonde-haired woman he had ever seen entered the reception area. Except for her hair, she could have been a twin to the receptionist. There was a certain glow about her. She walked over to him and said, "Hi, I am Dr. Alysia Xanthe. You must be Eddy Lebert."

Eddy struggled to his feet and mumbled, "Hello, Doctor."

"No need for formality here," she replied. "Call me Alysia, and of course I shall call you Eddy."

"Okay, Alysia," Eddy managed to reply. Her beauty stunned him. *Damn,* he thought, *if I can lose weight this is the kind of woman I would want to spend the rest of my life with. No forcing, just great sex.*

Alysia Xanthe smiled and Eddy knew he had to have her, but first things first.

"This way," she said, leading him into a sterile-looking steel and glass room with a large examination table in the center.

A number of gleaming scientific instruments sat next to the table. Eddy had no idea as to what they were for. He didn't care, either. He wanted the weight loss.

Still, he wasn't without caution. "Is this going to hurt?" he asked, a hint of fear in his voice.

"Second thoughts, Eddy?" The doctor smiled. "You will not feel a thing. Here," she said, handing him a gown and pointed him to a dressing room. "Disrobe, slip into this and then get up on the examination table."

Eddy disrobed, looked in the mirror on the dressing room door in disgust, and slipped into the skimpy gown, which did nothing to hide his bulk. Dr. Xanthe lowered the table so Eddy would have no trouble getting on.

"I will be back in a few minutes," she said.

He got on the table and stared at the ceiling, his thoughts ran the gambit from fear to joy. *If only this works.*

There was a knock and Dr. Xanthe entered the room.

"What's the process?" Eddy asked, still a bit nervous.

"I will take some measurements and then we will begin the procedure. You will be in a slight state of suspension but you will be aware of what is going on. You have an unusually large amount of body fat, Eddy," she said, as she ran here instruments over him. "I see an anomaly in your system."

"Is that bad?" he asked, fearful that she couldn't help him.

"Not at all, in fact it is very good. Now, Eddy, I am going to give you an injection so I can start the procedure. I promise you will feel no pain except for a slight prick of the needle." She injected him and asked him to count to ten.

He began to feel a little drowsy as he watched as Dr. Xanthe prepared a pump-like instrument with clear tubes on either end. Then she took a scalpel and made an incision near his belly. There was no pain.

The doctor inserted one end of the tube into the incision, the other into a clear tank. The pump began to hum and he could see the yellow fat leaving his body. While this was going on, machines in the table were doing things to Eddy's body.

An hour later, Dr. Xanthe smiled down at Eddy, removed the apparatus and waved a small instrument over the incision. It healed immediately.

In a few minutes, Eddy regained feelings. "What just happened?"

Dr. Xanthe licked her lips and smiled, then led him to the full-length mirror. The reflection he saw back was of a well-muscled svelte, young man.

"Do you like it?" she asked. "Are you satisfied?"

"Yes, I-I am."

"Good. Now Eddy, you must lie down again. There is still a recovery process."

"But I feel fine. In fact, I feel great! I really have to go." He was ready to show off his new body.

"That is not possible, Eddy, you need to stay." She nodded and Eddy Lebert was grabbed from behind and felt a sharp pinch.

When he awoke he was back on the table, strapped down and once again, tubes were inserted into his body. Dr. Xanthe stood over him. She was flanked by the beautiful receptionist and to his surprise, the cab driver who brought him to the clinic.

"What the hell's going on here? Let me go."

"Calm down," Dr. Xanthe said. "I will explain. You see, Eddy, we are not from this planet. Our world is far from here. We live on fat, human fat. This is among the most obese planets in the Galaxy—or at least your country is. So we set up shop here. You are not the first we have offered our treatment, but I must say you are the best. The anomaly in your system makes your essence extremely delicious."

"Yeah, if you live on fat, how come you aren't fat? Eddy demanded.

"Please, Eddy, we are not gluttons. Your fat will sustain us for the next six months."

"Then what, you find another sucker?"

"Eventually. Now, however, you are too thin for my tastes, pardon the pun. Eddy, we are going to fatten you up again. With the nutrients we feed you, you will become obese in another month and then we can feast again!

"We can do this for three years. Then, poor Eddy, you will expire. In your thoughts you said you wanted to spend the rest of your life with me. So dear man, you shall. I will be your woman until you die. But now, we must repair to dinner . . . please try to keep the noise down." She flipped the switch, and as the nutrients began to enter his body, the cabbie and receptionist wheeled the vat of Eddy's essence toward the door. Eddy never heard them leave; he was too busy screaming.

Sweet Spring Revenge

JESSIE CHANDLER

WELCOME TO SPRING in Minnesota.

I shivered as I stood in the parking lot of Jimmy Johnson's Best Pre-Owned Vehicles. Frozen flakes floated from the heavens. The forecast called for snowfall of over an inch an hour, along with winds that would freeze your nostril hairs together and rip the breath from your lungs. The storm wasn't supposed to let up until sometime the next day, after dumping fifteen to twenty inches of the white crap over the land of the North Star.

My breath came out in foggy puffs, and I tried to keep my eyes diverted from the plentiful butt crack exposed by ill-fitting polyester pants of the man bent over in front of me. Jimmy's head was buried once again in the engine of the purple '98 Geo Metro he'd sold me back in August.

I'd been laid off for over a year, and I now worked three pizza delivery jobs to make ends meet. If I hadn't been in desperate straits at the time for cheap but reliable wheels, I'd never have coughed up the dough for the Metro or the warranty I couldn't believe Jimmy offered, even if I had to pay some big bucks for it.

Jimmy, the lecherous shyster he was, had to be sorry he'd suckered me into his "JJ's Best Used Vehicle Warranty." He thought he was getting over on his customers by charging a bundle for a warranty he gambled would-n't get used often. Then I came along. Too bad I didn't know Jimmy was a one-man-freak-show and official perv when I signed my name on the Xeroxed line.

It all started with over-heating issues. Jimmy's solution: drive with the heater on in 90-degree late-summer heat. Then the tire on the passenger side sprung a leak. I told Jimmy he shouldn't have listed tires as a covered item on the warranty if he didn't want to fix it. He begrudgingly swapped the leaker with a nearly bald replacement. On the bright side, the tire didn't lose air any more. It would probably just explode when I was going seventy on the interstate.

Then the alternator went out. It took him two weeks to install the new one. When I finally picked the car up, he had an angry red welt on the back of his bald head and a black eye. I had to stifle hysteria when he told me the hydraulics gave out and the hood fell on his head. I didn't feel sorry for him. He deserved that and more. Last time I'd been in the office with him, he'd pinned me against the wall and mashed his filthy mouth against mine while grunting like a pig. I'm pretty sure he'd have tried to do a whole lot more if another customer hadn't walked in just then.

This was the fourteenth trip to the dealership for one issue or another. It was already dark when I'd arrived with the Metro sputtering mysteriously and losing power at highway speed. Bad news in this weather.

I pulled my black and red Mama Maria's Pizza delivery jacket tighter and stepped back, far enough, I hoped, to avoid the grope that by now I was certain was coming. I wanted to sue the creep for sexual harassment, but working three jobs took every ounce of willpower and determination I had. I could hardly find time to sleep, much less figure out a way to pay a lawyer and sue someone.

Jimmy backed away from the car and removed the metal rod propping the hood up. It slammed shut with a hollow thud. "Can't find anything that might be causing the trouble. You'll be fine."

"You said that last time."

"Honey, honey," he said as he jittered over and threw an arm around my neck before I could sidestep away. "You just trust old Jimmy here." He was a good six inches taller than I was, and practically had me in a headlock. I tried to pull away, but he held tight. The smell of pot and body odor clung to his jacket, filled my nose. My eyes watered as I tried to wiggle from his grasp.

His other hand shot toward me at chest level like a heat-seeking missile. He managed to hit his target and squeeze. I yowled and twisted, tried to knee him in the jewels but caught his thigh instead. Damn.

I wrenched myself from his grasp. "You're a disgusting bastard, Jimmy Johnson. And take a damn bath."

Jimmy chuckled, the sound as sinister as his leer. "You little wildcat." He swung his hips Elvis-style and massaged his crotch. "It's just a matter of time before I get you where I want you. You know you need it. And I'll give it to you good." He chuckled ominously with an unfocused look in his sex-crazed eyes.

I backed up, more than a little alarmed. "Get away from me, Jimmy. You're sick."

He actually reached down and unzipped his pants. "You know you want some Mr. Happy."

Over my dead body, I thought. *Or yours.*

I blinked at that. In the space of that blink, I must have completely lost my mind.

A stranger took over my brain, one that conned Jimmy into following me home. I told him I was afraid the car might break down in the now near-blizzard conditions, and he wouldn't want my frozen body on his conscience.

We pulled out of the car lot. I squinted at Jimmy's annoying blue-white headlights in the rear view mirror. Snow drifted in random patterns in the headlights, and the tires sliced through at least four inches of heavy slop. Visibility was terrible.

As I carefully drove, my new alter ego plotted. My ex was a *Cops* junkie. One episode featured police utilizing a PIT—Pursuit Intervention Technique—on fleeing cars to stop them by spinning them out of control, much like the bump and run in NASCAR. It looked easy enough.

I white-knuckled the steering wheel as we crossed the Mississippi River on Interstate 610. There wasn't another car in sight.

It was only a quarter mile to Jimmy's fate now. The objective, the ramp connecting one interstate to another, was just ahead. The land the ramp circled slanted sharply down to a deep drainage pond. Every time I navigated that curve in bad weather, I imagined how easy it would be for someone to go over the side and disappear into the deep, muddy water below.

I slowed to a crawl and exited. Jimmy impatiently rode my tail. There was hardly room for a toothpick between my bumper and his. You'd think he'd be a little more careful, especially in this weather.

My tires bumped along the inside edge of the lane. I cranked my window down, praying I wouldn't lose control, and waved Jimmy around me.

My breath whistled rapidly. As Jimmy's rear door passed, I hit the accelerator. My tires spun wildly. The engine roared. For a second, I didn't think I'd gain traction. Then the tires grabbed hold and the little Metro shot forward.

Jimmy stepped on his own gas pedal a little too enthusiastically and fishtailed. What happened next occurred in slow motion. My left front bumper kissed his right rear quarter panel with a satisfying crunch. His car slid further out of control as the Metro pushed it in a near circle, right toward the abyss. I kept the accelerator mashed to the floor. The engine screamed. I might have been screaming too.

I met Jimmy's gaze as the car swung around. The leer was gone. His eyes were wide, in shock or fear. Yeah, fear sounded good. I ripped one fist loose and gave him the finger as our cars parted.

The Metro shot toward the opposite side of the ramp. I took my foot off the accelerator and feathered the steering wheel. As the Metro was about to shoot off the ramp, the tires caught and I slammed on the brakes. The car did a 180, and came to sliding stop facing the wrong direction. My arms quaked and my legs were rubber. My heart nearly pounded right through my ribs.

The snow was so thick I could hardly see ten feet ahead. I cautiously turned the car around, and parked on the right side of the ramp. I crawled out on wobbly legs and slogged through the snow to the edge. Jimmy's car was gone.

"Hasta la vista, asshole," I yelled. Then I drove home.

Two days later, after nearly collapsing every time the phone rang, I saw a short article in the Twin Cities Tribune. It said the police and FBI had raided Jimmy's used car lot the day after the snowstorm of the century dumped twenty-two inches on the Metro. They carried away file boxes, computers, and other records. There were allegations against Jimmy for federal tax evasion as well as swindling customers and numerous sexual harassment complaints. They speculated Jimmy had been tipped off and skipped town.

I didn't know if I helped Jimmy escape or if I killed him. In my heart of hearts, I'm pretty sure it was the latter. Not long after the night I lost my mind, I sold the Metro to a shady dealer in North Minneapolis. I quit my three jobs and moved to Tuba City, Arizona. Now I deliver hoagies on a Vespa and wait either for a settlement to come from the harassment lawsuit against Jimmy Johnson's estate, or for the cops to show up and arrest me for murder. Whichever way it turns out, it was worth those fifteen minutes of snowy springtime revenge.

Banned in Grand Rapids

PAT DENNIS

WHO WOULD HAVE THOUGHT a book of hotdish stories would be banned?

The initial book reviews for *Hotdish To Die For* were something to brag about, starting with the review in the Minnesota Women's Press–"wickedly wonderful" to Armchair Interviews' comments—"Her quirky characters and twists of plot are very funny, the kind of story you tell people and they say, 'Sounds like Aunt Mary'."

The collection of six culinary short stories and eighteen hotdish recipes has sold nearly 20,000 copies, not bad for a self-published tome complete with typos and a recipe that leaves the cook going "huh?" when discovering an extra can of cream of mushroom soup left unopened on the counter.

I believe the book's success is its element of surprise. *Hotdish To Die For* is not what most readers expect, filled with typical Ole and Lena tales. It's more like Ole and Norman Bates. The consistent reaction of "ah, this book is so not what I expected" has had its benefits but it also created a few drawbacks. Like being banned in Grand Rapids, Minnesota.

It was late spring when my husband and I decided to vacation in Winnipeg. He would bicycle to Canada and I would drive to meet him. Along the way, I would hawk my book *Hotdish to Die For* at bookstores and gift shops. At the time, it sounded like a great idea. By the time I left the Twin Cities metro area, my salesman's pitch, and hopefully my buyer's response, was perfected. It would go something like this . . .

"Hi, my name is Pat Dennis. I am the author of *Hotdish to Die For*, a collection of murder mysteries where the weapon of choice is hotdish. And there are 18 hotdish recipes and . . ."

"Hotdish? Did you say hotdish? We'll take a dozen."

The actual sales were almost that easy, especially in Grand Rapids, birthplace of Judy Garland and home to one of the finest commercial rifle shooting centers in the nation. The first establishment I visited in the town was a-never-to-be-named-yuppie-gift shop. My second destination was the gift shop of the Itasca County Historical Society.

When I walked into *Never-To-Be-Named*, I immediately noticed all the really neat things I could never, ever afford. Clothing with words like Patagonia embroidered on the front jumped out at me. Sports equipment, often with price tags marked over a thousand dollars, glistened nearby. There were shiny mountain bicycles, handcrafted birch bark canoes, and high-tech walking sticks. Aisles of shoes, hiking boots, and socks made from virgin llama yarn sat next to hundreds of Native American artifacts, most of them made in China.

It was the sort of outdoorsy and back-to-nature stuff that only those that worked full time—plus most weekends—could afford. The inventory's sole purpose was to lure money away from wealthy tourists. And nothing goes *ka-ching* quicker in Minnesota than a product connected to hotdish.

As I held up my book to show the manager, she gushed, "We'll take a dozen." She quickly pulled out a checkbook. I handed over a dozen books, mumbled thanks and hit the streets, humbled by what had just happened. My next stop was just as easy. The folks at the Itasca County Historical Society chuckled at the book's concept and bought a dozen or so books. I thanked them and left smiling. I started to envision both wealth and a mega-shopping spree at Target.

Yessiree-bob, as soon I came back from our Canadian vacation, it would be the life of Willie Loman for me. I had become not only a comedian/writer, but also a successful saleswoman. Move over Jehovah Witnesses, I'm going to conquer the world, door-by-door.

Or so I thought before I checked my home voice mail that afternoon from my Canadian hotel room. There were three, separate messages from the folks at *Never-To-Be-Named*. Each one of them left the same, upsetting words. "How dare you sell us this book? *We would never carry this kind of book in our store! We want our money back right now!*"

My heart sank as I listened. Not only did *Never-To-Be Named* hate my book, they wanted their money back immediately, an impossible task for me to do. I was, after all, in another country.

To be honest, the fact that I had bragged about my book in order to sell it in the first place was akin to my being involved in a scam of gigantic criminal proportions. Underneath my padded amour of self-assurance and diva personality, is a rock solid foundation of shame, self-loathing, and lower than low self-esteem. I understood completely that if the folks in Judy's hometown hated it, there had to be a reason. And the word I thought of immediately was *bad*, as in bad writing, bad concept, bad human being—bad me.

Visions of the intellectual elite of Grand Rapidonians filled my brain. The Gore Vidal Petersons and Susan Sontag Nordlands of the north lit their cigars, popped open their cans of Grain Belt beer, and hungrily dissected the scribblings of Pat Dennis. All of them came to the same conclusion—*Hotdish To Die For* was a horrible piece of self-published trash.

I did not call *Never-To-Be-Named* back that day, or return any of their messages. I couldn't. I was too ashamed. Surely their vehement rejection had to do with the quality of my writing. After twenty years of therapy, any rejection of my writing is still a rejection of who I really am. But, I knew I would call them as soon as I returned home. If my church-going mom succeeded at anything, it was to rear a guilt-ridden, shamed-based, good girl.

Seven days later, I strolled into my little house, barely refreshed from what was to be a vacation. After a few hours of mumbling to myself, I gathered the nerve to telephone *Never-To-Be-Named*. Winter must have arrived four months early in northern Minnesota because the phone lines frosted over as soon I introduced myself. I politely informed the shop manager that the store could have their money back as soon as I received the books back. The woman agreed to send them to me and hung up the phone abruptly.

It took a few days for the package to arrive at my house. I instantly opened the box, fearing that the books were shredded and used as packing material. But I found the books intact, sitting perfectly inside. I also discovered the reason why *Never-To-Be-Named* hated *Hotdish to Die For*. Even I could read between the lines.

Their handwritten note stated, "We have read your book, now read ours." Enclosed was a bible.

Praise be to Jesus! They didn't hate my writing after all! Well, they did, but not in the way I thought they did. I quickly assumed *Never-To-Be-Named* had determined I was as evil as my protagonists or plotlines. The stories in the book contained not only swear words but the tales themselves gave very little hope for mankind. Wives killed husbands in my stories and I suggested that was often a good thing. Women lusted after ministers during church services while close friends longed for another close friend's death. And most Minnesotan of all, adult children wanted to kill their aging parents for the best reason of all—inheriting the lake cabin.

Surely if I, the author, could think of such things, I could probably just as easily do such things. Or so they must have thought.

Never-To-Be-Named didn't hate my writing! They only hated "the sin," and of course, "the sinner," but not the book itself.

Woo hoo! I didn't even mind the fact that receiving a Bible was sort of offensive. First of all, I already own a Bible, though I haven't read it in twenty years. Until I received their biblical reminder that I was not a Christian, I considered myself to be one, in my own self-defined way. I mean, who wouldn't want to be Christ-like? But then I would also love to be Buddha-like, and like a few of the other deities that keep hanging around. It's too bad their generous gift was wasted. I've already read the entire Bible and feel no compelling need to ever read it again. However, if there's ever a Holy Bible, the Sequel, sign-me up.

Still, that morning, I was joyfully delirious my writing wasn't rejected for the reason I thought it had been. My book and I were discounted by *Never-To-Be-Named* because they assumed I was going straight to Hell, via Winnipeg.

My bliss continued, unabated for at least fifteen minutes, until I noticed the light blinking once again on my answering machine. I recognized the caller ID. My heart sank as I listened to the recording and heard the words, "This is the gift shop at the Itasca County Historical Society. Would you call us as soon as possible."

Oh no! Not the historical society, too!

How could a small, self-published book about hotdish turn into Minnesota's *Farenheit 451*?

Doesn't anyone in the Northland have a sense of humor? I wondered. Feeling completely rejected and with great hesitation, I returned the museum's call. The conversation went something like this:

"Good morning, my name is Pat Dennis and I . . .

"Pat Dennis?" The museum worker interrupted quickly. "You're the author of *Hotdish To Die For*?"

"Yes," I admitted shamefully.

The woman rushed out her next words. "We don't know why, but there has been a run on your books. Can you ship us more immediately?"

Ah, life is good. And at times, so is hotdish.

Nature Takes its Course

SEAN DOOLITTLE

T HE VET WANTED NINETY-FOUR DOLLARS to put my daughter's cat Buddy down. Emergency service, he said, being a Sunday afternoon. I could hear the Vikings-Jets game in the background when I hung up the phone.

"Maybe it's best to let nature take its course," I said, and right away I wished I'd kept quiet. Nora immediately started sobbing, telling me to see how sick Buddy looked. I could feel Tina behind me, listening.

The cat looked sick all right. It had something wrong in its blood and had already beat the odds, living as long as it had. Now the poor damned thing had curled up in the towel closet, eyes all gummy, too weak to lift its head. When I glanced at Tina, standing in the hall with her arms folded, I could read the dark warning in her eyes: *You'd better do this right*

I pulled Nora close. She mashed her wet cheek into my leg. I could feel her small shoulders heaving under my hand.

By the time I had my coat she'd already made arrangements in her head. She wanted us to bury the cat in the little patch of woods on the vacant lot behind our apartment building.

I rubbed her back and told her I didn't think the vet would probably let me bring Buddy home, but Tina said, "Sure they will." She knelt down beside the laundry basket I was to use as a carrier and brushed away Nora's tears. "They'll put Buddy in a nice box with some padding and a lid, almost just like Great Grandpa Melvin. Do you remember?"

I wondered how Tina knew all that. Then I saw some old hurt in her eyes and didn't need to ask. I couldn't help thinking that the lot out back was private property, but I didn't mention that, either. I didn't mention any number of things. Tina stood up and touched my arm; it was the first time in awhile she'd touched me so tenderly.

"Okay, Buddy," I said. "Here we go."

Nora made sure he was tucked in and told him goodbye. Then she ran down the hall to her bedroom, crying again. She sounded like a pint-sized ambulance driving away.

Tina sighed and gave a weary smile. She kissed her fingertips and pressed them to my cheek. Then she followed our little girl down the hall.

I carried the cat out to the parking lot in the laundry basket. It was cold for September. The sky looked like steel plate. I put the basket in the passenger seat of my truck and got in behind the wheel. I still didn't have ninety-four dollars.

My brother Ward lives on five acres north of town. I drove up to his place and asked if I could borrow a hundred bucks—ninety-four for the vet, six for the gas to get me home again.

"You out of work?" he asked.

I told him I was working. He asked when I got paid. I told him I'd gotten paid at the job site Friday afternoon. Played poker Friday night.

He nodded slowly. "Guess you haven't told the wife that part yet."

"I was hoping to avoid it."

Ward didn't ask how I planned to do that when the rent came due. Or the next time Tina needed to go to the store. He only shrugged and said, "Why not borrow the .22? Cost you like four cents for the cartridge. Cat won't know the difference."

"I don't think Tina would go for that."

"Tina wouldn't know the difference, either."

I told him that wasn't the point. He agreed with me.

In the end, he carried the laundry basket from my truck around the side of the shed, where his own kids couldn't look out the windows from the house and see. I carried the little single-shot Winchester he kept on pegs in the shed.

The cat watched me over the top of the sight post at the end of the barrel. I couldn't shake the look I'd seen in Tina's eyes when she'd touched me on the arm. For a moment, I almost lowered the rifle and told my brother it was no good. But then I thought of the way he'd looked at me when I showed up asking for money again.

I squeezed my finger. The shot made a high sharp crack in the cold, ringing away over the cottonwoods. The cat flopped on the ground and then laid there, a dull gray rag at my feet.

Ward said, "Guess that does it."

I closed my eyes and said yeah.

I used my last two dollars, and all the spare change I could dig out of the truck, to buy a plain white cardboard filing box from the office-supply store on my way home.

By the time I got back, Tina had called the owner of the vacant lot for permission to use his ground, and Nora had written a poem called "I Love You Buddy" on a piece of fuzzy-edged school paper.

We stood in the trees around the hole I'd dug while Nora read her poem aloud, and for a little while we felt like a pretty good family. It seemed like everything would be all right.

Then Nora said, "Can I see him?"

And the bottom fell out of me. How had I failed to imagine this?

Because I didn't know a thing about a seven-year-old girl, that was how. Not even my own.

"Oh, kiddo," I said. "I don't know."

Tina misunderstood my panic and took Nora's hands. "Of course you can," she said. "If you're sure you're not scared."

Nora looked at the box beside the hole.

I jumped into the silence. "Maybe that's not such a good idea."

Nora looked at Tina.

Tina looked at me. "I think it's okay." She looked back at Nora. "What do you think?"

"Maybe Buddy would want us to remember him the way he was before." I could feel my dumb heart pounding.

Tina pulled me aside and spoke in a whisper. "What are you doing?"

"I don't know. I just think. . . ."

"This is important."

"I know it is. But wait. . . ."

"You said you wanted a second chance with us." I felt her grip leave my elbow.

Looking back, I should have told her everything then. About screwing up again, after all my promises. About what I'd done. I could have begged her to see that we'd grown up on a farm, me and my brother, where you didn't pay some chiseling vet ninety-four dollars to put a poor dying cat out of its misery. I could have insisted Buddy had something wrong in his blood.

But then Nora screamed, and I couldn't say anything. She'd gotten down on her knees and lifted the lid of the box while her mother and I had been arguing, and all I could do was stand there, alone, watching sorrow turn to horror at the godawful mess I'd made.

Hanging Luce

JAN DUNLAP

WHAT DO YOU DO when the woman you love turns out to be a killer?

It was Saturday morning, but I'd gotten up early out of pity for the little flock of redpolls sitting in the bare trees just beyond my back deck. My bird feeders were empty, so I dragged myself out of bed just after sunrise to feed the birds. Despite the mounds of mushy snow on my deck, I could feel the first touch of tentative spring in the air, which means I could inhale fresh air that didn't instantly coat my lungs with ice.

Yes sir, Bob White, I told myself, *spring is just around the corner.* And for a birder like me, that means just one thing: spring migration. I could almost feel the excitement of a new birding season beginning to build up inside me, sort of like the sap I imagined beginning to rise in the maples in my back yard.

Could I be any more of a nature nerd if I tried?

Thankfully, my cell phone chirped in my pocket, bringing me back to the more mundane reality of late March in Minnesota, which is that my naked toes were turning blue on my snow-crusted deck. I hopped back inside my townhome and pulled out the phone.

"I need you to come over right now," my fiancé Luce breathed into the phone.

All right! I thought, mentally pumping my fist. I couldn't think of a better way to wait for spring than a little snuggling under the blankets on a frosty morning.

"On my way," I told her, grabbing a jacket and my car keys. I stepped into the garage and froze. Literally. I'd forgotten about the bare toes. I grabbed the boots I keep beside the door.

". . . and I don't know what to do," Luce was saying. I suddenly realized she was sniffing, just like I realized I'd missed the first part of the sentence in my rush to get my boots on.

"About what?"

"The body," she said, definitely crying.

"What?"

"Are you not listening to me?" Luce's voice rose, a note of uncharacteristic hysteria in her tone. "I said the body on my deck. I don't know what to do with it."

A body on her deck.

"A dead body?" Call me stupid, but I just thought it might help to be really specific here.

Luce sighed into the phone. I could hear the tears in her voice. "Yes, Bobby, a dead body."

"Are you all right?" I demanded, tearing out of my driveway. My desire for snuggling had instantly morphed into all-consuming protectiveness. I may be a sensitive high school counselor when it comes to dealing with teenage drama queens, but when it comes to my fiancé, I can be a real caveman. Me, warrior; Luce, gourmet chef.

Even cavemen appreciate a tenderloin beef roast with cognac and peppercorn glaze now and then.

Luce sniffed. "I'm fine. I'm just really upset. I need you!"

My heart was breaking for her. I couldn't imagine how hard this had to be on her, to be alone with a body on her deck. "I'll be there in ten, sweetheart. Call the police."

"I can't do that," she whispered. "It's my fault."

"What do you mean?" I flew up the ramp to the highway.

"I killed him, Bobby."

I pulled the phone away from my ear and stared at it. "WHAT?"

"I want you to help me get rid of it," she said, pleading.

Holy crap. My fiancé wanted me to be an accessory to a crime. If this is what I got for being the early bird, I was giving it up. The redpolls could starve from now on.

"I'll be there in five," I told her and hung up.

The rest of the way to Luce's I spent in deep thought. Did I really know this woman I was going to marry? Did I want to spend the rest of my life with an executive chef who was proficient in the use of very sharp knives? Would I be watching my back for the rest of my life when we went birding together?

Apparently not.

I wasn't sure.

Probably.

I pulled into Luce's driveway and jumped out of the car. Not sure I could face her, I went around the house to the deck out back, and stopped in my snowy tracks.

She was right. There was a body on her deck. Although, technically, she was wrong. The body wasn't *on* her deck—it was hanging *above* the deck, its neck clearly broken.

I reached out and carefully lifted the body up from the deadly trap formed by the two swinging arms of Luce's birdfeeder. The little redpoll lay motionless in my hand, its delicate bones just a whisper of weight in my palm.

"I feel so awful," Luce, beside me, sniffed. "The poor thing was just trying to get a meal, and it slipped between the arms. I couldn't bare to touch it hanging there."

She turned her beautiful blue eyes to mine. "Thank you."

I walked over to a patch of wet earth beside the house and using the heel of my boot, scraped up a tiny grave. After I laid the redpoll in it, I pushed the dirt back over it, then walked back to where Luce was shivering on her deck.

I took her hands in mine and led her into the house, where I wrapped my arms around her. "Cold hands, but a warm heart, Luce," I told her. "Next time, tell me it's a bird first. I was pushing eighty all the way here."

"Eighty?" she said. "Are you crazy?"

"Only about you."

I kissed her, instantly deciding I was in no rush for spring migration this year. Now if I could only remember where Luce kept those blankets . . .

Another You

CHRIS EVERHEART

"**O**H, MY GOD! I just can't believe there's another you out there!" Selly's voice is as clear as fiber optic on her cell phone. She gets a new one every three months. Her mom and dad can't stand being behind the curve. "Do you think she's, like, your long-lost twin or something?"

I look at the photos she sent me. I feel cold. I want to throw up. I want to run away from Selly, but I'm alone here in my bedroom. She's two miles away. "I, uh . . ." I can't answer, can't talk.

Selly fills in the blank. "You should totally call that number and tell them that you're her and you want to cash in on the reward for finding yourself! God knows you need the money." She's always reminding me how poor I am. "And the picture's close enough."

She laughs. I stare.

I know the picture labeled "Last Known Photo"—an eleven-year-old girl with brown eyes and thick bangs who hasn't grown into her teeth yet. I hate her. I want to smash her face, punch right through the screen and tear her eyes out.

The photo on the right, labeled "Age Progression," looks fakey and blurry, like the face of a burn victim after a bunch of plastic surgery. Almost right. Nearly real. But not quite. Selly's right, though—it's close enough.

"Selly, did you show this to anyone else?"

"I *just* found it. Stupid Social Studies project. Missing kids," she sneers. "I mean, *who cares*, right? But this is *too good!* I'm gonna post it in my gallery next to your junior yearbook photo. Survey will definitely say 'Separated at birth.'" She makes the "secret" giggle, the one she gets when she knows something no one else does—halfway between a sheep and a parakeet.

"Oh, please don't," I say. "I don't want a bunch of people seeing this. It'll be all over the place. No one will shut up about it."

Long silence. "Fine," she sighs. "But you *owe* me."

She hangs up and I sit frozen. All I can hear now is my heart pounding. The blood rushes through my ears and the swirling makes the sound of my name—*Tabitha . . . Tabitha . . .*

"Bethany!" It's coming from outside my door, down the hall—Mom.

I don't want to leave the computer. I suddenly have so much work to do. Four years after I erased the last thread . . . I thought I was in the clear. Now *this* shows up. Someone is still looking for me.

Calm down. Deep breath. You can do this.

I try to calculate, but my head is spinning. How long will it take to hack into the Lost Children Coalition's database? Will I be able to find the source of the posting? Will it give me a name? Some great aunt or second cousin with a blood-tie cause, campaigning for a spot on Maury Povich. Parents murdered, twelve-year-old missing, presumed sold into the sex trade. But they don't *know*. They make up the worst stories to keep hope alive and get people on their side. Why won't they just leave it alone already?

"Bethany, supper's ready!" Louder.

I hold my fingers over the keyboard. I have to get it done now.

But if I don't answer, Mom will start flaking out. I can't afford another scene like the last one. I leave for a Saturday sleepover and she "forgets" to take her meds. Shows up at the school office Monday morning telling everyone that I'm not her daughter, that her real baby was stillborn.

And I don't have time to find another home—months of emails and photos and "long-lost baby girl" letters . . .

Stanford next year, full academic scholarship, Computer Science. Not enough girls in that field. I can write my ticket. Everyone says so. Just five more months . . . Hold it together.

"Bethany!" More frantic now.

"Coming! I'll be right there." I listen. No response. That's good. Keep her calm. Keep everyone calm.

And then there's Selly. Can I trust her? Did she really *just* find this? How long can she keep her mouth shut with something this humiliating? How long before it's in her gallery and on every cell phone in the school?

I stare at the corkboard above my desk, at the honor roll certificates, at the acceptance letters, at the digital printout photo of me and Selly, real heads with the same hairstyle, with cartoon bodies hugging. The caption in the rainbow above reads "A friend is" and below in the fluffy white cloud "ANOTHER YOU!"

I feel a soft rumble deep inside. I haven't felt it in a long time. It's scary. I should fight it, control it, talk it back to where it's been sleeping. But it's too late. And, anyway, I don't want it to go back.

The pressure grows. From a dormant seed way down in my gut it expands and fills my shape, pressing against the boundaries of my body and my mind. I recognize her. She pushes the fear right out of me. I feel bigger, stronger. She replaces my thoughts with her thoughts. Her voice sounds just like mine, her ideas bubble up inside my brain and every one is soothing.

She's thinking for me now, fearlessly. I let go, let her take control. She already knows what she wants. She only asks one thing: *How long will it take us to get to Selly's house?*

Spring Fever

BARBARA FISTER

To LOOK AT ME, you'd think "what would *she* know about anything?" I'm short, I'm fat, and hell, you work outdoors in this climate—might as well get used to it; every day is a bad hair day. I'm not getting a whole lot of sleep lately, either, being a grandma who did such a great job the first time around that I get to do it all over again, which is why I got Cheerios all over the back seat of my car and formula stains on my shirt. So yeah, what would a person like me know?

You'd be surprised.

Like, the lady living on the corner? Her own kids got no idea how senile she's getting. Maybe if they visited once in a while they'd figure it out. Going to be pissed off when they find out there's nothing left for them, that all her money's going to those outfits that send you pictures of starving kids so they can sneak into your pocket while you're wiping your eyes. Some database for five-star suckers got her name in it. She gets more of that shit every day. I tell her it's junk mail, that somebody's getting rich on it, but she sees those faces with the big eyes and gets a worried look on her face.

The neighbors next door, the ones so proud when their kid got a scholarship to a fancy college out east? He's laying on the couch, watching TV all day with the blinds pulled down. Flunked out in his first semester and now he won't go out the door, afraid to meet his friends, the ones too stupid to get into college, ones that weren't going to amount to anything.

Across the way, there's a nice-looking house with a new all-weather porch. Might get it cheap when it goes up for auction, which is going to happen any day now. Man dresses sharp, carries a briefcase around, calls himself a consultant, but he lost his job two years ago, couple of months before he lost his fancy cars and his girlfriend. Used to grab that mail from me, until he figured out all those skinny envelopes were reject letters. Never liked him anyway.

That woman next door, though, she got a new man, and he's a keeper. Shoveled the front walk all winter, repaired the front steps, helps out with the kids. Saw him with the youngest, that wound-up little speed freak, shooting baskets for hours yesterday. Got a nice smile, too. She don't want him, I'll give him a place to stay.

Pick any house on my route, and I know what's going on inside. Not 'cause I stand around gossiping; no time for that shit. The boss keeps saying "work faster" and since I do my job right, he just gave me six more blocks to cover. Asshole. I try not to let it get to me. Life's too short. Just six more blocks full of stories, way I see it.

Like this morning. Come around the corner onto LeMoyne and see the street full of cop cars, lights flashing, that crime scene tape like on TV. Hotshot detective strutting around in a nice leather jacket, pushing it back with his hand on his hip making sure everybody sees what he's wearing there, like he's saying "see? Mine's bigger than yours."

Everybody out enjoying the weather, watching the show. Happens every spring. First nice warm day, people go after each other.

When I handed the mail to Mrs. Percy at 3366, she couldn't wait to tell me. "That Byron DeWeese finally got hisself killed last night."

"Heard on the radio we set some kind of record last night, thirteen shootings."

"Wasn't no shooting. Got his head caved in. Blood everywhere they say. His wife got home from work and found him like that." She sniffed. "So she says. You know how them two was always carrying on. Night before last? Thought I'd have to call the cops. Maybe I should have. Might have prevented a tragedy."

Tragedy, sure. She was loving every minute of it. Everybody was. Not like DeWeese had a fan club around here.

"Must have been one of those friends of his," I said.

"Friends?"

"Always hanging by that house round the corner? You know the one."

"That crack house I keep talking about at the beat meetings? Plain as day what goes on there. Don't know why the police don't do something about it."

"Way DeWeese acted, you know that man was mixed up in some shit." Yolanda Marshall from next door had come closer to get a better view. "There been some wrong-looking characters coming by. Wouldn't want to owe them money."

"Why I keep my grandbabies inside when they come over, all the drugs and violence." Mrs. Percy shook her head sadly. "Not like it used to be."

"That man, 'bout time somebody staved his head in." Miz Wilson, the oldest resident on the block, had tottered across the street to join in. "Don't blame that poor wife of his, not one bit."

"People are saying it was gangbangers," I told her. Mrs. Percy and Yolanda Marshall nodded, proud of being in the know.

"He owed 'em money," Yolanda said, leaning forward to keep it confidential.

Miz Wilson closed her eyes and shook her head sadly. "Lord, lord. That boy was running drugs when he was ten years old. Proud of it, too. I was helping out at the school, heard him bragging in the playground. Him and his little friends spray-painted those symbols on my garage door. Gave him a whuppin, but it didn't do no good. His momma tried, but once they get in with the gangs, ain't nothing you can do. Might as well sell your soul to the devil."

By the time I got near the crime scene tape strung across the sidewalk, the neighborhood was buzzing about Byron DeWeese's on-and-off crack habit, his bad-news friends. His debts.

The front door of the house was open. Monica DeWeese sat outside on the front stoop with a blanket around her shoulders, her face blank, giving nothing away. I coughed to get the attention of an officer inside the tape. "Got some mail," I said. The hotshot detective hustled over and took it without looking at me. He walked away, flipping through the bills and flyers, ordering the cops to start canvassing the neighborhood, sounding bored already.

For a moment Monica's vacant eyes focused on me. Her lips parted, then pressed together, as if something had almost slipped out. She knew all the times I'd seen her with a busted lip or a black eye, times I'd watched her move slow because her ribs hurt.

She knew that yesterday I'd seen her working in the front yard. First warm day after a hard winter, you think about the future, start making plans. She was on her knees, pulling weeds and straightening up a line of white-painted rocks, each one about the size of a softball. Going to plant some flowers this year, she told me, edging the cleared earth with the stones that had been hidden in the weeds. From the other side of the tape I could see a socket where the rock closest to the steps was missing.

"I'm sorry for your loss," I said, loud enough for her to hear. She nodded, even though we both knew it wasn't a loss, then wiped her eyes with a crumpled tissue and wrapped the blanket closer. As I moved on to the next block, police were fanning out to talk to the neighbors. Hard cases to solve, ones involving gangs. Hardly worth trying.

They didn't ask me any questions. I mean, shit, what would a woman like me know about anything?

Red Cadillac

ANNE FRASIER

I PUSHED MYSELF AWAY FROM THE BAR and stood up. I was drunk. *Really* drunk. How long had I been there? I tried to remember what time I'd arrived. After the political rally. Just one drink.

I pulled my cell phone from my jacket and squinted at the digital numbers. Six hours ago.

I smoothed my skirt and straightened my spine. Adjusted the strap of my purse. Nobody was looking at me. Nobody recognized me. I spotted the door and aimed myself for it. Once outside, I gulped in air. It would clear my head.

My car. There it was, parked in the Minneapolis downtown lot where I'd left it hours ago. Unlock the door, slip inside. It took me three tries, but I finally got the key in the ignition. Driving always sobered me up.

I pulled from the parking lot and turned in the direction of home and Lake of the Isles. The car seemed to know where it was going, and for few moments I closed my eyes.

Just a long blink interrupted by a loud thump and bone-jarring impact, followed by the sound of shattering glass. I wrenched the wheel. Tires squealed as I pulled the careening car back on the road.

Get home. Had to get home. Couldn't be caught in an accident. Couldn't be caught drunk, not with elections in a month.

Through a small opening in the shattered windshield, I was able to make out the centerline. I followed it, metal dragging against pavement.

At home, I push the automatic garage-door button attached to the visor above my head. I closed the door behind me and stumbled from the car to the house and my bed, passing out before my head hit the pillow.

Early the next morning, the phone rang. I checked the caller ID. Arlo, my campaign manager. I considered not answering, but instead drew in a deep breath, tested my vocal skills, then hit the talk button, trying to sound as if I'd been awake for hours.

"Have you heard the news?" he asked.

"What news?"

"Turn on the television. Your opponent is dead."

I pushed myself upright, my back against the headboard. "Dead? How? When?"

"Last night. Killed by a hit-and run-driver." Arlo sounded excited. "His body was found this morning by a jogger. He was out walking his dog. Dog is fine, but Thomas Bachmann is history."

Something slipped from my hair and dropped to my bare leg. A small cube of thick, tinted glass. I massaged my scalp; more glass fell.

"You've got it in the bag," Arlo said. "Keep your nose clean for another month and you'll be the new governor of Minnesota."

I picked up a cube of glass and stared at it. I mumbled a goodbye and disconnected. In the bathroom, I threw up, slipped on a robe, then walked through the kitchen to the attached garage. For a moment, I stood there with my hand on the knob. In my mind, I imagined the car on the other side of the door. A red Cadillac convertible. My campaign car. My parade car.

Inside the garage, I felt along the wall for the switch, turned on the light, and circled to the front of the vehicle. The right fender was crumpled, the windshield shattered. On the passenger side was a star-like explosion with an indentation roughly the size of someone's head. Upon closer inspection, I found light-brown hair and blood stuck to glass fragments. Thomas Bachmann had light-brown hair.

My life was over.

From deep inside the house, I heard the slam of the front door, followed by humming. "Hello! Ms. Sarah? You home?"

My housekeeper, Vivian Moreno.

I stood there, frozen, unable to think, to move.

"Oh, there you are." Her eyes narrowed. "You okay? You don't look so good."

"I . . . I was in a wreck." I lifted a weak hand toward the damaged vehicle.

Her expression became more concerned.

"I hit—" I stared at the car, at the dented fender, the shattered glass.

Vivian finished my sentence: "A deer." She circled the car, surveying the damage. "I swear I hit a deer almost every year." She tsk tsked as she reached and tugged the tuft of hair from the glass, looked it over, then tossed it in the wastebasket near the cement steps. "My cousin Jesus owns a body shop. Does nice work. Cheap. I'll call him and he'll come get your little red Caddy. Have it looking like new in no time."

Her innocent suggestion offered me a way out. Maybe my life wasn't over. Maybe no one would discover what had happened. "With the election coming up I'd rather nobody hear about this," I said. "You know how the media is. Do you think your cousin would mind picking it up in the middle of the night?"

"No problem. I'm always asking him, when do you ever sleep?" She grabbed my hand. "Why, you're freezing. And shaking. You just go take a hot shower and I'll fix you some breakfast. By tomorrow, your car will be gone and in a few more days it will be back like nothing ever happened." She turned me around and pushed me toward the open kitchen door. "Stupid deer."

"Stupid deer," I echoed.

Three days later, I attended the funeral. Once it was over, once the pallbearers had slid the casket into the hearse, reporters spotted me and shoved microphones in my face. "What do you think about the death of Thomas Bachmann? What does this mean for your campaign? If you win, will it seem a hollow victory?"

"We disagreed on most things," I said, going over the prepared and memorized words, "but Thomas Bachmann was a good man, a kind man, an honest man, and his wife and children are in my thoughts and prayers. He will be greatly missed by not only the citizens of Minnesota, but the country as well."

Another microphone. Another question. "What about the hit-and-run driver?" a female reporter asked.

"I hope he comes forward." I looked at the camera and gave it my intense, passionate face. I could already see myself in the Governor's Mansion. I was imagining the big Christmas tree that was erected every year, like the White House tree, only smaller. "Thomas Bachmann might be dead, but his family deserves closure." I meant it. In the span of a couple of days, I'd almost convinced myself that I *had* hit a deer.

A few days later my car was back in the garage, smelling like fresh paint and wax. "What's this?" I asked, fingering the small cloth pouch hanging from the mirror.

"That's a mojo." Vivian stood in the open car door while I sat behind the wheel. "My cousin said something about the car being cursed." She looked embarrassed, and twisted a kitchen towel in both hands.

"Cursed?" The last thing I needed was a guy named Jesus telling me I was cursed.

"He said something about a place where you can check on cars . . . see what's happened to them."

"CARFAX?"

Her face brightened. "That's it." But her happiness was short-lived. "He said your car has been in other wrecks."

I wasn't the original owner. I had no idea of the car's history. I didn't care. But I could see she was holding back. "What else did he say?"

"He said it's been in two vehicular homicides."

"Okay, that's enough." I ripped the stinking bag of mojo from the rearview mirror and tossed it at the wastebasket. I missed, and Vivian scurried over and picked it up, holding it to her stomach as if to protect it from me.

"Throw it away," I said.

She shook her head.

I was about to rip it from her hands, when I noticed her terror. Let her have her silly superstitions. I made a disgusted sound and shook my head. "Keep it. Put it under your pillow at night or whatever. But I never want to see it again."

I won the election by a landslide. Would I have won if Thomas Bachmann hadn't been killed by that hit-and-run driver? Maybe not, but it didn't matter anymore. I was the first female governor of Minnesota.

The day after the election, a victory parade was held in my honor. I wore a light-blue skirt with matching jacket and a cute pillbox hat. White gloves that stopped just below the elbow. Arlo drove my Cadillac, and I sat in the passenger seat and waved to the people lining the streets.

Behind me in the back seat sat a Star Tribune photographer hoping to get a good shot for tomorrow's paper. I spotted a mother with a baby in her arms, the baby gripping an American flag on a tiny stick, and I was reminded of my favorite images of Princess Diana, most taken with her doting public.

"Stop the car," I said.

Arlo glanced at me, then back down Summit Avenue.

"Stop the car," I repeated.

He braked, and once the car stopped rolling I opened my door and stepped out, motioning for the photographer to follow. I hurried across the grassy divide to the mother on the sidewalk. I smiled to her, held out my gloved hands, and was presented with the toddler. I made some cooing sounds. The child looked surprised, then a smile blossomed and the photographer got the shot. I gave the baby back. "Such a sweet child," I told the bemused and proud mother. I could already imagine tomorrow's paper and my beautiful gloves and hat, the gorgeous baby with her little knit cap and red cheeks.

Something slowly filtered into my brain. An odd sound, like a deep growl of anger. Tires squealed. I turned to see people scatter. In the center of American flags and supporters was my car, red and shiny with a silver grill, barreling toward me.

I didn't feel the impact, but suddenly I was being propelled by the hood, my feet dragging the ground beneath the vehicle. I saw Arlo's face behind the wheel, his eyes and mouth wide.

Shut it off. Turn the key. Put it in neutral. Take your foot off the fucking gas pedal. I wanted to say all of these things, but I said nothing.

And then it was over. With jarring impact and a crunching of metal, the world stopped moving.

Why, that wasn't so bad.

I became aware of a crowd gathering. The mother with the baby in her arms. The photographer, who slowly raised his camera, a look of horror on his face. Arlo, who was somehow no longer behind the wheel, but standing near the front of the car.

"You're bleeding," I said.

He looked confused, and put a hand to the gash on his forehead. He let out a sob. "Call 911!" he screamed to anybody who would listen. "Somebody call 911!"

"I'm okay," I assured him.

He shook his head, his lips trembling, tears streaming down his face. It was then that I realized I was pinned to a tree. The car's grill, its smiling, grinning, laughing chrome grill, was embedded deep in my belly, slicing me in two.

"Well," I said, feeling the life leaving me. "Maybe I didn't kill Thomas Bachmann, after all." The photographer was clicking away, and I wondered if my lovely blue hat was still on my head. I lifted my gloved hand—and I waved to the camera.

From a Cold Place

BRIAN FREEMAN

JONATHAN STRIDE AWOKE TO CINDY'S KISS and the smell of soap and perfume mingling on his wife's freshly scrubbed skin. Her long hair spilled across his face as she bent over him. When she stood up, her lipstick left a smudge on his cheek, and she wiped it off with her thumb.

"It's seven o'clock," she announced.

Stride dragged his mind out of sleep into the cool morning air of the bedroom. When he reached for Cindy's hips to pull her into bed beside him, she ducked nimbly away.

"None of that," she told him brightly. "The early bird gets sex, the late bird gets a kiss and coffee. Deal with it."

"That better be good coffee," he mumbled.

Cindy winked and spun away, full of energy. His eyes followed her as she left. She wore a T-shirt and panties over her skinny frame, and her damp hair needed brushing. She bounced across the hardwood floor in oversized fleece slippers. His wife was a morning person. Stride wasn't.

He got out of bed, and the hot water of the shower revived him. He stayed under the spray while he shaved and cracked the bathroom window, enjoying the bite of the late fall wind. When he was done, he dressed and made his way into their tiny kitchen. He poured coffee and saw Cindy standing on the porch, where she watched slushy drizzle making streaks on the windows. It was still dark outside. Waves rumbled off the lake like thunder.

He came up behind her and slid an arm around her waist. She wore jeans now, and her hair was combed into straight, silky strands. He pulled her hair back and kissed her neck.

"Nice try," she told him. "I've only got five minutes. I'm teaching a class at the Y this morning." She stuck her feet into tennis shoes and sat down on the chaise lounge to tie the laces. "So how's the new kid working out? Maggie?"

Stride sipped his coffee. "She's smart. Doesn't miss a thing."

"But?"

"But there's always a breaking-in period with a new partner."

"It's only been a few weeks," Cindy said.

"Exactly. We're still getting to know each other."

"Is she too young?"

"She's young," Stride agreed, "but I knew that when I hired her. It doesn't matter. For a kid in her twenties, she's already a better detective than guys who have been doing this for ten years."

"She's cute, too," Cindy said. "I like that bowl hair-cut and the button nose. With a little makeover, she'd be sexy."

"I haven't noticed."

Cindy laughed. "You? Sure."

"I just hope she loosens up," Stride said. "She's so damn formal. I tell her jokes, and she doesn't even crack a smile."

"I've heard your jokes. Maggie's not the problem."

Stride shot her a look of annoyance. Cindy grinned and stuck out her tongue.

"Anyway, it's not that," he went on. "She hasn't learned the human side of the job yet. This is all science to her. It's solving a problem, figuring out the solution to a puzzle. I'm not sure it's sunk into her brain that we're talking about people's lives here."

Cindy stood up, balanced on her toes, and extended her arms upward in a yoga position. "Give her time. She's still more Chinese than American. That'll change."

"I hope so."

She dropped back onto her heels. "Gotta run."

"Yeah, okay."

Cindy kissed him again and left. He heard the front door close. Alone, he finished his coffee on the porch while the mixture of rain and snow continued outside. Somewhere over the lake horizon, the sun was up, but the black clouds barely allowed light onto the beach. He was hungry, but he decided to buy a donut on his way to City Hall and eat it at his desk.

Stride turned off the lights and deposited his coffee mug in the sink. He grabbed his keys and swung them on his fingers as he headed down the shadowy hallway. He shrugged on his leather jacket near the door. When he pulled it open, he was surprised to find Maggie Bei standing on the steps, waiting for him. Her wet hair was plastered in strands on her face. She wore a long brown trench coat, and her hands were shoved in her pockets. She wore flat, sensible black shoes.

"Good morning, Lieutenant," she said, with a slight bow of her head.

"Hey, Mags," he told her casually, closing the door behind him. "Weren't we going to meet at the office?"

"Yes, I apologize for coming to your home."

"Don't worry about that. You're always welcome. Cindy wants to have you over for dinner sometime."

"That would be nice," she replied.

"So what's up?"

"A new case came across my desk this morning," she told him.

"This morning? You've already been to the office? What time do you get there, Mags?"

"Usually about six o'clock."

"You don't have to be there so early, you know."

"I know, but I'm grateful for the opportunity, and I want to prove I'm worthy of it."

"Just don't expect me there with you," Stride said. He added, "What's the case?"

Maggie pushed her wet bangs away from her eyes. She hesitated. "I know it would have been better to phone you, rather than come here, but I thought you would prefer if I told you in person."

"What's going on?" he asked, his face creasing with concern.

"I was contacted by a patrol officer," she replied. "He responded to a call at a hunting cabin near Island Lake. It appears there was a break-in and a shooting. Mr. William LaSalle is dead."

*

Stride stopped at a red light at a deserted intersection. The windshield wipers squeaked as they pushed aside pellets of sleet, and the empty highways on the flatlands north of Duluth looked gray and lonely.

"Mr. LaSalle was a friend of yours, was he not?" Maggie asked. He heard the tentativeness in her voice, as if she was afraid of asking him a personal question.

"Yes, he was."

"I'm very sorry, Lieutenant."

Stride nodded. Ahead of him, the light turned green.

He glanced at Maggie, who stared at the road and not at him. "You don't have to call me Lieutenant. You can call me Jonathan or Stride, whatever you'd like."

Maggie shook her head firmly. "No, that wouldn't be appropriate. You're my superior."

"I'm your boss," he said. "There's a difference." He added, "Do you mind that I call you Mags? Would you prefer if I called you Maggie? Or Officer Bei?"

She turned her head with a question in her eyes, as if she thought he might be making fun of her. When she saw that he was serious, the rigidness in her face softened. "No. I like it that you call me that."

He smiled at her. He realized it was easier to think about Maggie and how to break through her Great Wall of China than it was to think about Bill. But his mind was caught in the past and wouldn't go anywhere else.

"I met him when I was a sophomore at UMD," Stride recalled, his voice soft. "I was engaged to Cindy. Bill was engaged to Diane."

Maggie didn't say anything. He wondered if sharing stories from his life made her uncomfortable. He went on anyway, as if he was talking to himself.

"The four of us were friends for most of college. We hung out together all the time. You know how it is when you're young. You think you can solve the problems of the world together over a pizza."

"Yes, I understand," Maggie announced.

Stride knew her college experiences had been more serious than his own. She'd protested loudly and publicly against the Chinese government, and she couldn't go home without fear of arrest. Home for Maggie was Duluth now, which had to be a foreign and intimidating place for her.

He told himself again that he was being unfair, expecting her to adapt to this life more quickly.

"I assumed we would all stay in touch after school," he went on. "Duluth isn't a big city, so you think you can't lose people. But you do. I became a cop, Bill became a lawyer. Our paths just didn't cross much. Same for Cindy and Diane. We'd get together once or twice a year, but it wasn't the same. You can't help but compare things in your head and realize you weren't as close as you once were." He frowned and continued, "It's been a bad season for Bill. I called him a couple times last month when I heard about him and Diane. We never connected."

"A bad season?" Maggie asked.

"Diane filed for divorce. Bill found out she'd been having an affair for several years with another man."

"That's terrible."

Stride nodded. "You think you know people, but you don't."

He drove onto the highway bridge stretching across Island Lake. The water was black and choppy, and the wind buffeted his truck. He had only been to Bill's hunting cabin twice, and it had been nearly five years since his last visit. He wasn't sure if he remembered the directions once he reached the north shore of the lake, but two miles later, he saw a patrol car on the shoulder of Highway 4. He turned left between the trees onto a dirt road and nodded at the officer behind the wheel.

"Who found the body?" Stride asked.

"His brother Randy," Maggie said. "Do you know him?"

"I've met him. He's five years younger than Bill." Stride added, "Tell me again how this went down."

"Randy LaSalle says he came to the cabin early this morning to hunt with his brother. He found the door open and the place in disarray. Items had been damaged and stolen. His brother was dead on the floor with a gunshot wound to the head."

"Where was the gun?"

"It's missing," Maggie said.

Stride looked at her. "No gun?"

"No." She hesitated. "Did you think we'd find it?"

"Yes, I did." He didn't explain.

Stride saw police vehicles parked in a clearing ahead of him. A hiking trail led to the lake, and the old hunting lodge was nestled among the birches. He remembered it. The cabin was rustic, a single room built from thick logs, powered by an oil generator and warmed by a fireplace. He had been surprised that a successful attorney like Bill hadn't chosen a more luxurious property, which he could easily have afforded. But when Bill came here, he said it was like visiting his childhood. Simpler times.

Stride got out of his truck, and his feet sank into the wet mud and dead leaves. A whole day of rain had left the ground sodden. Maggie headed directly for the cabin, but Stride veered away toward a dirty black pick-up truck at the end of the road, where he saw Bill's brother sitting with the door open and his face buried in his hands. Maggie looked at Stride to ask if she should accompany him, but he waved her toward the crime scene.

"How are you, Randy?"

Bill's brother looked up and recognized Stride. His eyes were a mess of red blood vessels, and tears streaked through the dirt on his face. "I just can't believe it," he said.

"Tell me what happened."

Randy wiped his nose on the sleeve of a Vikings sweatshirt. He wore an orange down vest and a baseball cap. "Not much to tell. I was supposed to meet Billy up here early, so we could be in the woods before sunrise. When I got here, the door was open, and I found him. Crazy."

"Did Bill spend the night in the cabin?" Stride asked.

"I guess so. The blood on the floor was—it was frozen. Billy had been lying there a while."

"What did you do?"

"I drove to a gas station and called you guys, then I waited at the dirt road to show the cops the way."

Stride nodded. "Did you call Diane?"

Randy's face twisted in anger. "Call her? No way. That bitch. They're still married, you know. She's going to get all of Billy's money. It's not fair."

"Yeah."

Stride extracted a pack of cigarettes from his inside pocket. He gestured at Randy, who shook his head. He tapped out a single cigarette and lit it. He limited himself to a couple cigarettes a day now, except when it was a really bad day. Cindy hated that he still smoked.

He studied Randy, who twitched like the shadow of a candle on the wall. Randy was small, like Bill, with wavy, sandy blond hair. Bill's own hair had grayed early, and Bill kept it short, the way a lawyer would. Randy had spent most of his life in the shadow of his older brother. Bill was the successful one, the married one, the stable one. Randy flitted from job to job and girl to girl.

"Where did you spend the night, Randy?" Stride asked.

"What do you mean?"

Stride exhaled smoke into the air. "I mean, where are you living these days? You lost your house a while back, didn't you?"

Randy's lower lip jutted forward. "The bank took it. I'm staying in a studio apartment downtown."

"So that's where you were?"

"That's where I was, yeah," he retorted. Belligerence crept into his voice. "What are you suggesting?"

"Were you alone?" Stride asked, ignoring his question.

"As a matter of fact, no. I live with a girl. It's her place."

"What's her name?"

"Rhonda."

Stride flipped open a notebook and handed him paper and pen. "Write down her phone number."

Randy shot him a sullen stare and scribbled numbers on the page. "I didn't shoot Billy. I'd never do that."

Stride nodded. "Didn't say you did."

He folded the paper and slipped it into his pocket. He turned on his heel and left Randy sitting in the pick-up. He stopped back at his own truck, finished his cigarette, and crushed it in the ashtray. With his arms folded over his chest, he studied the cabin as he walked toward it. The evidence technicians came and went around him, carrying cameras and plastic bags. He saw Maggie talking to the lead ev tech, Max Guppo, near the cabin door. Guppo, a five-feet-tall gassy cherub who looked like he'd swallowed a volleyball, gestured to Maggie with excited waves of his arms.

Stride studied the driveway and the mud and brush around the cabin. He eyed the hiking trail between the drooping pines that led toward Island Lake. Getting closer, he stared through the doorway into the matchbox interior of the cabin, but the gloom made it impossible to pick out details.

Then, with the burst of a camera flash, he saw a wooden chair, tipped over on its back, and a body on the floor.

He lingered in the door frame before going inside. The frozen air covered the smell of death and blood. He saw Bill clearly now, his eyes closed, his limbs sprawled on the cold wooden floor. He wasn't a large man, but his body looked shrunken, the way corpses do. He was dressed in a heavy coat, pants, and boots, but his hands were bare. The round entry wound on his forehead was surrounded by scorched skin. Clumps of white stuck to the tweed sofa behind him like cauliflower thrown from a child's plate. Brain matter.

Maggie stood next to Stride. Her golden face was as serious as ever. "Guppo thinks we have a problem," she said quietly.

Stride nodded but held up a hand, stopping her. "Give me a minute here, okay?"

"I am one lucky bastard," Bill announced to Stride.

The two of them, both twenty years old, sat on the ground at the end of the south pier jutting into Lake Superior. They had several empty bottles of Schell's beer between them. The overhead sun was bright, and the two boys wore sunglasses, tank tops, and shorts.

"Yeah?" Stride asked. "How so?"

Bill pushed his sunglasses to the end of his nose. "Come on, have you seen Diane?"

"Okay, you're right."

"Body like Cheryl Ladd," he said.

"True."

"Personality like Goldie Hawn," he said.

"Okay."

"She loves me," he said.

"She does."

"I rest my case. You are looking at one lucky bastard." Bill swigged the last swallow of foam and spit out of the bottle and laid it like a bowling pin next to the others.

"Have you guys set a date?" Stride asked.

Bill shook his head. "Nah, we're waiting until I'm done with law school and can hook up with a good firm. If you're going to marry a blonde goddess, you have to be prepared to treat her like the queen she is. Money talks, my friend."

Stride grunted without agreeing.

"What about you and Cindy?" Bill asked.

"Oh, we'll probably elope," Stride replied, taking off his sunglasses and squinting into the sunshine. "Go to Reno. Do the dirty deed. See how long it takes people to notice. We don't want to wait until we're done with school. Why wait if you know what you want?"

"Because poverty sucks," Bill said.

"We won't starve."

"Young cops make dirt, you know that, right?" Bill pointed out. "You're talking about a life of mac and cheese and Pop Tarts."

"I know that."

Bill shrugged. "I keep telling you, corporate law, Jon. We'll both be getting up at four in the morning, but you'll be retching over dead bodies, and I'll be driving a Cadillac. Do the math, my friend."

"Yeah, but is the money really worth it? You're going to spend your life writing small print on contracts that nobody reads."

"I don't care as long as I'm paid by the hour," Bill announced. "Lots and lots of billable hours."

"Is that what Diane wants?"

"Of course she does. She wants the house on the hill and the season tickets to the symphony in Minneapolis. That's what every woman wants."

"Not Cindy," Stride said.

Bill smiled. "Well, you better ask her about that, my friend, because you might find that she's got some other ideas."

Stride reached into the Schell's box and opened two more bottles of beer. He handed one to Bill and then clinked the neck of his own bottle against it. "Here's to the future richest lawyer in Duluth," he said.

"Here's to the future top cop." Bill drank, belched, and wiped his mouth. "I'll tell you something, Jon. Seriously. I'm not doing it for me. I want Diane to have everything, you know? I thank God every day that I have a girl like that. I love her to death. I don't know what the hell I would do if I ever lost her."

Stride clinked the necks of their bottles again. "Me, too, buddy. Here's to never losing them."

*

"Get somebody to call this number and talk to Rhonda," Stride told Maggie, handing her the paper from his pocket. "Find out what time Randy left her apartment."

"Right away, Lieutenant." She waited before leaving and added, "Guppo thinks that—"

"I know what Guppo thinks," Stride interrupted her. "Just be quick about that call, okay?"

"Of course." Maggie left him alone.

Stride stood in the middle of the cabin. He glanced at a wooden end table near the overturned chair. Two inches of Chardonnay had frozen in the bottom of a wine bottle. A crystal glass sat next to the bottle with another inch of frozen wine at its base. He picked up the glass with a gloved hand and held it upside down and then put it back on the table.

The fire on the wall next to him was long dead. A mound of fresh ashes lay under the grate. The wind through the door picked up gray flakes and blew them into the air like snow. He took a poker and pushed at the fluttery mound and saw a fragment of paper that had escaped the flames. He squatted down and looked closer and saw that it was a corner of a photograph. All he could make out was a splash of blue that looked like sky. The rest of the picture had burned away.

He looked at the scattered debris. A lamp had been pushed onto the floor, its white shade askew. He saw glass fragments from a broken vase. Beside the wall, a rickety TV stand stood empty—no television, just a small square of wood with less dust than the rest of the table. Bill's wallet lay open and empty beside the body on the floor. He shook his head in disgust.

The cabin had a large window that looked out on the lake. He stood in front of the window and watched the whitecaps on the open water. On the trail between the trees, footsteps came and went in the mud.

Stride had seen enough.

Before he left, he stopped and stared down at Bill one last time. For a few years, he had considered this man his best friend in the world, other than Cindy. Those days were frozen in his mind. He realized it wasn't an accident that he had sought out Bill less and less in recent years. Whenever he saw him, in his suit, in his house on the hill, it was a reminder that things had changed. They had each achieved what they wanted, but from the beginning, they had wanted different things. It was easier not to be reminded that they shared little in common now. He preferred to let the memory of their college friendship remain intact.

He wondered what Diane would say when he told her what had happened. If you don't really love someone, it's hard to understand that they love you.

"I wish you'd called me," he told the man at his feet, but they were long past the days when Bill would have turned to Stride for help.

He left the cabin. Maggie was waiting for him. "Did you reach Rhonda?" he asked.

She nodded. "Randy left her apartment at five o'clock."

"And the 911 call?"

"Six-thirty." She added, "Is that what you were expecting?"

"Yes."

He watched the discomfort in Maggie's face and was actually glad to see it there. Her dark eyes filled with confusion and concern. She stared at him silently as if to say, without saying, "Are you all right?"

"I'm fine," he told her, reading her mind. "Why don't you help Guppo wrap up the scene, okay? I need to talk to Randy."

Maggie nodded.

He slogged through the muddy road back to Randy's pick-up. Bill's brother watched him and chewed on his fingernails, then took off his baseball cap and squeezed it in his hand. He tapped his boot in the dirt.

Stride leaned on the open door of the truck. "I'm sorry you had to find him like that, Randy."

"Yeah."

"Did you talk to Bill last night?"

"Yeah, sure."

"Did he say anything?"

Randy didn't look at Stride. Instead, he craned his neck and studied the messy interior of his truck. "Like what? I mean, he just said we should meet here."

"That's all? Nothing else?"

"No."

Stride nodded. "Where's the gun, Randy?"

Randy's head snapped around. "What?"

"Is it in the lake? Is that where you threw it?"

"I didn't do this!"

"I know you didn't. I just wondered if Bill gave you any clue last night about what he was planning to do."

Randy opened his mouth and closed it without saying anything.

"You found Bill in the cabin," Stride went on. "He was dead. The gun was next to him. You took the gun and tried to make it look like a robbery gone bad. Why?"

"Hey, look, I didn't –" Randy began.

Stride cut him off. "Don't bother lying. Nobody's been here since it started raining except you and Bill. There aren't any other footprints or tire tracks. The gun was pressed against Bill's temple when it went off. You're lucky you had an alibi, Randy, because otherwise the only thing you would have accomplished with this stupid stunt is to make yourself a suspect in a murder. What were you thinking?"

Randy cursed. "Billy was the stupid one. That bitch wasn't worth killing himself over."

"Maybe not, but Diane was his whole world. Did he tell you what he was going to do?"

Randy shook his head. "He didn't say a word."

"Why did you try to hide it?"

"I didn't want to give her the satisfaction," Randy snapped. "I didn't want her to think that Billy would do that for her."

"It'll be worse for Diane knowing the truth. But stop acting like a hero. You didn't do this because of her. What is this about, Randy? Is it money?"

He shrugged and spat on the ground. "Okay, there's some life insurance."

Stride waited.

"Billy took out a policy years ago that made me the beneficiary," Randy said. "It's not much, but I could use the money, you know? I didn't figure they'd pay off if he killed himself."

"Do you know how many crimes you've committed here?" Stride asked him.

"Hey, I panicked. I'm sorry. But I thought I should get something out of this, not just Diane."

"He was your brother," Stride said, unable to hide the bitterness in his voice.

"I know that. You think I'm not hurting? We may not have been close, but I never thought he would do something crazy like this. If anyone was going to give up, I thought it would be me."

"Don't expect pity," Stride said. "You were just looking out for yourself."

"Everybody looks out for themselves. That's the way it is." Randy's face twitched in fear. "So what happens now?"

"Now I'm going to send a little Chinese cop over here, and you are going to tell her *everything* you did. Got it? Then you can hope like hell that the County Attorney decides to give you nothing but a slap on the wrist."

He stalked away from the pick-up without letting Randy reply. He gestured to Maggie, who jogged away from Guppo to join him at his own truck. It was too early for another cigarette, but he lit one anyway.

"Did he admit taking the gun?" Maggie asked him.

"Yeah."

"Guppo knew it was suicide as soon as he looked at the crime scene."

"Sometimes we get easy ones," Stride told her. "Don't get used to it."

"You suspected before we got here, though, didn't you?"

Stride shrugged. "I knew Bill." He added, "Take Randy's statement, will you? Run him through last night and the whole morning. Make sure he's not holding anything back on us."

"Okay, boss," Maggie said.

He looked at her in surprise. "Boss?"

Her eyes widened. "I mean, Lieutenant."

Stride smiled. "Boss is fine."

Stride sat in front of the fireplace. Cindy sat cross-legged next to him and leaned her head into his shoulder. It was almost midnight. He picked up a glass of Chardonnay from the carpet and swirled the wine and thought about the frozen dregs in Bill's cabin. Two-thirds of a bottle—that was how much had it taken for Bill to gin up the courage to pull the trigger.

"I'm sorry, Jonny," Cindy murmured, watching his face.

Stride didn't say anything as his eyes followed the flames. He wondered about the photographs that Bill had destroyed and whether they went all the way back to the days when the four of them had been together in college. He thought: how far do you have to go to erase the past?

"How did Diane take it?" Cindy asked him.

He shrugged. "Not well."

"I guess that's good," she said.

"I guess so."

"You're not blaming yourself, are you?" she asked. "Because you and Bill drifted apart years ago."

Stride nodded. "Maybe that's what I'm blaming myself for."

"Don't. It was the same with me and Diane. It's nobody's fault."

She was right, but that didn't change how he felt. He always found a way to take the blame.

"I thought Bill would have been a stronger man," Cindy said. "I never realized he was so vulnerable."

"People surprise you," he said.

"Well, when I run off with Guppo, you're not going to kill yourself, right?" she asked.

Stride laughed. "Guppo?"

"You never know, Jonny."

"No, I guess I won't, but let's not put it to the test."

She wagged a finger at him. "Remember, if you decide to run off with Maggie, I might kill you but certainly not me."

"Fair enough," he said.

Cindy's face grew serious as she finished her own wine and lay down the glass. "I just wonder where it comes from, you know?"

"What's that?"

"The impulse to kill yourself. To say that's the end. To give up."

Stride shook his head. "I don't know. Wherever it is, it must be a cold place."

Cindy said nothing, but she shivered. He felt a downward draft of air that made the fire flicker nervously. It was a reminder to him that winter was coming and that Duluth itself would soon be a cold place again. Above him, a brass clock chimed for midnight. Time had added another day to his life. He reached for Cindy and took her in his arms, but it didn't stop him from feeling older.

Wonderland

ELLEN HART

I DON'T REMEMBER MUCH about the year I turned twenty-five, just the life-altering stuff. Like my husband's death. And the trial that I'd expected to last for months but which, at the last minute, had been turned into a plea bargain. I was so deeply into an emotional blackout that I don't remember even looking up, truly taking my bearings, until several weeks after I was locked into the women's correctional facility in Shakopee. It could have been worse, I suppose, but because my lawyer was able to make a strong case for mental and physical abuse, because I'd never been arrested or even received a speeding ticket before, and most importantly because Dave's death was unpremeditated, I received a manslaughter charge instead of murder. Lucky me. Some days I thought I should have been locked up for life, other days I thought the whole thing was a joke, that I shouldn't be serving any time at all. That tells you a little about who I was seven years ago. And maybe a little about who I still am.

As long as I live, the stunned look in my husband's eyes the night he died will always haunt me. I loved him in my selfish, greedy, unexamined way, and thought I couldn't live without him. He was freedom, sanctuary, and a passionate man in my bed every night—all things I craved. The only problem was, it wasn't real. It was all a fairy tale, dreamed up by an angry, deeply lonely and impulsive girl. Sitting in prison all these years, I've had time to think about what I did, to divest myself of the sort of magical imaginings that got me—and poor Dave—into such a mess in the first place. I didn't think much at all seven years ago, but I sure did feel. Everything was life or death.

One of my first interviews in prison was with a therapist, a woman. I thought she looked like a pencil with hair, but turns out she was pretty smart. She stared at me for what felt like the entire first quarter of a football game and finally said, "Who *are* you?"

I knew she had all the general details. Age, twenty-five. Name, Emily Anders Lindstrom—but called by my nickname, Roady. Daughter of the artist Bridget Anders Lindstrom, and the rock musician Django Lindstrom. A half-finished degree in journalism from the University of Minnesota. A blond, fat nobody with a sullen look and a superior attitude. I was uncomfortable in her office chair and probably didn't hide it very well. I felt uncomfortable all the time back then, yanking on my clothes to try and hide my growing girth. I was pretty and knew it, but I also knew that most guys gave me a pass because of the extra weight. When Dave came along, he was like this big, amazing gift. He loved my size. He liked to cook and eat as much as I did. And since he was an amateur weight lifter—a bear of a man—he was always trying to bulk up. We were a match made in heaven—or maybe it was the Food Channel. They looked awfully similar back then.

But returning to the question of who I was, I remember just blinking at the therapist. I had no idea what to say. And that upset me more than I might have admitted. I mean, everybody knows who they are, right? Except, when it came right down to it, I didn't. I was no longer a wife. I was a daughter, but that was a direction I wasn't interested in pursuing. I didn't think much of myself, really. I remember muttering something about being stupid, a useless lump. And then I stopped talking. I simply refused to say another word. I was sent back to my cell and asked to think about the question, which it turns out, I did.

As I sat down on my bed, I remembered something a teacher had once said in one of my journalism classes. In his opinion the interview was *the* art form of the Twentieth Century. It had antecedents in the confession box as well as the witness stand, but it was perfected only recently. Anybody could maintain a pose or an image for a couple hours, according to that same professor, but after that, if you were still talking, still willing to invest the time, an interviewer truly had his interviewee in the palm of his hand. I knew that a good interview eliminated all the space fillers, all the bullshit. And that's what I wanted to aim for. I decided then and there that I was going to interview myself. I had nothing but time and I needed answers.

To get at anything real, you have to know what came before. Something important always comes before. There is no beginning, and I suppose no end to human connection. Until the sun blows up, or nuclear rockets rain down, or an asteroid hits the earth or a volcano spews crap into the heavens so thick that the light can't get through and we all die in a state of perpetual winter, there will be mothers and fathers, sons and daughters, friends and family screwing each other over. I know that's a bleak view of life, but in my experience, it's bedrock. We all, whether we admit it or not, live in the land of the bottom line.

So, here's the deal, the beginning of my downfall. I idolized my dad. Simple as that. He was everything to me. When he left, walked out, I felt like he'd walked out on me and only me. I was twelve, the oldest of his three kids, and his favorite—I was sure of it. Oh, we still lived in a big fancy house. I was still famous by proxy. My friends thought I lived this charmed life. There was my wild, intense artist mother. My hunky rock star father. We were the stuff that dreams were made of—rich, almost royalty.

That's the bullshit part.

Here's the real part.

My mother had mood problems. That's how the adults in the family put it. It was the reason, I found out later, that my father never pursued custody of my brothers and me. Everyone in the family—and I have a big family—said that it would push my mother over the edge.

My dad put the house in his name, employed a man to pay all the bills because my mother couldn't be trusted with money. He installed a chauffeur in the gatehouse because, again, mother couldn't be trusted behind the wheel of a car. But sometimes, when the financial manager wasn't in a good mood or couldn't be convinced of a need or was out of town on business, we failed to get enough money for clothes or birthday presents or whatever. I never wanted to bring too much attention to it because I was so incredibly embarrassed. I told my brothers to keep their mouth's shut. We'd simply make do. We were chauffeured everywhere, but at the same time there were holes in our underwear. It was insane.

I loved my mother. I needed her after my father took off, but couldn't have her. She was so erratic that I never knew who she was going to be at any given moment. She was fine, completely normal for long stretches, but then she'd fall into a depression so deep we would hardly see her for weeks. And then, just as suddenly, she would become so crazy energetic that she would demand that we all help her build a Rose Bowl float in the living room.

So that's a little of what came before my stay in Shakopee. I went on with my self-interview for years, until I got deep enough to finally see some important truths about myself and my family. But in all my meanderings, it always came back to this: For all practical purposes, my father locked me and my brothers inside a mansion with a madwoman and a chauffeur and never looked back. It was an existential triumph. People who live in the moment always leave chaos in their wake. I'm part of that chaos.

Welcome to Wonderland.

Capital Partners

LIBBY FISCHER HELLMANN

THE GULFSTREAM BUCKED AND PITCHED like an angry bronco. Grace had always been a bad flyer; now, at thirty thousand feet, her stomach plunged in direct proportion to the altitude. As the pilot called back to put on their seat belts, she gripped the armrests.

"Just a little turbulence, Gracie." Jay turned on his smile. "Nothing to worry about."

When Jay smiled, and he did a lot, Grace's doubts melted away. The curve of his mouth slipped sideways, his crow's feet stretched like tiny accordions, and a seductive twinkle came into his eyes. His smile was an amulet; nothing bad could happen when it flashed. It had been that way since they met. This time, though, the jet was like a roller coaster, and after a particularly steep drop, even Jay's smile lost some of its wattage.

"Sy said there's a foot of fresh powder. This must be why." He looked out the jet's small window. Nothing, Grace thought, except dark clumps of angry storm clouds.

"He probably said that so you'd drop everything and follow him out here." Grace couldn't keep the edge out of her voice. "He hates to be alone."

"He's got Dana," Jay said.

"Like I said, he hates to be alone."

"Don't worry, baby," he said soothingly. "We're almost there."

Almost there. How many times had she heard that? She'd known six years ago when they first met that Jay Montgomery was going places. His hunger and ambition was as intense as a neon sign. But Jay had manners. He was respectful. He never pressured. He was the perfect salesman. With her trust fund and his financial know-how, they'd quickly sailed out of upper middle class, coasted through well-off, and landed at rich.

The turbulence eventually quieted, just like Jay said it would, and the pilot made a smooth landing. The limo was waiting near the hangar, and they climbed in quickly—Grace had left Chicago without a coat—for the drive to the chalet. Chalet was actually a misnomer; she and Jay owned a six-bedroom home with a magnificent view of the mountains, especially at twilight when the purple dusk was sliced by the mellow lights of Vail.

Their housekeeper met them at the door. Grace could hear the crackle of a fire in the family room.

"Two messages, Missus," Lucy reported as if they'd only been gone a few hours, not months. "Dinner at eight with the Penningtons. And a call for Mrs. Montgomery. A Mr. Cole. He left his number."

Jay frowned. "Cole?"

"Yes, sir."

"Thanks, Lucy." Grace took the steps up. The chalet was larger than their Village brownstone, the London flat too, but space was important to Jay. Grace could be happy in one room, as long as the people and things she loved surrounded her.

They showered and dressed for dinner. Jay watched in the dressing table mirror as Grace applied her make-up. She was in her bra and panties. He wasn't smiling, but his expression was one she knew well.

"You're not having an affair, are you?"

"I have no idea who 'Cole' is," she replied. "Probably wants to sell me something."

"Just checking." He grinned, came up behind her, and nuzzled her neck. "I think we might be a little late," he said in a husky voice.

The limo dropped them at the Gilded Age, the newest restaurant in Vail. Grace walked past a fountain, which, even in winter, burbled cheerfully. Inside, the restaurant was only about thirty tables, but they were all filled. She spotted Sy and Dana Pennington right away. He'd commandeered the best table. Better than Cameron Diaz or Kelsey Grammar's, she noted.

Dana waved when she spotted Grace. She looked fabulous, Grace thought, in a shockingly blue après ski outfit. Smooth skin, not a wrinkle in sight. Dana had been Sy's trophy wife fifteen years ago—they met in Vegas—and her regular appointments with the plastic surgeon indicated she intended to stay that way.

Grace tried to like Dana, for Jay's sake, but Grace couldn't figure out how Sy put up with her. Maybe Dana was a winner in the sack. She waved and glided over, nodding at Dustin Hoffman who was involved in an intense conversation.

"You look fabulous, Dana," she chirped as she kissed them both.

Dana smiled prettily. "New trainer. He comes to me after Demi Moore."

Sy made a show of looking at his watch. "You're late. You gotta stop having all that sex." Sy guffawed as though they were all sharing a dirty joke.

Dana giggled too. Clearly, they had had a few. Sy was a stocky man, with gray hair that was too long, fingers that were too thick, and eyes that were too small. "They flew in lobster from Ecuador. I ordered for us, okay?"

Grace made small talk through the appetizers, her voice matching the tinkling silverware. Jay was reserved, but he usually let Sy take the lead. As usual, Sy quickly lost interest in the conversation, instead nodding at people he deemed worthy, then stuffing lobster down his gullet when it arrived. He was coming loose at the jowls, Grace thought. She actually felt a little sorry for Dana.

The waiter cleared the dishes, signaling the inevitable trip to the ladies room for the women. She rose and started across the room.

"Hey, wait for me," Dana rose unsteadily. Grace backtracked and took her arm. Dana plopped down at a silk brocade bench in front of a mirrored dressing table and pulled out her lipstick. When Gracie came back from the toilet, Dana patted the seat next to her.

"You've been a good friend to me, Gracie. You are my friend, aren't you?"

"Of course."

"No one likes me. They never did. Sy's kids . . . well you know. Second wife and all."

"Kids eventually get past that kind of thing."

"Not Sy's."

"Don't worry about it. You have a fairy tale life, Dana. We both do."

Dana giggled in a spaced out sort of way. "Including the monster at the door."

"What are you talking about?"

"I have a secret to tell you," she whispered theatrically. It would have been more effective had she not slurred the word "secret." "Something happened. I'm not sure, but I think it involves Jay."

"They are partners."

Dana shook her head. "This is different. But you can't say anything."

"Okay."

"Sy had a visitor today. They went into Sy's office. And fought. At one point, Sy shouted, "I don't fucking believe you.""

"Sy does have a temper."

"Like I said, this was different. After the guy left, Sy told me he's flying back east on Monday."

"Why?"

"He says something came up." Dana lowered her voice. "But I heard him make a call. Before he changed for dinner."

"And?"

"Well . . ." Dana eyed Grace. "Well, I sneaked into his office and pressed "redial.""

Grace raised her eyebrows.

"It was area code 202. Washington. The u.s. Marshall's office."

"What?"

Dana shrugged. "That's all I know."

Grace pretended to frown. "I can't imagine what it's about."

Dana ran her tongue around her lips. "You wont tell, will you? Not Jay? Or anyone? If Sy finds out . . ." She winced.

"Don't worry." Grace stood up. "We'd better get back."

Back at the table, Sy was gesticulating wildly. Jay listened with a weak smile. As Grace sat down, Sy's hand accidentally brushed her dress. "Oh, sorry, Princess."

Grace suppressed her irritation. Sy liked to call her that because she shared a name with Grace Kelly, and they both came from wealthy families on Philadelphia's Main Line. In fact, Sy usually couldn't make it through one evening without mentioning how Princess Grace whored her way to success. And insinuating that Grace did the same. Grace never bothered to tell him her mother named her for Grace Slick.

The next day Grace and Jay hit the slopes. With the foot of new powder, the skiing was exhilarating, and Grace forgot about Dana's confession until they went into the bar late that afternoon, and a man walked up to Jay. He was small and squat, with dark hair and a trimmed goatee. He was inappropriately dressed for Vail, Grace thought, in khaki slacks, a sweater, and loafers. When he said something to Jay, her husband shook his head and spun around, his face ashen. He caught Grace's arm and steered her to the door. "It's pretty crowded in here. Let's go somewhere else."

It wasn't crowded. There was even space at the tables. "Who is that?"

"I don't know," Jay said after a beat. "He thought he knew me. He didn't."

Gracie nodded, but her stomach clenched.

Jay was lying.

As she and Jay walked into another bar down the street, Grace asked, "Is everything okay, sweetheart?"

"Sure." He leaned over and kissed her. His color had returned. "This is vacation. No business allowed." But he had looked concerned. Even scared. And the man at the bar had a knowing look. Grace recalled her conversation with Dana.

"Damn," she said. "I left my makeup in the car. I'll meet you inside."

"You look ravishing, Gracie. You don't need makeup."

"You're my husband. You're supposed to say that." She smiled at him. Order me a pinot grigio okay?"

He nodded and went inside.

She went back to the first bar. The man was still there. She tapped him on the shoulder. He turned around.

"Who are you? Why did you approach my husband?"

The guy looked her over. "You're . . . Jay's wife?"

"I'm Grace Montgomery, yes."

"I'm Danny Cole. Short for Colleti." The man flashed a cool smile. "I see you got my message."

"Why did you call?"

He gazed at her then reached into a pocket. He withdrew a business card and wrote on the back. "Google this name." He handed the card to her. "I'm at the Arabelle until Tuesday. I'll wait for your call."

"You're pretty sure of yourself."

Again a phony smile.

She took the card, turned it over. The name on the back was Charlie Farina.

As soon as she got home, Grace googled Charlie Farina. She was surprised at the number of hits. Apparently, he'd been a bookkeeper on the East Coast, who, with his partner, George Siegel, had created an investment pool that turned out to be a Ponzi scheme. Some of their biggest investors were mobsters. But instead of facing prosecution when the fund collapsed, Farina turned states' evidence. His partner was sentenced to thirty years, but Farina went into the witness protection program.

When Grace clicked on Google Images, a chill ran up her spine. The only photo of Charlie Farina was over ten years old. His hair was dark, not sandy. His nose and chin were more pronounced—had he had plastic surgery?—but she knew those eyes and the smile that slipped sideways. Jay Montgomery.

Slowly she shut down the computer. She'd met Jay on a Metroliner between Newark and Philadelphia. He came from Indiana— Wheatfield—he said. His father died of a heart attack when Jay was eight, his mother sold the farm, and they moved to the Jersey suburbs. His mother worked two jobs so he could attend college. Eventually he got a job with a New York investment firm.

When they met, Grace was nearly forty and unmarried. They married six months later. It appeared now he'd neglected to mention the firm's biggest client had been the mob. And that he built a house of cards and left them holding the bag when it collapsed. Clearly the mob wanted their pound of flesh. And had somehow tracked him down.

Suddenly Sy's visitor and subsequent phone call to Washington made sense. Jay was now partnered with Sy in another investment firm, and they were doing it again. But this time Sy was running to the Feds before Jay could. The problem was that most of Grace's trust fund was invested in the firm.

The next morning while Jay was getting a massage, she checked her monthly statements. Regular returns, nothing exorbitant. Just a steady rise in value, all of it reinvested. She made a call to her accountant. She was getting her own massage when the call was returned. She called back and left instructions.

That night Grace made fierce, almost brutal, love to Jay. Afterwards, he traced his hand up and down her arm, his breath still coming hard and fast. "What got into you, baby? What we did tonight ought to be a crime."

She brushed her hand down his cheek.

The next day was Sunday. Feigning a cold, she kissed Jay goodbye, and he went to the slopes. She dug out Cole's card.

"Good morning, Mrs. Montgomery. How can I help you?"

At least he had the manners not to gloat.

She explained what she wanted. "Nothing fatal, you understand."

He was quiet for a moment. Then, "I think I have just the thing."

"What?"

"Nope. You can't know, see?"

"You're right. So how much is this going to cost me?"

He cleared his throat and gave her a figure. "Half now. Half on delivery."

"Oh my god! That's half my —"

"You'd rather lose it all?" He paused. "Also, I'm gonna need some of your husband's clothes."

She thought about it. "Be here in twenty minutes."

Her trainer came two hours later, squeezing her in on his free day, probably because she tipped so well. They were doing bicep curls when the front door opened. Grace made a point of calling out. "Is that you sweetheart? You've been gone for hours. Where were you?"

Grace heard the news from the detective who showed up to arrest Jay Monday afternoon. Sy Pennington was dead. The Gulfstream had crashed just after takeoff that morning. Grace clapped a hand over her mouth and sank into the couch.

Jay turned pale. "What happened?"

"We're still working it out, Mr. Montgomery. If you don't mind, where were you yesterday afternoon?"

"Me? Why?"

"Because one of the airport mechanics says someone fitting your description was at the hangar where the Gulfstream was parked."

"That's ridiculous. I was on the slopes all day."

The detective turned to Grace. "Is that true?"

She nodded, but her brain was working, thinking what a wig and the right clothes could do.

"What are you getting at?" Jay asked.

"Can someone vouch for you, Mr. Montgomery? Someone you were skiing with, perhaps?"

A wave of crimson climbed up Jay's neck. "Gracie had a cold. I—I was by myself."

"Wait a minute." Grace spoke up. "Are you accusing my husband of tampering with the plane?"

The detective's eyebrows shot up. "Are you?"

She flashed the man an indignant scowl.

"You see, Mr. Pennington was on his way to Washington to talk to the Feds. About your husband."

Now the tide of crimson flooded Jay's face.

"About what?" Grace asked, all innocence.

The detective explained. Grace pretended to be shocked.

Jay flailed his hands. "I didn't do it. Gracie." His voice was hoarse. "You have to believe me. Someone was impersonating me. Honest."

Grace folded her arms. She kept her mouth shut.

"Gracie, please. I love you. Help me."

She turned her back as they took him away.

The next morning Cole called. "Meet me in the coffee shop of the Arabelle by ten."

When Grace arrived, Cole was sitting at a table with an attractive woman. As she drew closer, she realized it was Dana Pennington. Her mouth fell open. What was Dana doing here? Grace thought fast.

Cole waved her over. "I believe you ladies know each other." He stood up. "The envelope, please."

Grace opened her purse and handed over a white envelope. Cole rifled through it then stuffed it inside his jacket. "Well, I guess I'll be on my way. It's been a pleasure doing business with you both." He smiled and headed for the exit.

Grace and Dana stared at each other for a long time. Then Grace said, "Sorry to hear about Sy."

Dana shrugged, and a small grin curved her lips. She was stone cold sober, Grace noted. "Yeah. Too bad," Dana said. "You get your money out in time?"

Grace nodded, remembering the call she'd made to her accountant.

"So did I." Dana watched Cole's retreating back. "But I'm not happy giving so much of it to him."

"Me neither," Grace said. "He played us."

"I suppose we should give him credit," Dana said. "He killed two birds with one stone, so to speak. Sy is gone, and Jay's behind bars." She eyed Grace. "But I know what you mean." She paused. "So what do you think about getting it back, Gracie?"

"The money we paid Cole?"

"Unless you'd rather let the Mob walk away with it."

Grace considered it. "It won't be easy. "

Dana nodded.

"And it's going to be dangerous."

Dana nodded again.

"We'd have to be partners," Grace said.

Dana flashed her a smile that wasn't really a smile. "Well, you know what they say about the devil you know."

Guest at the Wedding

KATHLEEN HILLS

WILL YOU MARRY ME?

"I've spent all day getting gussied up, the champagne is ready to pop, and the good Reverend has a golf date. Let's get on with it!"

He lifted my hand to his lips. "Yes, lets."

It was the wedding every girl might dream of, late afternoon sunlight on sapphire water, classical guitars, soft breeze creating apple blossom confetti, and a groom—a groom so kind, so lighthearted, so smart, so perfect in every way it could bring tears to your eyes. But I hadn't been a girl in a long time, and what I wanted most of all was for it to be over. I'd held out as long as I could for a quick and stealthy trip to the court house with a cab waiting at the door to carry us to the airport for a flight to Anywhere-But-Here, but it was a lost cause. A smile from that perfect, and persuasive, groom had cast its spell, and here I was, got up like the queen of the faeries, ready and only too willing to make a public spectacle of myself. A small sacrifice it was, to gain a lifetime of those smiles.

He'd arranged it all, from the agonizing choice of guests and hiring those guitarists, to the bouquet of yellow tulips being strangled in my sweaty grip. All I had to do was show up. I'd made only two requests: the wedding must be in the open, and we'd promenade that petal strewn carpet together. I'd drawn a firm line at running a claustrophobic church-aisle gantlet alone.

After the initial surrender, there was no point in holding back. Engagement ring, engraved invitations, newspaper announcement; all the trappings, right down to the white gown. No ambiguous sickly ivory, either. I stood next to my future husband and greeted our guests dressed in slinky silk so pristine in its whiteness that it could have guided ships to the shore. A brand new life deserved nothing less. Besides I looked good in white and could hardly fall any lower in the estimation of the world.

Maybe that was being unfair. My future in-laws were ecstatic, having long ago given up hope that Neil would find anybody he considered suitable, and his friends and relations had turned out in droves. My own family was a good deal less euphoric, but at least a smattering of them had shown up. They'd pulled the folding chairs into a sort of semi-circle, and sat huddled like a covey of quail in the wind. The better to pat one another on the back for their great valor in putting themselves through this ordeal. They weren't doing me any favors. My mother could hardly think that sitting there with a face like she was going to a hanging could be seen as furthering family unity.

A spasmodic clench of Neil's hand on my arm brought me back to the important parties in this situation. He and I. No one else mattered. I returned the affectionate squeeze and looked up to see him gazing, not into my eyes like a smitten sheep, but over my left shoulder, with a horror-filled stare and slack jaw that could only mean my insistence on the city park wedding had been a grave mistake.

I held my breath and turned. Low sunlight through splashing water let me see only the dark silhouette of a man, gaunt and rangy, coming toward us, not menacing, exactly, but purposeful. Something hazily familiar in his stride evoked a spasm of inexplicable sorrow. He rounded the fountain, and my heart settled back into my chest. Grandpa Jack. If any member of my late husband's family had to crash our festivities, his grandfather was the least threatening. He was also the last one I'd have expected to see. This might well be the farthest from home he'd traveled in his entire life. He hadn't even made it to Kevin's funeral.

I covered Neil's hand, still clutching at my forearm, with mine. "Don't worry. He only looks like something Stephen King dreamed up."

Grandpa Jack fixed yellowy eagle-like eyes on me, showing a mixture of ferocity and bleakness that made me think maybe I was being hasty in my estimation. He spoke formally for an old backwoodsman, apologizing for turning up uninvited, studied Neil for a moment, and extended his hand. "So this is your young man. Who'd have thought we'd meet again? I'm grateful it's in better circumstances."

I'd no idea they knew each other. But then Neil and Kevin had been friends a long time. Since before I knew either of them.

Neil took the hand, but his face hadn't regained its color. "I'm afraid you've mistaken me for someone else. I don't think we've met."

"You're way too modest. I recognized you in the paper. The engagement picture. That's why I'm here, really. Seemed like sort of an omen." Jack turned to me. "Your man saved my life."

"Mine too," I said.

He went on without acknowledging my chiming in. "I swerved to keep from hitting a deer and sunk Annabelle Lee so far in the bog I'd still be there if this gentleman hadn't pulled her out of the muck and got me on my way."

Beads of perspiration stood on Neil's neck, and his gaze flitted from Jack to me in confusion hardly befitting a super-hero. I explained that Annabelle Lee was Grandpa Jack's equally ancient motorcycle, not exactly in those words. Jack was a bit of a local celebrity, an infamous recluse who only emerged from the woods when he fired up Annie for his annual birthday ride.

The Reverend Mackay gave a final impatient nudge and strode off to await us at the vine festooned arbor.

"I only wanted to wish you the best," Jack said. "And now I've done it, I'll be off."

"Please, no. This is a public park, after all. And it's so good to see you. I'm glad you came. It means a lot to me."

It did. After the initial shock, his being there really did feel like an omen. Jack was old, not far from death himself; all that separated him from Kevin was a few more feeble heartbeats. He'd stepped out of the light of that fountain, frail and insubstantial, the embodiment of a connection of the past with the future—a messenger. I wasn't loony enough to think he carried a message from Kevin, but I was taken by a strange feeling that his grandfather's arrival was, if not a portent, important, that it made a difference.

Maybe it was less mystical than that. Jack hadn't gotten a hundred and twenty miles from home on old Annabelle Lee. It was remotely possible that he'd been recruited by Kevin's family to bestow acceptance and forgiveness by proxy. Not that I needed it, or them. I had a right to a life whatever they thought. I had a right to replace the life Kevin had ripped from me.

Neil's cousin and his wife took their places, ready to bear witness to our glorious union. Jack shook his head again at my request that he stay and patted my cheek. "I'm so very sorry." Sorry for what, he didn't say. I would choose to believe it was for the viciousness of his descendents, for their ostracism of me, all but blaming me for Kevin's death simply because I'd grabbed the lifeline Neil had thrown. He walked off, his rolling gait so like his grandson's that I felt the eerie sense of recognition again, along with a stab of the grief that I thought had been strangled in its infancy.

I forced my gaze from him and reminded myself that Kevin had walked away, too, with no thought for me. He'd left me. Deliberately and irrevocably.

The Reverend faced us and nodded smartly. Neil reclaimed my arm. As we set out together forever, it was hard not to skip to the strumming of the guitars. Any lingering impediments to our happiness were dispelled by the unexpected guest. I brushed against my groom's shoulder and felt a shudder that made me almost laugh aloud. The world's most confident man was charmingly nervous. He'd avoided this moment for half a lifetime. I would make sure it was worth the wait.

We reached the arbor, and I struggled not to squirm under the weight of the eyes on my back. I fought the impulse to provide the spectacle they craved; to turn, fling the tulips in the air and shout, "Yes, I'm getting married! Yes, I have only been a widow for six months! Yes, even as I buried my husband, I was falling in love with his friend. Would you rather have me suffering alone? Would that make you all happy?"

That wasn't fair either. I think too much of myself. Kevin left us all. It hadn't been easy for anybody, even Neil. Especially Neil. He'd suffered for years, loving me from our first meeting, never showing a sign. Moving a thousand miles away to avoid the pain of seeing Kevin and me together. Never forgetting me. Denying his love to keep from destroying our lives. And he had to live, as I did, with the knowledge that the torture that drove

Kevin to his death was something he didn't let us in on. Not a word had he breathed to his friends or his wife. My husband didn't trust me enough, or love me enough, to tell me that he wanted to die. That was the source of the worst agony, and the greatest anger.

But, unlike me, Neil had been strong. Strong enough to stifle his feelings to protect his friendship, and strong enough to admit to them when Kevin was gone. In his bravery he enveloped me in so much love that I couldn't help but return it.

The Reverend Mackay cleared his throat. "We are gathered here in the sight of —"

Everyone on the planet. The eyes bored into my spine. I sidled nearer to Neil, near enough to feel his warmth and absorb his strength. I felt his trembling, and moved closer still.

How like him to stop to upright an old man's motorcycle from the mud and never mention it. He might have made the six o'clock news! Grandpa Jack's annual birthday ride through the back roads of the north woods generally merited a few minutes of feel-good footage on Channel Four or a newspaper photo of the leather helmeted octogenarian charging through autumn leaves . . .

"I, Neil, take you . . . " I felt a small buzzing in my brain, and I shook my head to clear it.

"Forsaking all others. . . ." That was the crucial part. I would happily, eagerly, forsake all others and devote my life to loving this wise and gentle man, to being safe in his arms.

His hands felt damp and cold. His whispered "*I will*" went straight to my heart.

The buzzing grew louder, so real that I wondered if Neil also heard it; his gaze had strayed from my face toward the rose hedges.

Once again he stared, pale and stiff, at his late friend's grandfather.

Grandpa Jack was not far off, seated on a bench, turned away from us, facing the lake. He sat with his hands on his thighs, as Kevin had so often done. Jack's birthday trip hadn't made much of a splash the previous October, I remembered. Other news had pushed the need for human interest filler right off the page—news of the thirty-nine year old man, off for a day of grouse hunting, who'd left his car near a railroad bridge, walked to its center, and leaped to the riverbed 90 feet below. No, there were no apparent problems, no history of depression. He left a seven word text message of goodbye, a wife of sixteen years, and a devastated family, as well as a multitude of grieving friends, one of whom was, that day, returning to his home in Chicago from a business meeting in Winnipeg— or perhaps he was only a few miles away helping an old man with a good memory for faces get his motorcycle on the road.

God, how I hated that old man now. The swamp opened at my feet, grown deeper, slimier, blacker in its half year of waiting to reclaim me.

"Do you take Neil for your lawful wedded husband, to live in the holy estate of matrimony? Will you love, honor, comfort, and cherish him from this day forward, forsaking all others, keeping only unto him for as long as you both shall live?"

I gripped my never-to-be husband's hand harder, unable to quiet its shaking. The buzzing stopped.

The question of what I would have done if I'd had a real choice haunts me to this day.

The silence stretched on.

The tulips landed in the grass and I heard my mother's sharp indrawn breath.

"No." I said.

Obsessive Behavior

DAVID HOUSEWRIGHT

THEY TOSSED MY ROOM after the fifth day. Actually, Josie searched it while Meg banged my brains out in her living quarters in the back of the hotel. I would have preferred Josie. Meg had bluer eyes, blonder hair and bigger breasts, but the lovely, doe-eyed Josie gave off a girl-next-door vibe that more than once made me reconsider my life choices. It was easy to see why Johnny the Boy Scalise had fallen for her, why he had trusted her with the combination to his safe.

Josie hadn't found anything in my room. That's because I had brought nothing that would have identified me as a PI; I didn't even bring my guns. Still, I had taken a chance letting Meg seduce me. Josie was sharp—all three of them were sharp—yet they lacked experience, otherwise they would have known that the smart move was to go for the cell phone in the pocket of my sports jacket that Meg had stripped off before leading me to her bedroom. They would have seen all those numbers in the call log with the 312 prefix for Chicago and they would have been frightened. If they had re-dialed the last number I had called, they would have been have been frightened even more.

I didn't want the girls to be frightened. I wanted them relaxed, calm. Only Johnny the Boy had crossed me up. He had told me to sit on the girls until he arrived. That was six days ago and still no sign of him. You simply cannot hang out for that long at Meg and Josie's Hotel, Restaurant and Bar—that's its actual name—without making people suspicious. The joint was located in Alma, Wisconsin, a 19th Century-style European village filled with inns, bed and breakfasts, art galleries, gift shops and restaurants that was perched on a narrow strip of land between the Mississippi River and a 500-foot-high limestone bluff. It catered to tourists chasing walleye or the fall colors, birders attracted by the nesting grounds of bald eagles, and rail buffs enticed by the thirty trains that passed through the town each day. Yet while many people came and went, as a rule they didn't linger for long. But still there I was after nearly a week, keeping to myself, and neither fishing, birding, nor trainspotting. Of course, the girls were alarmed. I would have been alarmed, too. Especially if I was on the lam with 3.2 million of a gangster's ill-gotten dollars.

I liked the girls very much, had liked them even before I met them. Johnny had called them whores, skanks, bitches. They weren't. They were professional women, graduates of Northwestern University; they could speak five foreign languages between them. Brenda worked in public relations, Cassidy was an economist and Linda was trying to parlay an art history degree into a career in high fashion as a hair stylist. Just about everyone I met while searching for them spoke of their kindness, their generosity, their unbridled sense of fun. Their only crime, it seemed, was falling in with the wrong crowd.

Brenda had taken up with Johnny the Boy, Cassidy with his Number One henchman, and the third—Linda—she was their roommate. Things went from bad to worse almost immediately. Cassidy was sent to the emergency room when the henchman lost fifty large betting on the Bears in the 2006 Super Bowl—he had to take his frustration out on someone. The incident so appalled Brenda that she broke it off with Johnny. At least she tried to. Johnny refused to take no for an answer, ignoring the restraining order forbidding him to go anywhere near Brenda, threatening her friends with rape and murder if she didn't wise up, and scaring off every lawyer that tried to come to her rescue.

This lasted for nearly a year. Then poof, the girls were gone. The cops couldn't find them, although they didn't look very hard, and neither could Johnny. It became apparent that the girls were living under fake IDs that were as solid as anything provided by the U.S. Marshall's Witness Security Program because three years of relentless effort by some very good bounty hunters couldn't put a dent in them.

To pull off a magic act like that, they would have needed help. So I went to a guy I knew who specialized in disappearances. Johnny's boys had interrogated him, too, and got nothing, but he owed me a favor and to pay it off he told me a story. It was about three beautiful princesses who had begged—literally begged—a good wizard a traveling bard had spoken about to help them escape from an evil monster. The wizard liked the princesses very much, plus it didn't hurt that they had a boatload of treasure. The wizard hid them in the forest until he was able to conjure a spell that rendered the princesses invisible. It was the finest work he had ever done—his masterpiece—and he boasted that no one would ever find and hurt the princesses again.

Which was good enough for me. Except Johnny the Boy started demanding results. I explained that while I had great faith in my craft, it was unlikely I could do in a short time what others couldn't accomplish over a period of years and he should forget the whole thing. Johnny didn't see it that way.

"They claim you can find anybody," he said.

"That's not entirely true."

"It better be."

Johnny the Boy suggested that I try harder and then started listing the names of family members and friends that might suffer due to my lack of success. I didn't think for a moment that he was bluffing. I understood Johnny's obsession. If it should become known that three girls fresh out of college had ripped him off and gotten away with it, well, a lot of Johnny Boy's rivals would look upon it as a sign of weakness, something you just didn't show in his line of work. Already there were rumors that Tony the Ant and Jimmy Legs were preparing to move on him, which was why Johnny the Boy so rarely left the fortress he had built for himself on Lake Michigan.

I didn't like it, but I went back to work in earnest, accumulating every piece of information about the girls that I could. See, the key to finding someone who is hiding in plain sight is the past. People are creatures of habit. After spending a lifetime doing a specific thing in a certain way, it becomes extremely difficult, if not impossible, to change. A fugitive who was an accountant, goes back to being an accountant; a used car salesman might give up cars, but odds are he'll sell something else. The girls had been footloose and fancy free for over three years now. Possibly they were sliding back into their old lives, whether they had meant to or not. Possibly they were making mistakes.

I catalogued the magazines the girls had subscribed to, and bought the subscription lists to all of them. I compiled the names and addresses of the business organizations they had joined and secured a list of members. I examined the membership directories and subscription lists of every public-relations-related association and newsletter I could find. I searched the motor vehicle licenses and registrations of forty-nine states and the criminal records of every county in all fifty states. I hired an information broker and had her hunt through bank accounts that had been opened IRS the past three years. I paid an IRS agent under the table to check on any female who was either depositing large sums of money in an account on a regular basis or passing large sums from one account to another. The most time consuming thing I did was look up the names of every woman between the ages of twenty and thirty who was issued a license by a State Board of Cosmetology somewhere in the U.S. in the past three years. Then I cross-referenced it all. It took me three months to find Karla's Kut & Kurl, opened just nine months earlier in Alma. Once I had that, it took three hours to find Meg and Josie's Hotel, Restaurant and Bar.

I drove out there. I popped into Karla's Kut & Kurl for a haircut. I recognized Linda instantly. She was all sweetness and light and she gave me the best haircut I ever had. While she was working a young woman entered the shop. With tears in her eyes she hugged Karla, thanked her profusely and told her that she was the kindest person ever. After the woman left I asked Karla what it was all about.

"She had a problem," Karla said. "I helped. No biggie."

I pressed but Karla wouldn't give me any more. I liked her for that.

After the haircut, she told me if I was looking for a meal or place to hang my hat, I couldn't do any better than Meg and Josie's place across the street. She leaned in and whispered.

"We're friends, so if you tell them I sent you they'll treat you just as shabbily as they do me."

The hotel registration desk was on the left as you entered the front door; the bar and restaurant were on the right. The restaurant had a nice lunch-hour trade; I didn't see a single empty table. Brenda met me at the door with a menu in her hand.

"I'm Josie," she said. "Can I help you?"

"Karla sent me," I said.

Josie hooked an arm under mine.

"Would you like to sit at the bar?" she asked.

She led me there before I could reply. She sat me on a stool and waved over the woman who was tending bar. Cassidy smiled as brightly as Brenda.

"Meg," Josie said. "This young man is a friend of Karla's."

"Oh," Meg said. "Are you married?"

"No, I'm not," I said.

"Neither is Karla."

For the next ninety minutes, they joked with me as if I was someone they were trying to set up with their little sister. That and the meal made it the most enjoyable lunch I could remember.

All during the drive back to Chicago I tried to think of how to avoid telling Johnny the Boy what I knew. There was no way. I liked the girls very much, but I had family and friends that I liked more. I told him everything. He asked about his money.

"They own a hotel," I said. "They own a hair salon. I don't know anything beyond that."

Johnny's henchman grinned.

"They'll tell us before we're done with them," he said.

I didn't like the implication, but what could I do?

Johnny the Boy gave me $50,000 in an envelope. That in itself made me nervous. Johnny wasn't the kind to give away fifty-K unless he intended to take it back. He then said he would pay me another ten large to go back to Alma and watch the girls until he arrived. It wasn't a request and I didn't take it as such. I drove back that night, settling into a room third floor front. The stretch of the Great River Road that passed through Alma was designated a National Scenic Byway, although there wasn't much to see from my window. Just the river, railroad tracks, a boat ramp, Lock and Dam Number Four and directly across from the hotel, the neon lights of Karla's Kut & Kurl. But that's where I spent most of my time, watching, waiting.

The rest I spent in the restaurant and bar. I came to know the girls quite well, mostly from customers—they didn't talk much about themselves. My favorite story was about how they had organized protests to keep the mayor from awarding the snowplowing contract to his brother-in-law and then, two weeks later when they learned the mayor's wife was diagnosed with breast cancer, hosted a fund-raiser to help pay her medical bills.

It was about 11:30 on the evening of the sixth day when they called me out. The bar was empty—there wasn't much nightlife in Alma during the middle of the week. I was sitting at the bar nursing a draft. Meg stood on the other side, a bar towel in her hand. Josie was still my favorite, but Meg had risen considerably in my estimation since the evening before. Josie sat on my right, Karla on my left.

"Who are you?" Karla asked.

"Kent Kramer," I said

"We know that," Josie said. "Why are you here?"

I didn't answer.

"You know who we are, don't you?" Meg said.

"I know who you are. I just don't know what names to call you."

"Darn it," Karla said.

"Does Johnny Scalise know?" Meg said.

"Yes."

"I knew it," Josie said. "I knew this day would come."

"Darn it," Karla said again.

Josie rested her head on the top of the bar.

"Now what?" she said.

As if on cue a man wearing a black suit, black shirt and black tie entered the bar. He paused at the entrance, found a table near the door and sat down facing us. All of us watched him intently. Karla gasped. Josie reached out and grabbed my arm. Meg had the presence of mind to circle the bar and walk up to his table.

"Good evening," she said. "May I get you something?"

"Seven and seven," the man answered.

Meg returned to the bar, mixed the drink and served it to the man.

"Thank you," he said.

We all watched him sipping the drink. He pretended not to notice. ESPN was on the monitor above the bar and he fixed his gaze on it and did not look away.

"What should we do?" Karla asked.

"Wait," I said.

I took a long pull of the beer. Josie became agitated.

"I'm not waiting," she said.

I took her hand.

"Please," I said. "Wait."

ESPN went through two commercial cycles while we waited. Finally, we all heard the ring of a cell phone. The man reached into his pocket, took it out and answered it.

"Yeah," he said. He paused. "All right."

He returned the phone to his pocket even as he rose from the chair. He walked across the bar. As he approached, he slid his hand under his suit jacket. Karla gasped again. The man smiled at her reaction. He produced an envelope from his inside pocket.

"You Kramer?" he asked.

I nodded. He set the envelope on the bar in front of me.

"Compliments of Jimmy Legs," he said.

I took the envelope and put it in my own pocket. I didn't open it; I didn't count the money that I knew was inside.

"Everything all right?" I asked.

"All right for us, not so much for Johnny the Boy," he answered.

"What took so long?"

"Johnny got it into his head that it was unsafe to leave his place in Chicago. Took a lot to lure him out. If he hadn't known about the ladies here, if he hadn't been so obsessed . . ."

The man nodded his head at the girls and left the bar.

It took a few moments before the four of us started breathing again.

"What just happened?" Josie asked.

I got up from the bar and turned toward the three girls.

"You can probably go home now if you want to. Questions will be asked, but . . ." I raised the palms of my hands upward and shrugged. Afterward I gave the place a parting glance. "I really like it here."

I moved to the door. Josie intercepted me. Her dark eyes cut off a chunk of my heart; I could feel her tucking it away in her pocket. She hugged me and kissed my cheek and said thank you.

I left and I never went back, although I've thought about it often.

Damn Cat

CAMILLE HYYTINEN

IF CIRCUMSTANCES WERE DIFFERENT, Anna Cameron would be enjoying the scenic drive from Minnesota into Wisconsin. Mid-April could bring just about anything from snow to sunshine, and today she was blessed with the latter.

Her heart was heavy despite the beautiful day, because her father was dying. It made the freshly-born bright green buds that were popping out on winter's bare limbs almost painful as she thought of the strong man who loved and supported her from little on, lying in the darkened living room in a hospital bed provided by Hospice. He was old with a bad heart and his time had come, but gosh it was difficult to accept—for both Anna and her mother.

Anna was leaving family of her own to spend time with her father and help care for him in his final days. It was a juggling act between her and two other siblings. She felt she didn't quite measure up to their expectations, being they lived closer with no children and were there to help more often than she. The guilt was everywhere—from her sixth grade son who had no one to help him with his homework to a husband who wanted her home and not one hundred fifty miles away.

Her father, however, was foremost on her mind . . . a man like no other.

Born in 1912, he was in his fifties when Anna was born. The conception was a result of take-out hamburgers, according to her mother. A surprise child, but loved very much, Anna was a tomboy and constantly in a tree when she was young—whether reading a book or hiding from civilization. The man was concerned she'd fall and break her neck, so he built her a platform to sit on high in the sky. An animal lover along with her older sister, they'd adopt everything from stray cats, which he had a distinct dislike for, to injured birds and bunnies. The cats were initially banned from the house but before long took up residence in Dad's favorite chair and continued to be part of his life even to this day.

Oddly enough, Angel was the current cat's name, but the old man called it Damn Cat and it seemed to take to that moniker as well. The cat had a bad habit of rubbing between a person's legs when they walked, trying to trip them up.

Since the old man had become ill and bed-ridden, Angel stayed close by, lying at the foot of his bed and keeping a close watch. Anna grinned, thinking about the cat she and her mother had found on her property years ago that was now Dad's Angel.

Jean Cameron was preparing lunch as Norman snoozed. She had just administered his pain medication so he would be out for at least an hour. She was exhausted and glad her youngest daughter was coming to help. As she chopped onion for the chicken salad, tears rolled down her wrinkled face, but not from the onions. She often thought of better times. Jean tried to keep the crying to a minimum and never let Norman see her upset, but sometimes it was very difficult.

She heard the back door open and quickly wiped the tears away with a piece of paper towel. *Anna must be early*, was her last coherent thought.

The young man dressed in black with a bandana covering half his face almost sent Jean to the floor in a faint. She steadied herself with the counter, eyes coming to rest on the onion chopping knife, then looking at the stranger in her kitchen.

"Do what I say and no one gets hurt. Understand, bitch?" He pointed a gun at her face.

It had been quite some time since anyone called her the B word . . . The knife was no match against a gun and she wasn't stupid enough to think it was.

"You alone?" His eyes scanned the kitchen as he moved closer.

Norman coughed in the living room and called her name as if on cue.

"Who's that?" He moved fast and was right next to her in an instant. Reaching behind her, he grabbed the knife before she had a chance to react.

"It's just my husband. He's sick—bed-ridden. He won't cause any trouble." Jean could hear her voice tremble and wondered if this was how she and Norman would meet their maker.

"Okay, okay, lady. I want your money, jewelry, anything you got of value. Where's it at? Right now. I want it right now."

Jean went to the hutch in the kitchen. All of the cash along with the bills due to be paid were in the top drawer. "I don't have any jewelry. Only cheap stuff. But here's all the money." She opened the drawer for him.

He scooped it up and pocketed it. "Give me your wedding ring."

Jean hesitated. It had been on her finger for fifty-three years. "It's not worth much. Why would you even want it?"

"Do what I say, lady. And don't ask questions." He held out his hand.

Jean twisted the ring off her finger and deposited it into the robber's hand, a single tear sliding down her cheek.

He smiled. "Good girl. Thank you. Now . . . take a kitchen chair and come with me."

Jean dragged a chair, following the man into the living room where thankfully Norman had fallen back to sleep.

Spotting the stranger, the cat left its post and ran off into another room.

The robber instructed Jean to sit in the chair while he bound her hands behind her and tied a gag around her mouth. She noticed his hands were trembling as much as her own.

"Since you cooperated, I'll let you live," he offered. "But don't tell anyone. Don't call the cops. If you do, I'll be back, understand?"

Jean nodded and mumbled behind the gag in her mouth. He didn't tie the ropes very tight and the gag wasn't even gagging her. He was new to this . . . she could tell.

"Have a good day," he said smiling, and left her alone with a snoring Norman who was none the wiser.

Jean looked at the clock on the living room wall—11:45. Her daughter would be here any minute and she prayed the man would be long gone by the time Anna showed up.

A crash resounded in the kitchen.

Silence, except for Norman's oxygen machine, filled the empty space.

It was a little before noon when Anna pulled into her parent's drive-way. The day was bright and warm and as she extracted her suitcase from the trunk, she mentally prepared herself for the depressing state her father was in. The Hospice nurse would be coming today and it would give Anna opportunity to get her mother out of the house, if only for a little while. She worried about her mom almost as much as her dad. Life was certainly not easy these days.

Trudging up the steps, suitcase in tow, she entered her childhood home, almost tripping on a stranger lying face down, throw rug bunched to one side, out cold.

Shock registered and panic quickly followed, adrenaline coursing through her veins. "What the . . . Mom, Dad," she called, racing through the house, expecting to find the worst. As she ran she pulled out her cell and dialed 911. "There's been a robbery . . . or something. He's still on the premises. Hurry!" She recited the address and dropped the phone as she entered the living room and discovered her mother, very much alive, but very frightened.

"Oh my God! Mom . . . what happened here? Oh my God." She untied her mother and removed the gag.

"Oh, honey. I'm so glad you're here." She hugged her daughter. "We're okay, don't worry."

The sound of sirens rapidly approaching brought them back to reality.

Both Anna and her mother met the police at the door. The stranger was just starting to come around, moaning and rubbing his head. Before he could regain full consciousness, handcuffs were slapped on him and his rights were read.

The cat had been sitting stoically in one corner watching everything, and sauntered over to rub on Anna's legs. She bent down to pet it and coo. "Hi Angel. How's my Angel cat . . ."

The would-be robber scowled, suddenly remembering how he met this untimely demise. "Damn cat," he muttered as the cops led him out the door and shoved him into the back of a waiting squad.

Slater Maxwell

E. KELLY KEADY

THE FIRST BLAST OF ARCTIC AIR that steals the air from your lungs is always the hardest, but that's part of living in Minnesota, I said to myself unconvincingly as I left Once Upon a Crime Mystery Book Store. Flipping up my collar reminded me about the job, but not as much as the two slugs that shredded a fair amount of the muscle in my right thigh, making me wince as I walked up the stairs. I did better on level ground so I picked up my pace on the sidewalk with my new purchases clutched in my left hand, wrapped in doubled layered bags to keep them safe from the fine light snow that had been falling for the past twenty-four hours. The next stop on my usual Friday night routine, kitty corner from where I stood on Lyndale Avenue, was the CC Club.

Technically a dive bar by most objective standards, but on another lonely Friday night, it was my book club for a couple hours. I was quickly approaching fifty with the last fifteen as a widower and the past three years away from the job on disability, so I was hardly in a position to be picky about the company I kept. Grabbing the door and opening it, I let the stale bar air slowly consume me and pollute any fresh molecules that clung to my rumpled clothes.

Although the barflies melted into the rustic pine and red leather interior, the bartender's bright shiny demeanor stood out like a sore thumb. Todd, or Todd Johnson, as he instantly introduced himself to every new patron who passed through the entryway, was new to the CC Club. Everyone else was measured in terms of election cycles to describe when they first became regulars to "The Club." There were a lot of Reagan's, some H.W.'s, a couple Fords and Carters and one Nixon. Only the Obamas smiled back at Todd Johnson. Me, I'm a Reagan, having my first scotch in the club back in 1981 after Reagan got shot then spending the ensuing nights at the edge of my new barstool watching the life and times of John Hinckley as told by Ted Koppel. This was long before Todd Johnson had any idea that he would have to pick up a second job to help support his nine children. But I liked Todd, even when his smiling face, tailor made for greeting kids as they entered grade school, spoiled any self loathing I had built up over my day.

"Hi Detective Maxwell, I mean Slater! What can I get you this fine night?" asked the beaming Todd Johnson.

"It's dinnertime," I mumbled.

"How about a scotch?"

"Same thing," I said completing our ritual.

"Old or new?"

"Just bought a couple new books, so better give me an old scotch, please."

I looked around.

A typical Friday night before the twenty-somethings took over the bar for beers and fries. Silent Tom laid his head back on the bar with a cup of coffee in front of him after blowing his disposable income, and a little indisposable income, across the street on Captain Morgan and Cokes, pretending he was an Obama rather than a Herbert Walker Bush.

Crazy Di was back in her corner across the bar by the window with her double Manhattan garnished with four cherries on a sword, not a toothpick, never a toothpick, but that's another story. Di's face was weathered, not from Minnesota's arctic air, but from a lifetime of smoking. She always demanded to watch Larry King and only responded to "Lady Di" or "Your highness," two monikers with which Todd Johnson would usually add a gentlemanly bow. She definitely was a Reagan, even though she could pass as an Eisenhower.

I felt confident that the interior plastic wrap protected my books, so I set them on the bar even though Silent Tom might unexpectedly wake up, order a Cap'n' Coke, and Todd would be foolish enough to pour him one.

Now it was dinnertime. My first sip of Macallan warmed my mouth then soothed my throat before trickling down to fill my stomach.

As I started my second sip, Todd Johnson shouted over my shoulder, "Hello Detective McCambridge!"

"Hello!" barked the voice behind me.

"Todd Johnson," the bartender said, beaming, "The usual?"

"No, I'm on the job," stated the new patron.

"Todd," I added.

"I know his name, Detective Maxwell."

Whenever Minneapolis homicide Detective Jim McCambridge called me 'Detective Maxwell', a title I have not used since my disability kicked in, I understood that my brain needed to find that 'on' switch again.

"Are you going to buy me a drink at least?"

"You have a full one right in front of you."

"I'm hungry tonight."

"Okay," said McCambridge hesitating as he stared at the bartender.

"Todd," I added again.

"I know," the Minneapolis Homicide Detective said before overemphasizing, "Todd, get Detective Maxwell another scotch."

Two Macallans. This could be a really good night or a really bad one.

"Slater, I need to run something by you."

"I'm all ears."

"Is there somewhere else we can talk?"

"It's me, you, Todd, Silent Tom, and Crazy Di. How much more intimate can it be?"

"I heard that," snapped Crazy Di jabbing the sword that still had one cherry on it at Maxwell.

"I mean Lady Di," I corrected myself and lifted my scotch toward her.

Obviously uncomfortable, Detective McCambridge and I had gone though this dance before but really, who was going to rat him out about police procedure? Crazy Di . . . I mean Lady Di? He knew this as well as I did, but I guess he felt he had to at least make the objection before asking for my advice.

"We have a guy downtown I'm following up on for a . . ." he said, looking around to see if anyone realized what they were talking about, "10–109."

"A homicide," I whispered.

"Cut it out Slater. The guy is a cold blooded killer, but he has an air tight alibi."

"What is it?"

"His girlfriend swears he was over at her place all night."

"What happened?"

"The victim and the perp lived together. The perp says the victim was drinking heavily and passed out. Since the perp had sleep apnea, he assumes the victim choked to death on his own spit in his sleep."

"Who found him?"

"The victim's boyfriend. He said the roommates hated one another."

"Where was he?"

"His work confirmed his timeline. The time of death does not work for him."

"And the roommate's girlfriend?"

"She admits that her boyfriend complained that the deceased was a freeloading drunk that had not paid rent in the past six months, but she swears he was with her in St. Paul the whole time. That's where we found the perp. There's also a possible hate crime scenario, because the girlfriend says the perp is not a big fan of the Rainbow Coalition."

"Where was the perp's car?"

"At the girlfriend's."

"Does the girlfriend have a car?"

"No."

"Did the perp or the girlfriend say how long they were at her apartment?"

"Yes. They said they had not left the apartment since they heard about the winter storm warning, and that was hours before it started snowing.

"Did you check the perp's car?"

"Yes, it was snow covered," said an irritated Detective McCambridge thinking he had wasted his time and eight dollars on Slater's scotch.

"How did you know it was his car?" I asked.

"I scraped off the windows and verified the VIN numbers."

"Scraped off the windows?"

"Of course, you dolt. Your Minnesota winters are not only going to ruin all my clothes, but I've gone through three scrapers this year because they get 'borrowed' all the time."

It was time to enjoy a long drink from one of the Macallans waiting for me.

"I'm wasting your time and mine," said Detective McCambridge as he turned from Maxwell.

I wondered if I could get a third scotch out of him.

"Todd."

"Yes, Slater."

"You've lived in Minnesota your whole life, haven't you?"

"Wouldn't have it any other way, Slater."

"You betcha," I added.

"Slater," started Detective McCambridge as he zipped up his coat, "I'll let you know how it turns out."

"Wait," I said before taking another long drag from my Scotch . . . just a few more humiliating moments . . . "Todd, do you have a garage?"

"Yeah Slater, but with you know, with the junk, kids' bikes and stuff, only my wife's van fits in the garage."

I finished the rest of Macallan number one too fast to enjoy it, but the possibility of a third was on the horizon.

"Slater," said Detective McCambridge.

I ignored the detective.

"Where do you park your car Todd?"

"In the driveway outside."

"All the time."

"All the time," said Todd as he looked outside and for the first time sounded less cheerful than his usual demeanor.

"So whenever it snows, your car is outside," I repeated, eyeing my second Macallan and sensing McCambridge's ever increasing impatience.

"Of course," the Minnesotan admitted.

"So you have to clean off your car every time that it snows?"

"Of course," admitted Todd. "Theresa would do it, but I usually get out there early."

"Slater," said McCambridge sternly, "I'm on the job. I am not here to play games."

"I will bet you another Macallan that Todd will break your perp's alibi," I offered, thinking that I may have strung my old friend on a bit too long.

"Another Macallan?" said McCambridge.

I nodded slowly. The fly stuck in the web.

His former partner laid another ten bucks on the bar, but kept his hand on the money.

"Todd, which is harder after a snowfall? Cleaning a car off that you had been driving around just before it snowed, or a car that had not moved for hours before it snowed?"

"Slater, that's kind of a dumb question."

"Why Todd?"

"Same reason I pull my wipers up after I've been driving around in the snow."

With the third scotch in the bag, I enjoyed the first sip from Macallan number two.

"What do you mean, Todd?"

"If I'm driving around in the snow my car is warm, and if I keep my wiper blades down and it is still snowing, they will freeze to the windshield."

"What do you mean?"

"It's not rocket science, Detective Maxwell."

"I know, Todd." I answered reaching his limits, "but my friend here is not a Minnesotan like us."

"With most snowfalls this time of year, like this last one, the temperature is below freezing, so if your car has been running, the snow melts when it hits it, but will freeze later when the car cools down."

"Todd" I started winding down my Socratic lesson, "if your car had not been running before it snowed, and let's say it had not moved hours before it started to snow, say like it is tonight, would you have to scrape it off?"

"No. Slater you know that, it's too cold. I'd just brush it off the car. The car is too cold for the snow to melt and refreeze."

"And again, if you have been out driving right before it snowed or while it's been snowing?"

"Slater?" said the fed up detective.

"You scrape it off," insisted Todd Johnson.

"You scrape it off," I repeated knowing Todd would soon deliver the third McCallum.

"Jim?" I said.

McCambridge took his hand off the ten dollar bill.

"Todd," I finally acknowledge, "You solved a murder case tonight."

"Maybe what you guys do isn't so hard after all," said the bartender.

"Thanks, Slater," said Detective McCambridge leaving the Club.

"Thank you, Todd," I said moving McCambridge's ten dollar bill to the bartender, knowing I needed another scotch like I needed another hole in my peg leg.

Once Upon a Rhyme

LINDA KOUTSKY

"We don't read and write poetry because it's cute. We read and write poetry because we are members of the human race. And the human race is filled with passion. And medicine, law, business, engineering, these are noble pursuits and necessary to sustain life. But poetry, beauty, romance, love, these are what we stay alive for."
—JOHN KEATING, in the movie "Dead Poets Society"

CHAPTER ONE

"BUT THE BOOK'S GOING TO THE PRINTER TODAY!" I exclaimed. "I know, I know," Margo said, "He was adamant. He said he'd cancel appearances unless we slipped in this last-minute poem. He insists it's crucial to the book. It's short so it won't throw off the page count. We could even drop the colophon on the last page."

Margo, the typically easy-going managing editor at Pettingill Press, was just as exasperated with Jerome A. Chadwick as the rest of the staff. From the minute his second manuscript was accepted he turned into a problem author. He disregarded edits, added and removed poems on every draft, complained about the margins and tabs, and now he was threatening to cancel events our publicist had been lining up for months. On top of it all, he was a clumsy wreck who broke something every time he came into our offices. After he was here last week we had to replenish our first-aid kit's band-aids because he knocked over a vase of flowers and cut himself. But even though he drove us crazy, we all had to agree with a reviewer at *Publishers Weekly*, that "Chadwick grasps humanity by the collar and shakes out gems."

My only direct experience with Jerome was on his cover design. Initially he wanted an all white cover with his title and name in 14 point American Typewriter. As Pettingill's book designer, I told him that wouldn't help sell books because covers needed to look good small, and in black and white for ads, but he wanted to see it anyway. A lot of people give their input on cover design. Our marketing staff wanted the cover to reflect a regional influence since he had a loyal local following. An intern who idolized Jerome suggested using a photo of his hand. The publisher thought it should look post-Kerouac. Authors give their input too, but their best creativity is reserved for *writing* the book. My job is to use principles of design with artwork and typography to grab a potential buyer's attention amidst the vast sea of titles. For Jerome's *Word Search* I designed several covers before we all agreed on one.

Melanie heard us talking and came out of her cubicle, calendar in hand. "Fine! Let him cancel events. I swear, some authors don't want to sell their books." Jerome did have good sales with his first book and we all hoped that continued. "I'm waiting to hear back from one more bookstore then I'm done with him. I've set up readings all over town. He e-mails me on the hour with more requests and keeps asking about his marketing materials—the postcards and bookmarks were just designed this week!" Melanie pivoted on her patent-leather heels then looked back at us and said, "I don't know if he does this to you guys, but he signs every note to me with 'hugs and kisses.' I don't know if he's just difficult or if he's stalking me. My boyfriend Rodney tends to thinks it's the latter. All I care about is that we have books on time. We can't have events without books."

Shaking my head, I said, "Okay, give me the poem. I'll see if I can take up some line spacing earlier in the book. The courier's coming in an hour. Jerome's not going to see another proof." Margo waved her hand in agreement. For the initial galley, printed for reviewers well before the actual book, I set the text in Minion, one of the most popular typefaces in book design because of its classic proportions and high readability. Now I'm wondering if that was a premonition—Jerome has us scurrying around like his own worker bees.

CHAPTER TWO

"Thank you all for coming to tonight's reading. We're pleased to have Jerome with us to share from his just-published book *Word Search*." The crowded room broke into applause as Jerome stumbled up the stairs to the podium. He smiled and held his book high. As he pulled the promotional bookmark out it brushed against his index finger causing a small papercut. He sucked his finger then told the audience, "I have been lucky to work with such a fine publishing house. They put up with my perfectionism, catered to my whims, and I do believe that eventually I worked my way into their hearts. You know who you are—hugs and kisses. The first poem I'd like to read tonight is the last one in the book. It was put there moments before the book went to press. I hope you enjoy it."

EMERGING

In crisp air they rise.
Loose from earth's hold,
outstretched and grown wise,
vanquished from cold.

Each warming sun ray
melts longing's pain,
erases past days,
laments coming rain.

All hearts, blossoms too,
need love, crucial thing,
it bursts from ground's dew.
Enter now—spring.

Jerome lowered his head, put both hands on the podium, and closed his eyes in reverence. The crowd remained still—like at a symphony, no one claps 'til it's over. He gently swayed as if feeling the power of his own artistry. Then Jerome fell dead to the floor.

CHAPTER THREE

"Those of you gathered in this room today have been chosen to participate in our new Writers in the Prisons program. This is your opportunity to write a short story or poem with a visiting artist. Yes, Rodney? I see your hand's raised."

With a loud voice and a shaking fist Rodney said, "A poem is what got me *into* this mess! He was after Melanie all the time. Then when I saw that hidden message in the first letters of his poem I knew why. I poisoned the bookmark. How did I know he'd actually cut himself with it that night? I hate poetry . . . serves him right."

COLOPHON
The book *Word Search* was designed in the offices
of Pettingill Press. The text is set in the typeface Minion
with poem titles in Anything You Want.

DISCLAIMER
This story is a work of fiction and the product of the author's
imagination. Any resemblance to actual persons or events—
I swear on a Gutenberg bible—are purely coincidental.

ACKNOWLEDGMENTS
The author wishes to thank all the authors she's ever
worked with in the past (and hopefully future), as well
as her coworkers at a real publishing house, for their
expansive sense of humor and kind understanding.

Luck

WILLIAM KENT KRUEGER

cNALLY TOOK A STOOL WITH A GOOD VIEW of the pool table. The guy behind the bar was new. McNally had heard that Eddie, the bartender before the war, had been killed at Guadalcanal. Head blown clean off his shoulders. He ordered a shot of Cutty with a beer back and settled in to watch the show.

At the pool table, the hunchback wasn't winning yet, but McNally knew that he would eventually. He was hustling a Marine, or a guy who'd recently been one, judging from the Semper Fi tattoo on his forearm and the sharp, cold way he eyed the pool table and the hunchback. A long scar ran down the Marine's neck like a rope. The Marine wore his shirttail out. If McNally was any judge of character—and like most petty crooks, he was—somewhere under that shirttail, the man was carrying a gun or maybe a big knife.

It took four games before the hunchback made his move. The Marine had been calling him names, taunting him with "cripple" and "freak," to keep him rattled, and the hunchback made like he'd finally had enough and blew his top. He was down a hundred bucks at that point. He slapped four crisp Franklins on the table and told the Marine he was willing to bet it all on the next game. The Marine laughed and said okay by him. The hunchback insisted on seeing the money, and the Marine obliged and, with a snaky grin, accused the hunchback of being even dumber than he was crippled. Big mistake. The hunchback cleared the table, took what was probably the Marine's whole roll, and, leaning on his cane and limping slow, walked away a winner. With a look deadly as a bayonet, the Marine watched him go.

McNally went out ahead and was waiting in the alley north of the bar. When the hunchback passed, McNally stepped out and caught him by surprise.

"Hey, Bobo, what's shaking?"

It was a bitter cold night, the threat of snow in the air, and Bobo wore a big camelhair overcoat. Probably cost him a C-note easy, McNally figured. The moment McNally made his presence known, a little .32 materialized in the hunchback's hand, aimed at McNally's belly.

"Whoa, Bobo. Just me. Ed McNally."

"Call me Bobo again and I'll kill you," the hunchback said.

"Sure, Arthur. No problem."

The hunchback scowled up at him. "Heard you were dead. Heard somewhere in the South Pacific."

"Guess you heard wrong," McNally said with a laugh.

The hunchback didn't reply, but from his expression, McNally assumed the man wouldn't have minded at all if what he'd heard were true.

"Just got out," McNally said. "Just back in the old neighborhood for a quick visit. Things sure have changed."

The hunchback put his gun away and started limping again, his cane making a little clack every time it came down on the sidewalk. McNally fell in step beside him. He was sorely tempted to mimic the awkward gait of the cripple. McNally had grown up making fun of Bobo in exactly that way.

"Some things haven't changed," McNally observed. "You still shoot a mean game of pool. Still taking the suckers."

"A guy's gotta make a living," Bobo said.

"Judging from that coat you're wearing, you're living pretty well. Say, don't you worry about pissing off guys like that Marine tonight? Ain't like before the war, you know. Guys like him, they're used to killing. He'll slit your throat in the blink of an eye. Hell, guy like him, he'd enjoy it"

"Been dealing with guys like him my whole life," Bobo said. And he cast a sidelong glance at McNally.

They walked down Gower Avenue and turned onto Boyle. It was late and just beginning to snow and the streets were mostly empty. McNally recalled the old days, the hangouts, the corners where they'd pinched fruit from the stands of the Guineas, and the alleys where they'd hung back in the shadows, eyeing the cars parked on the street, figuring which would be the easiest to boost. In the summer, the neighborhood had smelled of hot cement and bad sewers. In the winter, it was dingy with soot-covered snow. He thought about all the years he and the other kids of the neighborhood had spent getting into trouble there. A lot of those guys were dead now, killed making the world safe for democracy. But not McNally. McNally had watched out for McNally and let the other guys die for democracy.

"I guess you had it pretty easy here," McNally said.

"Easy?" Bobo stopped and swung around to face McNally. "Listen, if they'd've taken me, I'd've gone. And if you think being me is easy, I'd love to have you walk in my shoes for a day."

Forget the shoes, McNally thought. But I'd take that coat.

"Just meant that you were lucky not having to go. Hell, you were always lucky, Bobo."

"I said don't call me that."

"Right," McNally said.

He was feeling again the burning resentment he'd always felt toward the hunchback. God had more than evened out the measure of hardship that came with Bobo's crippled body by giving him the most incredible luck. His skill at the pool table, for example. Who would have suspected, looking at that grotesquely humped body, the grace he was capable of when leaning over the green felt? Not the men whose money he took, certainly. And McNally had never heard of the hunchback ever once being jumped by somebody who'd lost a wad to him playing pool. What was that if not sheer luck?

But Bobo's luck was about to change. McNally was going to see to that.

They came to the old brownstone apartment building where Bobo had lived all his life.

"You're ma still here?" McNally asked.

"She died," Bobo replied. "Year ago."

"Sorry." Though he wasn't at all. Another stroke of luck for Bobo had been a mother who, despite his deformity, had loved him fiercely. McNally's old lady, on the other hand, would have thrown her son out if he hadn't been drafted.

They stepped into the light of the single bulb that dimly illumined the entrance to the building. Bobo hesitated before unlocking the door.

"Look," he said to McNally, and his demeanor had changed. Softened. "A lot of the guys in the neighborhood won't be coming back. The truth is I never liked you much, McNally, but I'm glad you made it home safe. You need something to get yourself started again, let me know, okay?"

"Don't worry about me." McNally tried not to let his sudden anger show. Who the hell did this cripple think he was, feeling sorry for McNally? "I got something in the works."

The hunchback nodded, but didn't make any move to head inside. In the dim light, as the snow began to fall harder around them, he looked up into McNally's face with genuine concern.

"It's not luck," he said.

"Huh?"

"The difference between you and me, it's got nothing to do with luck. We're like magnets, McNally. What comes our way, we bring to us. That Marine tonight? He's like all the guys I hustle. The only thing in his heart is taking and so he got took. You see what I'm saying?"

But McNally didn't. All he saw was the cripple in the warm camelhair.

Bobo shrugged, as if giving up on McNally, and said, "Anything else?"

"Naw," McNally replied.

They stood a moment, looking at each other like monkeys in separate cages.

"Guess I'll see you around," Bobo said.

"Guess you will," McNally replied.

The hunchback turned his attention to the door and the key and the lock, and McNally took the opportunity in that moment of distraction to bring out the iron pipe he'd slipped up his sleeve before entering the bar that night. He brought it down against the back of Bobo's head, and the hunchback slumped and fell in a heap in the open doorway. McNally quickly dragged him inside and turned out the hallway light and the entrance light. In the dark, he frisked Bobo and found the wad of money the hunchback had won from the Marine. Then he took off his own shabby jacket and replaced it with the hunchback's fine camelhair overcoat.

The hunchback groaned, as if coming around. McNally considered hitting him again, maybe doing him in for good, but decided against it. He liked the idea of the cripple waking up and realizing the way things stood.

"Your luck's finally changed, Bobo." McNally ran his hand over the smooth, warm fabric of his new coat. "Mine, too."

He opened the door and saw a light in an upstairs apartment across the street and someone at the window there, watching. He picked up Bobo's cane and stepped outside into the night and the snow. He hunched himself in the way he used to when, as a kid, he'd cruelly mimicked the cripple, and he made a show of limping along the sidewalk. In this way, feeling better than he had in a long time, he headed straight toward the mouth of the shadowed alley, where the Marine with the long scar and the big knife crouched and waited.

A Darker Shade of Green

LORI L. LAKE

FROM A SECOND-STORY WINDOW, Ralph Abernathy peered through bleak spring rain and watched a man in a dirt-brown cowboy hat flip open the lid on the recycling bin. He took a final slurp from a jumbo soda and tossed it in the container, straw and all, then wiped his hands on his shirt. He strutted along the walkway like a rodeo star.

This wasn't the first time Ralph had seen him dump trash in with the recycling. Why was he so lazy that he couldn't cross the parking lot and use the regular garbage can?

Without thinking of consequences, Ralph hastened through the back door and down the stairs. "Hey," he called out.

The man glanced back, but didn't stop.

Ralph raised his voice. "Hey, you. In the cowboy hat."

Now the man spun around and looked at him quizzically.

"Yeah, I'm talking to you." Ralph made his way down the path between the condo buildings. "I'm concerned about something and wanted to mention it."

The cowboy waited, a smirk on his lips. As Ralph approached, he realized the man was much shorter than he'd appeared from above, not taller than five-five, maybe five-six at most. The man had been unnaturally brown when Ralph had first noticed him around the complex, but his tan was fading now. His shirt was rumpled, his jeans stained here and there. Instead of cowboy boots he wore ratty graying tennis shoes. Only his hat looked at all crisp. Ralph thought the rest of him appeared seedy and unkempt.

"Whatchu want, old man?"

Ralph was taken aback by the rudeness, but he chose to ignore it. "Well, sir, I wanted to give you some information about the Minneapolis recycling program."

"What?" He drew out the word, *whuuuh-ut*, which made him sound ignorant.

"I'm just asking that you follow the rules for sorting garbage from the things that can be recycled."

"Y'all can go screw ya-self."

"Whoa. Now don't be that way." He gave what he hoped was a sincere smile. "Please, hear me out. It's real simple. Soda pop cups and fast food bags need to go into the garbage can. You can't recycle containers that food and drink have been in."

"I can do anything I want. Now buzz off."

"But—"

With a leer, the cowboy said, "You the pimp daddy for those lezzies that live here?"

Ralph was so surprised by the man's utter lack of respect that he couldn't speak. As Ralph sputtered, the cowboy walked away.

"Wait a minute," Ralph said in his best military command voice. "Just wait one damn minute. You must not be from around here. Where are you from?"

The man hastened back and jabbed his index finger in Ralph's face. Alarmed, Ralph held his ground.

"Ain't none of your business where I'm from, ya old geezer. You don't get to know a ding-dang thing about me. You can just move your skinny little self back to whatever hole you done crawled out of before I get a notion to kick yo' ass."

"So it's going to be like that, huh?"

The cowboy gave a smug nod. He grinned, revealing some of the worst teeth Ralph had ever seen on someone so young. Did he go to sleep sucking on a baby bottle full of soda? How could his teeth get so cracked and brown? Disgusted, Ralph stepped back. Until the cowboy opened his mouth, he'd been an average-looking, blue-eyed fellow, not so different from the young soldiers Ralph had commanded in the 1970s. Maybe malicious words, over time, had rotted away the teeth they had to pass over as they entered a world of people who deserved better treatment.

Defeated, Ralph retreated to his daughter's condo. He'd been staying with Flora and her partner since both winter and his chemo treatments had ended. He and Flora hadn't been close over the last few years, ever since his wife had died. Mostly the rift had been on account of him not knowing how to deal with Stacy or her relationship with his daughter. But when Flora heard about his prostate cancer, she'd come to him immediately. He thought about how sweet it had been to reunite with his little girl, and he had to admit that he'd eventually taken a liking to Stacy.

Right now the gals—he thought of them as "the gals" even though they were both in their mid-forties—were on a three-week European spring holiday. He intended to take good care of their place for them so when they returned home, he'd have earned his keep. He'd already installed a new water faucet in the kitchen, and almost every day he replaced another worn wall outlet. Next up he wanted to refinish a table, but that was a complicated project he wasn't quite ready to commit to. Some days were better than others. Today he'd started out with energy . . . but now he was pissed that he'd wasted it on that miserable excuse for a human being.

With a sigh, he sank down in a recliner, his thinning hair and shoulders damp from the rain. He wondered again about the cowboy. What was his name? Did he even live in one of the condos? Maybe he just walked through periodically to dump his garbage. He hailed from somewhere down south, but Ralph had no clue where. All he could say was that the mystery man gave Southerners a bad name.

The following day Ralph felt more energetic than he had in weeks. He was even able to keep down a full breakfast. He felt so good that he drove off to the grocery store and bought himself a steak, baked potato, sponge cake, and some frozen strawberries. He didn't often make such an elaborate meal, but he had the sense that he'd turned the corner. At long last, he prayed his health and vitality were returning. Every day he'd been feeling stronger.

Later in the evening, after his tasty meal, he watched TV, then rose to prepare for bed. It hit him that the garbage and recycling trucks were due in the morning, so he went around the condo and gathered up what needed to go out.

Outside the air was icy, and he wished he'd slipped a coat on. He left Flora's recycling basket near the recycling alcove and carted the two bags of trash across the dark parking lot. As he retraced his steps, he saw the cowboy at the end of the sidewalk near the street. Picking up the basket full of cans and newspapers, Ralph chose to ignore the jerk. One of the big containers was full, and he closed that one. The other had only a paper box in the bottom—and the cowboy's soda cup. Irritated, Ralph leaned the lid against the wall. As he bent to pick up the basket, an arm reached over his head and slam-dunked a bag into the recycling drum.

Ralph couldn't believe his eyes. He straightened up and examined the cowboy's sneering face. "I thought I made it clear that greasy burger bags can't be recycled."

"Whatchu gonna do about it, old man?" His voice was taunting, almost gleeful.

Ralph struggled to control his temper. What an asshole, he thought. This man isn't worth my precious time. "Never mind then. Guess I'll just report you."

Ralph didn't expect the sudden change in the cowboy's demeanor. The expression on his face sent a stab of fear through him. He looked ready to attack. Ralph took a deep breath and relaxed his stance, trying to control the tense feeling in his chest.

The cowboy stepped closer. "My daddy used to take out dumbshits like you."

"Doesn't sound like you had a very nice father."

"Screw you! My daddy could kick your ass right now."

Ralph's heart kicked into overdrive. Was this punk really threatening him? Over a bag of McDonald's trash? He hadn't survived the NVA, the VietCong, and the jungles of Vietnam without well-honed instincts, and right now, every alarm bell he'd ever heard in his days as a soldier was clanging. Quietly, he said, "Back off, son."

"Heh—or you'll do what?"

"I'll take care of myself."

"Yeah, right." He leaned in some more.

"Back off, buddy. I don't want to hurt you."

Now the cowboy was laughing hard, his mouth open, corroded teeth shining black in the ambient light.

"I said get away from me or you'll be feeling some unexpected pain."

The cowboy kept laughing. He turned his head slightly and shifted as though he meant to leave.

Ralph saw the fist coming. He stepped aside. He brought his own fist to his chest and struck out with the side of his wrist. The hard bone in his forearm caught his attacker in the throat. The cowboy let out a gurgling sound and doubled over. Ralph tried to step away, but the man charged forward, head-butting him against the recycling containers.

Ralph brought his knee up hard. With a grunt, his opponent rose up a bit, then made a strangled whinny. He wrapped an arm around Ralph's shoulder and tried, ineffectually, to land a punch.

One sharp blow to the cowboy's face, and it was all over. He gave another gurgle and relaxed, dead weight against Ralph's chest. Ralph got an arm under the man and lifted him, straining under the weight. He dumped him headfirst into the recycling drum. The man didn't move. Tangled up in the bottom of the container, he looked a lot smaller now.

"I told you not to go after me, son." Ralph breathed deep, catching his breath with effort. "You should have believed me when I said you'd be the one feeling pain." He picked up his basket and dumped the contents in the bin. "You can sleep it off there, pal. In the future, back off when someone requests it." He smacked the lid down, expecting that any second the man would suddenly rouse and shoot up and out, but all was quiet.

Ralph backed away to the foot of the condo stairs and waited.

Nothing happened.

He took the basket back up to his daughter's condo and returned with a flashlight. Shining it down into the recycling container, he saw that newspapers covered most of the cowboy except for an arm and the side of his face. There was a streak of blood coming out of his nose. One inert blue eye stared up at Ralph.

Ralph dropped the lid and backed away. He stepped on something, looked down, saw it was the brown cowboy hat. He picked it up and stuffed it into the other recycling container.

Back in Flora's apartment, he started to shake. Was the guy really dead?

He'd seen plenty of dead men in the jungle, and the cowboy definitely looked dead. Ralph's stomach hurt and his good meal roiled inside him. He resolved not to throw up. He made a big pot of coffee and sat at the window, waiting.

At four A.M., Ralph was roused by the beep-beep-beeping of a garbage truck. Bleary-eyed, he watched a worker manhandle the recycling bin out of the alcove, struggling with the weight of it. At the curb, the worker used a hand-control on the side of the truck to attach the bin to the hydraulic side-loader. The container rose slowly in the air and dumped the contents.

Ralph watched him roll the empty back and wrangle the second container. With a sigh, he muttered out loud, "Now that's my kind of recycling."

Beauty is in the Eye of the Newt

JESS LOUREY

THE AMPHIBIAN DARTED ACROSS THE TABLE. Its movement was rhythmic: right foot forward, right hip forward, ungainly tail; left foot forward, left hip forward, ungainly tail. It traveled quickly and with a drunken grace. The creature's back was moist gooseflesh, bumpy and slick to the touch.

It would have leapt off the table in fear if Penelope Church hadn't pinned its prehistoric appendage with her finger at just the right moment.

"Is it poisonous?"

"Not unless you swallow it." She pinched the thick tail between her forefinger and thumb and held the newt in the air, revealing its shocking yellow underbelly. The craven abdomen was unmarred except for a chicken-scratch birthmark near the right front leg. "He found this in his car?"

Len shrunk back from the arching animal. "Yeh."

"Was its skin wet-looking, like it is now, or dry?"

"Does it matter?"

She dropped the creature gently into a terrarium that she had pulled from storage. "If we're going to work together, Mr. Phelps, you'll have to excise your habit of questioning me. If I ask, it matters. Do we have an understanding?"

"Sorry, ma'am. Of course. The skin was wet when I picked up the lizard . . ."

"Newt."

He drew in his breath. "Newt. When I was handed the newt, the skin looked wet, but it was in a bowl with a skim of water and a sponge. I'll call to find out what condition it was in when he took it out of the Beemer."

"Excellent." She looked at him for the first time since he had brought her the news and the creature. A broad smile tipped her eyes. "And tell him I'll take the case."

Len Phelps tapped his forehead steadily against the steering wheel. He couldn't lose this paycheck. If he did, he'd be back on the street. He'd been deep into the sauce when the lady found him. She was plain-looking, tall, with one of those pear-shaped bodies that didn't do much for men. With some make-up and a curl to her hair, she might have turned a head or two, but she didn't bother frosting her cake.

"Excuse me." It hadn't been a question. The crisp and sweet melody of her voice had been an unexpected counterpoint to her appearance. "Are you in need of a job?"

Len remembered laughing, an empty, bronchial sound. "The boys you're looking for are farther down the street. Try Larkspur Avenue."

"I'm looking for an assistant. I think you'll do just fine."

He closed one eye so the other could focus on her. The brick wall of the bar he had been thrown out of pressed coldly against his back. "What kinda work are we talking about?"

"Let's get you some hot food and strong coffee, and we can discuss that." Again, not a question. Len had followed her. It's not like his dance card was full, and a hot meal sounded better than a kick in the pants. After four over-easy eggs, hash browns, toast, and coffee so good it tasted like love, Len had agreed to become Ms. Church's assistant.

He would get the run of a small loft apartment above her offices. For the first time in four years, he'd have a place to hang his coat. The bathroom was not much larger than a phone booth but had a door that closed, and the place came with a hot plate, a microwave, and a black-and-white TV. It was heaven on earth.

He'd also receive a weekly stipend, enough for food and other necessities, in exchange for being Ms. Church's gofer. In the four weeks he'd been on the job, his duties included handling the mail and the phone, collecting information, and running errands. He'd shown the initiative to grab food for Ms. Church on a couple occasions, though she never seemed to eat much. He didn't know where she slept, either, though he suspected she spent some nights in her office. She'd be rumpled-looking, leaning over her computer or one of her musty books when he'd come down in the morning. The office sheltered walls of books, but they were overshadowed by the hundreds of plants crowding every open space and brawling for light from one of the seven windows skirting the bottom floor. The greenery gave the offices a humid, earthy smell distinct from the concrete and metal world outside.

Len hadn't touched a whit of liquor since he'd moved in. He felt like the man he was supposed to be, as if Ms. Church had plucked him, spinning, out of the toilet and put him back on his life's track. He wasn't going to mess that up, even if that meant asking some twitchy paper collar how wet a newt's skin had been when he'd caught sight of it.

"He wouldn't tell me about the li- . . . the newt's skin. Said he wants to meet with you first."

Ms. Church raised one elegant finger and continued clacking on her keyboard with her other hand. Len shrunk into himself.

She tapped the last key and looked up. "Mr. Phelps, your degree was in accounting, was it not?"

"I, well, I don't . . . yes." He rubbed self-consciously at his bracelet, the only jewelry he wore.

"No need to look so frightened. When I saw you outside the club— do you remember that first night we met? You didn't carry yourself like the other drunkards. You have that slouch specific to the man who spends much time with books, though you don't like to read. You haven't expressed interest in a single volume on my shelves. And you take great care with your hands, much more than your head or your feet. There is only one career that requires much reading, but not of words, and where hands are paramount. Number crunching."

"But I . . ."

"And I knew from the first sentence out of your mouth that you were college-educated, probably from Washington State, by the lilt of your voice."

"Seattle University."

She clapped her hands. "Well that's wonderful news! A Jesuit accountant!" She chuckled. "And when we become more comfortable with one another, you'll have to tell me your real name. But there is no need to rush. You have absolutely no news about our newt?"

Len's hands felt oversized and obvious, so he shoved them deep into his jacket pockets. He wished the rest of him fit in there as well. "Not to speak of. The gentleman said he would rather talk to the detective he had hired."

"I am she. As of today, our client's wife has been missing for thirteen days?"

"Yeh. Today's newspaper says the police've scoured the house and all the vehicles front to back, inside and out, and they have no leads. They're reprinting the husband's story that his wife left a note saying she was leaving town and to not bother looking for her." Len felt good sharing what he had uncovered in the paper. His words came out fast, like a hundred lucky dice. "Her car was discovered in long-term parking at the airport, but she didn't board any planes under her given name. Her credit cards haven't been used."

"Any large bank withdrawals reported?"

"None, but the husband said she could have been squirreling away cash. He told the police and the papers that he had her on a hefty allowance. Two grand a week."

"And he thinks she was cheating on him?"

Len averted his eyes. "He hasn't said, not in so many words, though he refers to a 'mystery friend' his wife had. He'd be doing himself a favor if he fingered her lover, because the police are eyeballing him as their number one. The husband's always the chief suspect if the wife goes missing, if you believe the newspapers. But he won't come right out and sully her name . . ."

"Or his reputation."

". . . by saying she was cheating. But that's what the smart money is on."

"And it would be a simple missing person case if not for our friend the newt."

"It showed up in his car yesterday. His wife had a one-eyed newt that she loved so dearly, she took it with her when she ran out on him. Guess the critter belonged to her brother, who died in a car accident last spring. Now, almost two weeks after she disappeared, the same kinda animal appears in his car. Same color, same size, except this one has both eyes. The husband hates newts, said he could never stand them. He feels like his wife, or maybe this 'friend' of hers, is harassing him, trying to double-shame him. He's on pins and needles wondering what's going to happen next. You can tell it's taking its toll. He's as nervous as a giggle in church."

"He still thinks we can find his wife."

"He thinks if we find her, we'll find the person who planted the newt."

"Then there's only one thing we can do. We must visit our client. Is now a good time for you?"

"Yes."

"Excellent."

"Which do you think is stranger, Mr. Phelps? Truth or fiction?"

Len clicked the turn signal. The station wagon had come with the job, and he could use it for odd jobs, including chauffeuring Ms. Church around. As near as he could tell, she didn't drive. "I've seen strange things in my lifetime, things you couldn't get your head around."

"Exactly. What man *does* is always so much more bizarre, or violent, or unexpected than what he *thinks*. Why do you suppose that is?"

Len adjusted himself in his seat. "I've never gave it any thought."

"If you consider the whole uncharted realm of the imagination, you would be inclined to believe that humans could write some truly horrific and fantastical tales. But reality always trumps fiction. And do you know why?"

Len shook his head in the negative, but she didn't seem to notice. She was looking out her window as the car sped past two children playing hopscotch on the sidewalk. Len glimpsed orange and gold leaves skittering across one of the kid's feet and wondered what Ms. Church was seeing.

"Because the brain and the animal can't occupy the same space. When writing, the author's mind silences his beast within, but when in the physical state, the animal in us holds sway and can quiet the mind with a single snarl. A writer can never think as darkly as a man will act."

Len was quiet. Sometimes when listening to Ms. Church he felt like he was trying to take a snapshot of the entire earth while standing on it.

"I think our turn is here, Mr. Phelps. Our client lives in the Forest Harmony development."

Len veered into the gated community for the second time in as many days. Edina was a tony suburb of Minneapolis, but this development within it was recent and had the boxy, high-ceilinged architecture favored by the new rich. "It's the yellow mansion right up here."

"Of course."

"Do you think you'll be able to find his wife?"

Ms. Church sighed. "I'm not certain if she'll ever be found, Mr. Phelps, but I do know the origin of our newt. If you would be so kind as to use your cell phone to call the Minneapolis Police Department and ask for a Detective Cannery. Tell him you're my assistant. Bring him up to date on our limited dealings with this case, and ask him if he would be willing to share what he knows of the case of our missing Mrs. . . ."

"Aubrey. The wife's name is Elizabeth Aubrey."

"Yes. It's been splashed some on the news, hasn't it? Ask him what he knows of Mrs. Aubrey's will."

"You think she's dead?"

"I know she's dead, Mr. Phelps. The newt told me."

Len didn't bother ringing the door bell when he finished his call and came in. Ms. Church had requested that he be as quiet as possible, so as not to interrupt her conversation with Mr. Aubrey.

The house was antiseptic and oddly barren, despite being well-outfitted with glossy oak furniture, paintings in ornate gilded frames, and rugs designed to look oriental but mass-produced in some third-world factory, if Len was any judge of it. It felt like no one had ever lived here, or if they had, they glided through like ghosts without sitting in the chairs or glancing into any of the mirrors lining the long hall.

Len found his boss and Mr. Aubrey in what he supposed was a sitting room, three doors down from the entry.

"Have a seat, Mr. Phelps! Mr. Aubrey and I were just discussing his business."

The man in question was the color of cooked pork, and his cheeks were drawn. He didn't look up at Len. "I own a metal fabrication plant in St. Paul, the largest in the five-state area."

Ms. Church continued on as if her conversational partner were sparkling with wit instead of miserable. "Wonderful! You must work quite a bit with steel."

He looked at her peculiarly. "I suppose. Not directly, of course. I spend most of my time in the office. Haven't been back since my wife disappeared."

"It was her company?"

Mr. Aubrey's hands had been playing a silent march on his thighs. He stilled them. "Elizabeth's father's, actually. She didn't want much to do with it, so I took over once he passed. She was happy to shop and travel. Me, I need to keep busy."

"Had she traveled much before she disappeared?"

"Yes! She'd just returned from Barbados. One of our employees was out for vacation days the same period of time." Mr. Aubrey darted a significant glance at Len, one man to another.

"Mmm. And it was the night of your annual office party that she disappeared."

"We hold it in the fall," he said apologetically. "Easier to book a place, and it's at the end of our busy season. It was at the St. Paul Firehouse Restaurant."

"Very fancy! It must have been a good year for the business." She leaned forward to touch him companionably on the knee, and didn't acknowledge his flinch.

"It's the only time of the year some of our workers get into a suit, myself included." He tried to smile at his weak joke, but his lips weren't on board.

"I'm sure that's true, Mr. Aubrey. Now, I understand that you've hired us because you're disturbed by the appearance of a creature in your vehicle."

"A newt."

"Yes. Taricha granulosa, to be precise."

Any calm he had gathered around him dissipated. "I'm certain it's my wife, taunting me! She knows I despised the brute she had, every single minute it lived under our roof. Isn't it enough that she's left? She has to sneak back and leave lizards in my car?"

She didn't bother to correct his nomenclature. "I'm sure it's very disconcerting. Will you show me the vehicle you found it in?"

"This way."

Len and Ms. Church followed him to the four-car garage. The building housed a boat, an SUV, and a black, four-door BMW. Mr. Aubrey indicated the latter.

"Do you mind?" Ms. Church asked, indicating the car. She opened the door and sniffed tentatively. Nodding her head once, she leaned down to run her hands under the driver's side seat, and then under the passenger's. "Your car is damp."

"I suppose. I got it detailed a couple weeks ago. It hasn't dried properly since then."

"You got your car professionally cleaned before or after your wife disappeared?"

His face hardened. "After. I thought at the time she was on another one of her trips."

"With her newt?" Ms. Church's eyes twinkled, but Len was sure he was the only one who saw it.

"She loved that monster."

"I see. Can I peek into your wife's closets? I'd like to see what she took."

"Certainly."

They returned to the house and Ms. Church made a careful survey of both closets in the expansive master bedroom, zipping apart hangered clothes, looking in pockets, even getting on all fours to examine shoes top and bottom. The minutes ticked away, and still she searched. When she finally made her way out of the closet, she had a dust bunny in her hair and an odd smile on her face. "We have our answer, Mr. Aubrey, both as to where your wife has gone and how the newt got into the car."

Len noticed a particular expression crawl across Mr. Aubrey' face, melting it like glass. "Wonderful. Please. Tell me."

"I'm afraid I have one more loose end to tie up. Can you come to my office tomorrow, say 2:00? We should be able to finish this business then, and you can pay off your account."

Mr. Aubrey had regained what little composure he'd been afforded. "Your reputation must be well-earned, Ms. Church. I'll see you tomorrow."

Len drove them away silently, questions knocking around his brain like loose apples. He kept them to himself.

"Mr. Phelps, can you describe our husband to me?"

He expelled a pent-up breath. "For someone who hired you to find his wife, he didn't seem too eager find out what you knew when push came to shove."

"No, but that was to be expected," she said distantly. "What did you notice about his appearance?"

"Middle-aged guy, maybe late 50s. Nice head of hair, though it looks store-bought. Wrinkles around his eyes, but not the kind you get from smiling. Casual dresser, for such a rich guy."

She grinned. "Well done! And his knees?"

"Excuse me?"

"Did you see how worm the middle of his pants were, and how creased at the lap and back of the knees? Our husband has been bending a lot today, and that can only mean one thing: he's going through his possessions, and he's deciding which to take and which to leave. Let us hope his curiosity overrides his good sense, or we may never see him again."

"You think he killed his wife, then."

Her excitement faded, and she suddenly looked very tired. "I know it."

"Shouldn't you call the police?"

"I will, Mr. Phelps, but I'm afraid this is no longer a matter of urgency. Now tell me what the will said."

Ms. Church slid her microscope aside and absently studied the newt in its terrarium. There wasn't much to see. The creature just stood there, as far as Len could tell. It didn't even have whiskers to twitch. Neither animal nor woman looked particularly bothered that it was 2:30, and Mr. Aubrey had not yet shown. Except for a call to a friend of Mrs. Aubrey's deceased brother and another to the police, she had not spoken all day.

"Mr. Phelps, if you could visit any country in the world, which would it be?"

"I like the u.s."

She turned her full attention on him. "But you liked Japan when you were there, did you not?"

He forced himself not to register surprise. "I did."

"How long were you in the armed forces?"

"I did my four years." He couldn't stop himself. "How'd you know?"

"Not much reason for a Jesuit accountant to be in Japan other than being in the forces. As to how I knew you were there, that bracelet you always wear speaks volumes. The lion-head amulet could be found in many parts of the world, but if I'm not mistaken, the band is decorated with the singularly chartreuse seedpods of the Glaucidium palmatum, which is found only in the mountains of Hokkaido and Honshu, Japan."

"You're a horticulturalist?" The question felt personal.

"Of a sort." When the knock came, she did not act surprised. "Will you let Mr. Aubrey in, Len?"

She had never before called him by his Christian name. He wondered if it meant she was nervous under that cool exterior, or if they were just getting civil.

Mr. Aubrey entered with the sour scent of desperate bravado swirling around him. He took the seat Ms. Church offered, and drew back when his eyes met the newt's. "I can't believe you still have that horrible thing."

"On the contrary, Mr. Aubrey. You should be thrilled I still have it."

"I'm sure I don't understand."

"Your wife's will. It read like a diary, I'm sorry to say. Are you familiar with it?"

His face puckered like an ugly hole. "Who knows what her most recent will said? A cheating woman's mouth can't be trusted."

"That is an accusation you have yet to make with the police listening. Would you care to invite them?"

"I'm actually leaving town. I need a change of scenery."

"Then I hope you've been saving your allowance too because you'll soon be short of cash. Your wife's will explicitly states that should she die a death of unnatural causes or disappear for a period of more than 14 days, all her assets are to be frozen. As you know, that includes Hendershott Metal Fabrication, of which she was full owner, despite your having run the company since her father's passing."

"I'll fight it."

"I presume you will. And I imagine you'll be left with the house, cars, and any assets you accumulated in your eight years of marriage. Minus legal fees, of course. And minus your job. Mrs. Aubrey made it unequivocally clear that should a suspicious fate befall her, the company is to go co-op, with all current employees owning a share, less one. You. You are to be summarily fired."

"That's ridiculous!"

"Oh no. I saved ridiculous for last. Your wife had a good sense of humor, I take it. She has willed $2000 a week to whoever takes care of her newt, for as long as it lives. Her will offers you first crack at the job."

"But her newt is dead! She had it in her pocket when I . . ."

"When you knocked her out and put her in the hydrochloric acid, Mr. Aubrey? Or did you just strangle her until she lost consciousness before dumping her body in? That was the part I couldn't figure out, and I'm sure her corpse is dissolved beyond identification, so you are the sole keeper of that secret. The acid burns on the sides and bottoms of your dress shoes were the giveaway. It can be a little messy to dump a body into a vat of acid, even if the body is unconscious. If it were me, I would have thrown the dress shoes away afterward, but I appreciate your thriftiness."

"This isn't her newt! I tell you, her newt had one eye! The woman destroyed my life when she was alive and now she's haunting me from the grave." He let out a sob and buried his face in his hands.

"Her filing for divorce was hardly the end of your life, Mr. Aubrey, though it certainly would have required you to downsize your life given that she controlled all the assets. A smart man wouldn't have killed her so close to receiving the news, however. Her attorney was kind enough to forward me a copy of the document along with the will." Ms. Church gently slid the terrarium over, her voice growing thoughtful. "Newts are amazing creatures, Mr. Aubrey. They can regrow limbs, tails, even eyes. If you look closely at this newt's right eye, you'll see it's of fresher and brighter skin than the left. A recent growth, one you would have missed if you had never looked closely at the creature. A call today to Elizabeth's brother's old roommate confirmed it. If I held the creature up, you'd see a very unique black x marking his front leg, the same x the friend remembers on the original creature. This is your wife's newt. You failed at your attempt to get rid of both of them at once."

Mr. Aubrey looked up from a million miles away. "What now?"

"I recommend you retain a good lawyer and then turn yourself in to the police. If you confess, they might be inclined to be more lenient."

"I can go?"

"I have no power to keep you."

He lurched out of his seat like a man about to be ill, not bothering or remembering how to shut the door. Len got up to close it behind him. "Think he'll go to the police?"

"No."

"So he'll walk?"

"That's my best guess, though I did what I could with the police. They've been watching his movements since we left yesterday in the hopes he'll incriminate himself. When he left his home to come here, they removed the acid-burned shoes from the master closet. Without a body or a witness, though, we don't have much." She looked at Len with heavy eyes. "There are a quarter million unsolved homicide cases in the u.s. at any given time, Mr. Phelps. I'm afraid justice is a fool's dream."

He was silent for several long moments as he weighed the truth of her words. There really were only three points left to put to bed. "How'd the thing live so long without food or water?"

"He's a terrestrial newt, and the leftover water from Mr. Aubrey's car detailing must have provided enough moisture. As to food, a newt can go several weeks without eating. It's a miracle the car cleaners didn't find him, though Taricha granulosa are tricky little climbers."

"And the hydrochloric acid?"

"That one's rather too simple. Hydrochloric acid is commonly used to pickle steel, as any metal fabricator could tell you. As soon as I heard Mr. Aubrey's line of work, I had a good idea of what he had done with his wife's body, and the unique burn patterns on his shoes confirmed it. Not much call for wearing your best shoes to visit the acid vats unless you happen to be disposing of a body after a formal dinner party."

And the final point. "Mr. Aubrey didn't pay his fee."

"No, his wife did. We'll get paid a $2000 a week for caring for this charming amphibian, until we can get it back to Mrs. Aubrey's family."

"Beautiful."

Ms. Church smiled, and it was transformative. "Beauty is in the eye of the newt, isn't it, Mr. Phelps?"

Beware the Flying Moose

MICHAEL ALLAN MALLORY

Tank McShane was a total badass. He didn't take crap from anyone. Usually he was the one dishing it out. He was pretty hardcore; he loved to watch people crap their pants when he put the screws to them, such was the measure of his badassitude. McShane was hired muscle, a professional debt collector for non-traditional loan servicers, a one man monster truck rally. Burly, thick-necked, spiky-haired with a predilection for brown suede, he was built like a perverse cross between a rhinoceros and a bulldozer. Nothing pleased him more than an excuse to get in your face—and ruin it. That being said, there was one chink in this doombringer's armor.

McShane was superstitious.

"Is there a problem?" McShane studied the woman across the table from him. Madam Wanda was taking too long. The psychic usually didn't waffle like this. Not a good sign.

She scowled into her crystals with searching dark eyes, her palms pressed flat against the violet tablecloth. "There's something I don't understand . . . one image I can't figure out. But it means danger."

Slouched against the padded chair back, McShane sat up with interest. "What kind of danger?"

"Life threatening," she said with emphasis. Wisps of her long black hair curled by lips pressed into a tight line.

"What image?"

She hesitated.

He leaned closer. "Wanda?"

A preparatory breath. "This'll sound weird, okay? Keep that in mind."

"Spit it out."

"A moose,"

"A moose?"

"Specifically, a flying moose."

"Excuse me?"

"I told you it was weird."

"A flying moose?"

"Yes, that's the image. I see it over and over. You're in danger from a flying moose."

"What the hell does that mean?"

She shrugged. "I'm not sure except the threat is real. It could seriously hurt you, even kill you."

"The moose."

"Yeah."

McShane leaned back, shoulders as wide as Lake Superior obscured the chair. "Geez, Wanda."

"You know how it works. Sometimes the visions are clear, sometimes not, like making out shapes in a murky pond."

He raised a skeptical eyebrow. If he didn't respect Wanda's ability he would've walked right then, but she'd been uncannily accurate in the past, so he decided to cut her some slack. "Anything else you can tell me? Like more details?"

"That's all I got."

"Well, if that's all you got," he spoke softly, adjusting the sleeve of his brown suede jacket. He stood up and started for the door.

"One thing, Tank," Wanda added in a cautionary tone that stopped him in his tracks. He looked at her expectantly. "There was another impression. I can't quite put my finger on it. I think it's a way of avoiding the danger."

"I'm listening . . ."

She moistened her lips. "Compassion. Compassion will save you."

His gaze was dead on. "Yeah, I'm not really known for that. In my line of work compassion is a liability."

"Be careful, Tank."

He snorted. "I'll be fine as long as it doesn't start raining mooses."

For the rest of the day and for part of the next, the psychic's warning lingered in McShane's mind, though it was crowded out by the more pressing concerns of butt whuppings he planned that week for deadbeat clients.

When the end of the month came with no moose incursions of any kind, he began to wonder if his skeptical friends weren't right about Madam Wanda. Experience told him not to dismiss her warning lightly, but it did seem the odds of him running into a moose in the heart of the city were remote. Perhaps Wanda's psychic antenna was mixed up this time; even she had admitted her vision of the threat was murky at best. Which was all McShane needed. He liked the world black and white. Shades of gray weren't in his color palette.

By Wednesday of the fifth week he'd all but forgotten the warning, intent on tracking down a weaselly-ass clown named Eddie Van Dorn. Eddie owed a boat load of money to Big Lenny DeMarco and his payments, as they say, were in arrears. McShane had to either collect the debt or do a head-splitting fandango on Eddie's skull. With any luck he could do both. First, he had to track down the skinny little dipwad.

"Don't know where he is," Ink Kragen told him at the C.C. Lounge, a biker bar and pool hall in the Frogtown neighborhood of St. Paul. Ink was called Ink because of the impressive array of tattoos covering him, everything from mermaids, dragons, swords, sea serpents and catchy slogans. No moose though, McShane was careful to observe, though Ink's baggy clothing didn't allow for a thorough inspection. "Eddie hasn't skipped. He's got a sick wife and no ambition. He's got no place to run."

McShane loosened his turtleneck. His thick neck chafed under confinement yet he liked the sleek look of a black turtleneck under his short suede jacket. Navy slacks and black Docker shoes completed the look. They added to his mystique, he thought. Of course, many people would argue that a human pile driver who could go ape shit on you at the drop of a hat had enough mystique about without needing help from his wardrobe. "Any idea where he is?"

Ink took his time sizing up his next shot. He stepped around the pool table and leaned over the green felt. "Try the old Tapps Brewery on seventh. The other day Eddie was yammering about some guy he'd hooked up with. New business angle. I thought he said he was meeting the guy there this afternoon. Looks like a sweet deal."

"'Zat so?"

"Oh, yeah, he was stoked."

"Sounds like Eddie's about to come into some money. Good to know. Thanks for the tip."

Ink grunted back something incomprehensible, preoccupied with making the four ball in the corner pocket.

Tapps Brewery had been closed for over thirty years. The complex of six large brick buildings dominated the entire block and was an eyesore which had been slated for teardown and redevelopment several times without success. The old brew house had sloping, multi-tiered roofs, a connected power plant and bottling house. Row upon row of broken windows made the campus look like a war zone. The neglected grounds were littered with old beer cans, bottles, paper and the discard of countless visitors over time. Overgrown weeds burst from nearly every crevice in the broken pavement. McShane circled the complex in hopes of catching a glimpse of Eddie. Eventually he decided to enter the abandoned property near a sagging chain link fence. Driving cautiously, he wormed his way through the hulking brick ruins.

A sparkle caught his eye. The sun glinted off the side mirror of a parked car. Someone was here. McShane pulled up close to the old brew house and shut off his engine. From his glove box he removed a Glock pistol. He carefully closed the car door so it wouldn't make noise. For a big man he moved quietly, stepping cautiously through the mine field of broken glass and rusty metal to avoid announcing his presence. Peering around the corner of the brew house, McShane saw two men talking a short distance away. One, a chubby man with thinning brown hair, sported an open Hawaiian shirt over a white T-shirt and Chino slacks that emphasized his beer belly. He was showing another man the contents of the trunk of his Buick LaSabre. The man was Eddie Van Dorn, whose wiry body angled over the trunk.

McShane wasted no time. He stepped into view. "Hello, Eddie, funny I should run into you."

The color drained from Eddie's face. The pants crapping had begun. He shuddered back a step and darted his eyes around for a place to run.

"Don't even think about it," McShane brandished the Glock and closed in.

"Holy shit!"

"Who's your friend, Eddie?" McShane asked, facing the wide-eyed Hawaiian shirt dude. "And you are?"

"J-Jacob."

McShane peered into the trunk. HDTVs, GPS devices, boxes of smart phones, and video game consoles lay like presents under a Christmas tree, all ripe for the taking. "Looks like I interrupted some business between you two."

"No problem. I can wait my turn."

"Jacob, get your ass out of here."

You didn't have to hit Jacob over the head with a brick. He hastily closed the trunk lid, tossed Eddie a you-poor-bastard look, jumped into the old Buick and skidded off for parts unknown.

"Hey, Tank, how's tricks?" Eddie grinned a toothy, overwrought smile. His hand trembled as it ran through his slicked-back hair.

McShane pistol-whipped him across the head. Eddie yelped and clutched his face. "Don't be a douche bag. You know what I want. Where's the money?"

"I don't have it."

"Why am I not surprised?"

"But I'll have it soon!"

"How soon?"

"Real soon."

"Wrong answer." McShane slapped Eddie upside the head with his free hand. He pocketed the Glock. Using his hands was much more satisfying. McShane seized the frightened little man by the shirt and pulled him in close. "Last week you said you'd have all the money by Tuesday. Yesterday was Tuesday and I didn't hear from you. Imagine my disappointment."

"I know! I know! Something went wrong. The guy who was supposed to give me the cash skipped. That's why I'm here! Jacob and I were working out a deal where I bought discounted electronic merchandise to resell.

But you scared him off!"

Eddie's feet scuffed against gravel as he dangled from McShane's tree trunk arms. "Tell me you're not blaming me for not having the money. That would piss me off."

"N-no, no, not at all," Eddie could barely rasp out the words. The crazy dance was happening in his eyes.

"Good." McShane slammed Eddie into the brick wall. "You don't give me much of a choice." McShane cracked his knuckles with a predatory grin.

"No. . . ." Eddie backed away but was stopped by the brick wall. McShane ate it up.

"I may not kill you, Eddie. Depends on my mood. But you're gonna get a bad case of hurt."

The sound of far away street traffic echoed off the empty buildings as McShane let the import of his words sink in. Panic flashed in Eddie's face. His eyes darted for an escape route. Like a cornered rabbit he bolted, though not far. Within four strides he tripped and tumbled hard to the pavement.

"It's just not your day," McShane said as he pulled up Eddie by the shirt collar, then shoved him into the side of a nearby aluminum shed. The metal wall reverberated like thunder.

"Gimme a break," Eddie wheezed, rubbing the back of his head. "I've had a shitty summer. Lost my job and Darla had hip surgery. We got no insurance. That's why I borrowed the money from Lenny."

McShane hitched his shoulders. "Life's a bitch, Eddie."

"You gotta give me more time, man! For Darla. Have a heart, Tank."

McShane's eyes narrowed. What had Madam Wanda said? Something about mercy. No, it was compassion. He let the thought pass. "You should know, Eddie, I ain't got a heart." He closed the gap between them with clenched fists, eager to start a master class in badassery.

"Wait!"

"Wait this, dickhead."

Tank McShane drove forward with attack dog savagery and pummeled the crap out of Eddie, then slammed him violently into the shed again. The ten foot sheet metal wall thundered with a deep resonance that pleased McShane. He also liked the way Eddie bounced off, so he hurled the poor schmuck into the shed again and again with bone jarring force that stirred up the dust on the roof and jangled the shelves inside.

The world went quiet.

Crumbled at the base of the shed, Eddie hugged his gut. A pair of monster hands yanked him to his feet.

"Say goodbye, loser."

"No! You said you weren't gonna kill me."

"You dumb bastard, I lied."

The light started going out in Eddie's eyes.

With one last powerful shove, McShane rocketed Eddie backward into the shed with head-banging force that shook the metal shed and collapsed the human torpedo to the ground. McShane stepped in to deliver the coup de grace when—

Crack! Thud.

Something bashed onto McShane's head. For an instant he wobbled before dropping down to kiss the concrete.

When Eddie's head cleared he saw Tank McShane on the pavement, eyes open and staring lifelessly skyward. Eddie struggled to his feet and edged closer to the inert goonasaurus, nudging him with the edge of his shoe. No reaction. No pulse. Dead. Definitely dead.

"Whaddaya know?" Eddie tried to make sense of the sudden turn of events. Then he saw it, a dozen feet away, an old paint can on its side. He could see inside the can, which was stuffed to the brim with rusted metal parts, rocks, and god knew what, all fused into a hefty-looking anti-Tank missile. Eddie turned his gaze toward the sloping corrugated shed roof. Some workman must have left the paint can up there long ago, he realized, where it spent decades in the scorching sun, heavy rains and subzero winters morphing into a skull-crushing man killer. All the shed slamming had loosened it and tipped the can over the edge.

Eddie went to the body, removed a fat wallet from the suede jacket and found the Glock. "You won't be needing these," he said, standing up with a groan. He began to walk away, stopped and looked over his shoulder.

"What the hell."

He went back and unleashed his rage, kicking the body in the ribs, six, seven, eight times. Out of breath, he said, "Is that what you were gonna do to me, Tank? How's it feel? Oh, that's right, you're dead."

Eddie managed a satisfied smile and shuffled toward his car. When he neared the paint can he gave it a grateful tap with his foot. The can rattled in a wide arc before coming to rest with the label face up, the logo plainly visible now, a logo of a bull moose in profile. The slogan beneath it read: "Paint as tough as all outdoors."

A Fairy Tale for the Incarcerated

DAVID OPPEGAARD

FIRST OFF, YOU'RE INNOCENT. Of course you're innocent. You're innocent and you've been wrongly accused. Perhaps framed. You've slipped through the legal cracks and now you find yourself behind bars for a good, long stretch of time, fighting boredom and simmering with the rage of the unfairly incarcerated. During the day, you never laugh and you clench your jaw too much. At night, you grind your teeth as sleep fails to bring you even a modicum of comfort. You dream of all the women you've known, one after the other, and they float naked through your mind, just beyond your shackled reach. You dream of going to the bar, mowing your lawn, strolling through the mall as you shop for a new pair of shoes. Anything that involves opening a door and stepping into sunlight whenever the hell you feel like it, whenever the urge moves you.

And then, one fine evening, there's an earthquake. A mid-sized earthquake, big and tremulous enough that it knocks down a few walls in your prison and cuts out the power. You wake covered in dust and rubble, unsure of exactly what's happening. Men are shouting in the cells around you, though this isn't anything new—the men like to shout. What is new is the smell of fresh air that's blowing through your cell, a mixture of juniper and freshly cut grass. It occurs to you that the darkness of your cell has taken on a new hue this evening and that one wall seems different than the others, that in fact it is speckled with pinpoints of light that may actually be stars.

You search through the rubble strewn floor of your cell, find your shoes, and put them on. You sprint off into the starry night, thinking only of escape.

Other prisoners have this same general idea. The power has not yet come back on and you see men flitting though the darkness like moths, or bats, and they make no sound as they hurtle toward the outer perimeter wall. It's as if everyone's been released into the yard for a rare hour of nighttime exercise and is hell bent on making the most of it. You run as hard as you can yourself, your lungs expanding and contracting like bellows, fanning the fire in your blood.

Beams of light cut through the night, shattering the blanket of darkness. The enraged voices of guards can be heard as they begin to sweep through the crowd, tackling the slower runners to the ground. One throws a stun grenade into a group of prisoners that's made the mistake of believing in the strength of numbers—the grenade explodes in a deafening roar and knocks a dozen runners to the ground. You hardly see any of this, though— these events are merely things quickly noted in your peripheral vision for examination later, if there is a later. You have eyes only for the perimeter wall, which is missing a big chunk of wall, and as you approach it you leap over the fallen blocks of stone with the agility of a young Barry Sanders. You dart through the gap with your head down, ignoring the shots fired behind you as they zip through the air like deadly hummingbirds.

You cross an empty field and enter a forest. It's a densely thicketed forest with plenty of foliage and chirping crickets. You stop for a moment to get your breath back, to pinch your cheek and make sure this is all really happening. Your legs are trembling, electric, and a well-earned sweat dampens your forehead. You hear an owl hooting in the distance. You hear a dog barking, and then another.

They're tracking you.

They're following you into the forest.

So you push on, moving as fast as you can through the forest's scratching undergrowth. The barking remains constant behind you, but grows no louder. You come to a river that rushes through the forest like a winding, watery road. You take off your shoes, tie them together by the laces, and twist them around your hand so that you won't lose them. Then you jump into the river and let its rushing waters run you far, far downstream. You travel all night this way, floating on your back as your head bobs above the dark water, feeling at least half-drowned, and in the morning you wash up on the golden shores of a sandy beach.

The beach is not altogether deserted. A short ways downstream, a trout fisherman is casting his fly into the river, whipping his fishing pole back and fourth in a beautiful, hypnotic way that causes your waterlogged mind to focus with a new clarity. The fisherman sees you coughing and sputtering on the shore and steps out of the river himself, water running off his hip waders in splashy little rivulets. His eyes widen as he gets a better view of you and there's something familiar about his face. He's your grandfather.

No.

He's your father. He's your father and he's sorry for leaving, sorry for abandoning you so young. He had no other choice—everything would have been lost if he'd stayed.

Your father takes you back to the small, quiet cabin he lives in now, secluded from the entire troublesome world. The cabin smells like pine sap and Cavendish pipe tobacco. As you change into some dry clothes (which smell like your father used to smell) he fries up some of the fish he's caught that morning along with some greens and chopped carrots. You eat at his small wooden table, now set for two, and you tell each other the stories of your tangled lives. After dinner, the two of you leave your plates on the table, grab cold beers from the fridge, and go sit out on the cabin's front porch, where you drink in silence as you ponder the green forest buzzing all around and inhale the rich smell of dirt in the air. Prison is far behind you now, and so is the heat and pain you once found in the noisy world, the long list of mistakes you made in ignorance and desperation. You are glad the river has brought you here. You will stay and thrive quietly in this tranquil place, living with the father you'd thought lost forever.

You will know trouble no more.

Clothes Make the Man

SCOTT PEARSON

o catch a killer on a traffic stop . . . that would be cool. Officer Peggy
Roberts had the thought as a black car heading south ran a stop light
on Hamline Avenue. She'd just listened to the dispatcher send a squad to
a homicide a few miles north of the intersection. She accelerated, taking
a right off Larpenteur, to follow the car.

Probably just a coincidence, she thought. *This isn't* Law & Order: Falcon
Heights, *after all.* But when Roberts checked in with dispatch, she learned
that right after the 911 caller found the half-dressed body of his neighbor
lying in a puddle of blood, stabbed repeatedly, he'd spotted a dark car leaving the scene. Still, that didn't narrow things down much. How many dark
cars were there in a five-mile radius around the murder? And it seemed to
Roberts that at any intersection at least one car rolled through a red every
few cyclings of the lights. When had red lights become just a suggestion?

The black car, a late-model Lexus, was just a block ahead of her, and
Roberts quickly caught up. The driver appeared to be alone. Roberts
updated the dispatcher with the license plate number, a description of the
car, and her location, then turned on her flashers. Back-up was on its way,
just in case. The driver slowed and pulled into the parking lane, but kept
moving as if hoping she would drive by. When she pulled in behind the
Lexus, the driver gave up and stopped.

Roberts put her car in park and rolled down the window. The muggy
July air immediately battled with the AC in her squad. When she heard the

Lexus idling, she turned on her PA. "Please turn off your vehicle." The engine stopped immediately. After checking for bystanders and seeing the area was clear, Roberts stepped out of her squad. She was sharply aware of the delicate balance of adrenalin and training her job demanded and felt a sheen of sweat gather on her forehead as she walked slowly toward the Lexus. She kept her left hand on her weapon, though she left it holstered. A little blue hybrid swerved by, giving her plenty of room.

The Lexus was obviously well-cared for, probably washed every week, waxed to a mirrorlike sheen. Through the rear window she could still see only one person in the car. As she walked by the trunk, she reached out with her right hand and gave a downward shove to make sure it was closed all the way—and to leave her prints on the car, which could be useful evidence if the driver took off. Peering in through the rear side window, she saw nothing suspicious in the backseat. She stepped to the rear of the driver's door and heard the window electrically lowering. Roberts leaned forward to get a look.

A slight man in his early fifties sat behind the wheel. He wore a dark gray suit coat, tie tight around his neck. His hands held the wheel at ten and two. His perfectly combed sandy blond hair looked like each strand had been individually cut to the prescribed length. Roberts' unruly red hair was tied back in a thick braid. He glanced up at Roberts over his rimless glasses without speaking. She knew he couldn't see her eyes through her sunglasses. *He's a timid little guy*, she thought. *Doesn't look like he just stabbed a woman to death.*

"Good afternoon, sir. I'm Officer Roberts. You ran a red light back at Larpenteur. You're lucky there was a break in traffic, people could have been hurt."

"I'm terribly sorry, I . . . I don't know how I missed that."

"I'll need to see your license, registration, and insurance card."

"Of course." He hesitated. "My wallet's inside my coat."

She nodded and watched closely as he reached his right hand into his coat, which he left buttoned, and pulled out his wallet. He opened it up, pulled out his ID, and handed it over. Roberts took it and examined the details: Charles Reller. The photo and physical description matched the driver: five-five, 140 pounds, blue eyes.

"The rest is in the glove box."

"Please get them, Mr. Reller."

He leaned to his right and popped the glove box open. He fumbled around with one hand to grab the documents and handed them over. "I'd like to get this taken care of, I'm late for work."

She took the documents without looking at them. "At two in the afternoon?"

"I was at lunch."

"Did you consume any alcohol?"

"Just one drink."

"You're sure it was only one?"

"Of course. I don't drink and drive."

"But you did run that light." She gestured with her right hand. "Please step out of the car and over to the sidewalk, sir."

Reller sighed, undid his seatbelt, and got out of the car. She followed him off the road to the sidewalk. "I assure you, this a waste of time."

Roberts glanced down at Reller. She was a good two inches taller than him. "Are you declining the test, sir?"

"No, let's get this cleared up."

"Thank you, sir. Please stand with your arms at your sides, heels together. Good. Lift your right leg in the air and count out loud slowly until I tell you to stop."

"One, two, three . . ."

As Reller counted, Roberts leaned in to look closely at his suit. If he had stabbed that woman, she'd find blood spatter. She saw nothing, but the dark houndstooth pattern would make seeing small drops difficult.

"Six, seven, eight—"

"You can stop, sir."

He stamped his foot down and opened his eyes. "With all due respect, officer, can I please get my ticket and go? I have meetings."

"I'd like you to take your coat off, hold it in one hand, and spread your arms wide."

"What? I've never seen anyone do that."

She knew she was pushing it, but she wanted to see his white shirt, which would really show the blood. "Tell you what, sir . . . if you pass again, I'll let you off with a warning."

He blinked a few times. "Thank you. If you say I ran a light, I'll accept that, but I'm not a drunk driver." Reller unbuttoned his coat, shrugged out of it delicately, and straightened his tie. Then he hooked the collar over two fingers of his right hand, and spread his arms.

"Close your eyes, please, sir." Roberts looked him up and down. "Touch your nose with your left index finger." She shook her head. The shirt, and his artsy silk tie, were as pristine as his car. *And I already let him off the hook for a citation.* "Thank you, sir, you can put your coat back on." She watched him slip into it and button it back up. Then she smiled.

"Okay, are we finished here?" He didn't bother to hide his impatience. "I really need to get back to work."

She pulled her sunglasses down her nose and stared at him with her bright green eyes. "That's a great tie, Mr. Reller. A Van Gogh painting, right?"

"What?" He fiddled with it although it was already straight. "Well, yes, it is."

"It almost kept me from noticing what a lovely blouse you're wearing, but I did catch just a glimpse of the buttons on the left."

The color drained from his face. He straightened his glasses.

Roberts tilted her head to the side. "What happened? You didn't notice your mistress was wearing your shirt until after you stabbed her to death? Lucky for you she's your size."

Reller looked around as if trying to find some place to sit. He trembled slightly as another squad pulled up.

Roberts nodded, still smiling. *Catching a killer on a traffic stop . . . cool.*

Night Trip

MARY MONICA PULVER

"**W**HERE ARE WE GOING? she asked.

"Shut up," he said.

"But we've been driving around for . . ."

"Shut up!"

It was late on a hot summer night, and there was no other traffic on the highway. They had been driving for some while, the anxious woman and the worried, angry man.

"I told you he was smarter than he looked," she remarked after awhile.

"Fat lot of good it did him, didn't it?"

"But now it's murder and the cops will be really looking for us."

"Shut up!"

"I won't shut up. I want to know what we're going to do now."

"Ah, we wanted to leave this burg anyhow, right? We'll move to some other place, you'll dye your hair back to its natural color, and I'll get the eyeglasses you're always saying I need, and we'll lay low for six months, a year. We can afford it now, can't we?"

She frowned and looked away.

He waited, throwing occasional impatient glances at her, increasingly angry. Finally he burst out, "You stupid broad! You left the money right there, didn't you?"

She nodded, still not looking at him.

"How could you forget the money? Forty grand, you were standing there looking at it!"

"I was looking at *him*! He was laying on top of it, bleeding all over it. How was I supposed to . . . I couldn't touch it! Oh, you're so smart, why didn't you pick it up?"

"I was too busy wiping everything down, making sure we didn't leave anything behind! Of all the damn, stupid, yellow . . . I told you to get it, all you had to do was that one thing . . . Christ!"

There was a faint rumble of thunder, and he leaned forward to peek at the sky through the windshield. It was blackest night, no moon and not a star in the sky. The blacktop was two lanes wide, without patch or flaw, running between high, sloping grassy banks. There had been no oncoming traffic for a long time, and no city or residential lights were visible anywhere.

"You bring the statue?" she asked.

"Sure, but so what? It's not worth forty dollars."

"We fooled him, we can fool somebody else."

"Maybe."

"Sure. The real thing hasn't been found, has it?" She began the difficult task of bringing him out of his crappy mood. "He can't be the only sucker with more money than brains we can pawn this off on. Someone who thinks he knows all about art." It was a sweet con, selling something legit to a man who thought he was buying something stolen. That's why he wouldn't go to the cops about it. You don't say you have the original, you don't say you stole it. You just let the mark figure it out for himself.

"Say," she said before she could stop herself, "you didn't damage it when you cracked his head open with it, did you?"

"Nah, I'd have to hit something harder than his head to damage that figurine."

"Yeah, yeah, that's true." Still, she'd check it out when they stopped for gas. She looked out the windshield at the dark road, the endless grassy banks. "Where are we?"

"Shut up."

"We're lost, aren't we? If you'd let me drive, like I said . . ."

"I tell you, we're not lost! We're heading . . . north, parallel to the freeway."

"The freeway runs east and west."

"Good, that means we'll cut across it pretty soon. We'll take it west, I think. How'd you like to stay awhile in Omaha? Nobody knows us in Omaha."

"No, we need to go home first, pack some things. My diamond earrings, my good silk suit . . ."

"There's people with guns and badges waiting for us at home."

"How can there be? You wiped everything!"

"Not the money. You were supposed to bring the money, remember? And you helped me count it, remember? And you left it right there with our fingerprints all over it. Remember?"

That silenced her.

He turned his headlights up to bright, but that only broadened their view of the empty road and the endless grassy banks that flanked it. He turned them down again.

She had a sudden vision of a narrow black line in a huge emptiness, their car a tiny bright bead moving very slowly along it. To dispel the image, she said, "How about when it starts to rain you let me drive?"

"It ain't gonna rain."

"Sure it is. Didn't you hear that thunder? It always rains when it turns hot all of a sudden like this." She remembered how cool it had been that morning, how sorry she was she didn't bring her beautiful leather coat. Sorry twice over, now it appeared she'd never see it again.

"It won't rain," he repeated stubbornly. "It rains when it's hot and all of a sudden it gets cool, not the other way around."

"Hot, cold, whatever. Thunder means rain."

But the thunder did not repeat itself. He drove a while longer, then began to look for a place to turn left or right, or even around. "This road is getting us no place," he grumbled.

"Can't you drive any faster?" she asked.

"I'm going the limit. Better not speed, no need to draw any attention to ourselves."

"There's nobody out here to pay attention! We haven't seen another car in . . ." She frowned, thinking. "A long time."

"We're going up some kind of hill," he said. "I can't see what's on the other side. Better wait."

But the hill, a gentle incline, went on and on.

"Come on, admit it," she said at last. "We're lost and getting more lost every minute."

"We're not lost!"

"So where's a sign saying how far to the next town, or turn here to pick up the freeway?"

"How the hell should I know? If you'd just shut your goddamn mouth for a minute!"

Thunder spoke again, louder.

"There!" she said. "I told you it was going to rain!"

"You told me, you told me! You told me that mark was good as bought and paid for! You told me this was gonna be the best con we ever ran!"

"And it would've been if you hadn't got all impatient and started pressing and gave him cold feet! I always could read a mark better than you, I warned you to back off and give him time. But no, you got all paranoid and wondering if this wasn't a setup against us . . ."

"Shut up!"

The silence lasted longer this time. The road continued to rise gently before the headlights, and there was no other traffic.

"We can't be going north," she said at last. "If we were going north, we would've cut across the freeway by now."

"I know, I know."

"So what do we do now?"

"If you'll find me an intersection, I'll try another direction. Or a gas station, so I can stop and ask which way to go." He glanced at the gas gauge. "And fill up, too."

"Fill up? I thought you filled up earlier today." He always filled up on the day they did the sting.

"I did fill up. But we're almost on empty."

"You couldn't've filled up! Or we wouldn't be out of gas already." She looked out the side window. "I think we should stop at the next place we come to, to ask where we are and where's a gas station."

Still frowning, he nodded agreement, then said, "Look, a light."

"Where?"

"Up ahead, on top of that rise, looks like a farmhouse." The engine sputtered and died. "Just in time, too," he remarked, pulling onto the shoulder. "Come on, let's go ask Farmer Brown if we can use his phone or borrow some gas." He left the key in the ignition and the headlights turned on.

But she looked at the dim light on top of the rise just ahead and felt a sudden reluctance. "You go. I don't want to break my ankle climbing up that hill."

"So stay, see if I care." He got out, slamming the door hard. Before he was all the way across the road he had vanished into the thick darkness.

It really is dark out there, she thought, and looked out and up to reassure herself that the light hadn't vanished, too. No, it was still there, a dim and reddish glow. *Got their shades down*, she decided, and settled back to wait.

It wasn't like them to get into fixes like this. They'd worked together successfully for almost a dozen years, him short and thin and clever, her tall and buxom and bright enough to play dumb convincingly. They shared a taste for money and a talent for taking it illegally. Their doubling up on a mark had worked from the start. People were, on the whole, jerks, in her never humble opinion. Stupid and greedy. This was the first time in a long time it had gone wrong—and it had gone spectacularly wrong. But it wasn't her fault, it wasn't! She shifted angrily in her seat.

With the engine shut off, the air conditioner wasn't working and it had become stifling in the car. *Christ, I'm hot!* she thought, rolling down the window in search of a breeze. And though thunder rumbled again, the air was perfectly still. There was an industrial stink to it that put her in mind of an oil refinery. She inhaled deeply anyway and wondered how long he'd be gone.

Almost before she completed that thought, the door opened on his side and he was back. He fumbled for the key and started the engine.

"Hey," she said, "I thought we were out of gas."

"Not yet." Tight-lipped, he pulled back onto the highway.

"So what did Farmer Brown say?" she asked, her eyebrows lifting as he pushed the accelerator down hard. There were drops of sweat running down the side of his face, and he was breathing hard.

He didn't answer right away, and when he did, it was to ask a question she had never thought to hear from him this late in the game.

"Do you love me?"

"What?"

"Do you love me?" he repeated doggedly. "Even only just a little?"

She wanted to laugh, but something in his voice was scaring her. "Are you kidding?" she asked just in case he was.

"No." He wasn't looking at her, but down the dark, empty road, and he was holding the steering wheel so tight his knuckles were white.

"What makes you all of a sudden wonder if I love you?"

"It's important."

Maybe this was a joke. He liked to play jokes to show her how much smarter than her he was. So she turned the tables on him. "Do you love me?"

He shook his head. "Not really. You were one hot baby when we first hooked up, and you're smarter than you look, but I don't love you. I don't think I ever loved you." He shrugged and frowned and said carefully, as if it were important he get it right, "I think maybe I used to think I loved you."

Stung by this careful candor she shot back, "Well, I never once thought I loved you!"

The car's engine began to miss, and he pumped the gas pedal. "Never?"

"Well . . ." He was scared, she could tell. They had been together a long time, but she could remember their early years together very well. How handsome she had found him, how charming, how smart and clever. She had bragged about him to all her girlfriends. "Well . . ." she hedged, and he grinned at her.

The car's engine smoothed out.

"What's this all about?" she asked.

"I want you to think about what happened tonight," he replied. "After—well, after. I ran around wiping things off while you made oh-icky noises at our friend bleeding all over the money on the desk. We ran down the stairs because we were scared to use the elevator, remember? Then out the back door, down the alley, you behind me calling for me to wait up, remember?"

"Sure I remember! So what? There was that siren coming closer and we thought maybe it was the cops. Be just like you to run out on me, wouldn't it?"

"No, it wouldn't. And I didn't, did I? So we jumped in our car and we almost sideswiped the geezer in the Buick when I laid rubber getting us out on the street."

She was starting to smile. "And you ran a light on Highland, and I was laughing because when I looked back the siren was on an ambulance and we were taking crazy chances for nothing."

"Right," he said nodding. "Then what?"

"What, 'then what?' You were going like a bat out of hell, dodging around cars, must've been doing ninety miles an hour . . ." She stopped short. A brilliant flash of lightning lit up the interior of the car, but her face was already astonished. "Hey!" she said. "There was that truck . . ."

"And we ran right into the side of it," he said. "I broke the steering wheel right off with my hands and . . ." He touched the middle of his chest with trembling fingers. "The steering column went in right about here. And you, Miss Seatbelts Mess Up My Clothes, you went through the windshield."

"No!" she said. "That couldn't've happened! It was a dream or something. A nightmare. Because . . . because here we are."

"Yes, here we are." The car's engine sputtered again, and this time died despite his frantic pumping. He didn't steer it onto the shoulder this time, but let it coast to a stop on the blacktop.

"What are you doing, you dope?" she scolded. "You can't leave it in the middle of the road!"

"Yes, I can."

"So what do we do now? Wait for someone to come along and back-end us?"

"No one's going to come along. We have to get out and walk." He gestured forward, up the road.

"I can't walk in these shoes! You go ahead and walk, and when you get somewhere, send someone back for me."

"When I get there, they won't come back here. And anyway, you can't just sit there, you don't want to be in this place when the sun comes up."

"Why not? You think I'm gonna go for a walk in the dark? I'll wait for someone to come along."

"No one's going to come along. The way out of here is to walk. Now come on, we have to stay together, it's the rules."

"Who's rules?" she demanded.

But he opened the door without replying and, in an uncharacteristic show of manners, came around to open the door on her side.

"Haven't you figured it out yet?" he asked. "We're dead."

"No, we're not." She got out and pirouetted around him. "See? I'm alive." She reached out and touched him on the shoulder. "And you're not a ghost, see?" But her face was frightened.

"Listen to me: we're really, truly, for honest true, dead. They finished scraping what was left of us into rubber bags about two hours ago."

She puckered up as if to cry.

"Don't start," he warned her.

"I can't help it, you're scaring me."

"Then that makes two of us." He took her by the shoulders. "Come on, let's get started. "We want to keep on moving. If we want to get to heaven, we have to walk. We won't get tired, they promised."

"H-heaven? We can walk there from here? How far is it?" She peered ahead into the darkness but didn't see the glow in the sky that would mean a city nearby.

"Not close," he admitted. "You see, we weren't exactly nice people all our lives, so we got set down a long way from the gates. They gave us this car, but only as much gas as we had love, and it wasn't enough. So we walk the rest of the way, okay?"

"No," she said, but automatically, and she started to walk beside him up the road. She took his hand. "How far is it?"

"Four hundred and twenty million, seven hundred and eighty thousand miles, less whatever we drove in the car."

"She yanked her hand back. "*What*?!? That's *crazy*! Who told you that?"

"The people in the house back there?"

"Oh, yeah? How would they know? Who were they, anyway?"

"Just Lucifer and some of his friends."

Spring Peeper

PETER RENNEBOHM

"They lost a greener out at the Arboretum," the caller had said.

"Excuse me?" I replied.

The cop on the line wasn't going to make it easy. "A greener," he repeated. "You know, one of the volunteers."

At the time, I did not know. Two hours later, after a thirty-minute drive west from Minneapolis, the cop's explanation made more sense.

I turned off Hwy 5 onto Crimson Bay Drive, and was met with a gentle, winding road that led to the University of Minnesota's Landscape Arboretum. As it was a glorious early April day, I relished escaping from my stuffy downtown office.

A small gatehouse appeared half-way down the road. An elderly gentleman stepped out and waved me to a stop. As he leaned into the open window, I smiled knowingly. VOLUNTEER was printed in bold letters across the front of his emerald-green T-shirt. *This would be a greener*, I thought.

"Good afternoon, sir," the old gent said.

"Hi, there." I flashed my badge and asked for directions to McQuinn Hall.

As I pulled away, I replayed the original phone conversation with the Chaska cop who'd said, "File says you're to be contacted along with campus police."

He was correct. I was under contract to the University of Minnesota—

an independent contractor, retained as a security consultant to *investigate all on campus incidents requiring police action*; in short—to protect the University's interests while assisting local authorities. Public relations and liability issues were of utmost concern. The Arboretum and its 1200 acres, while some distance from the St Paul campus, was Minnesota's premier public garden and horticultural research center.

I parked in a shaded lot across from the main building and reviewed my notes: Orville Gunderson—age 83, resident of the Masonic Home for the Elderly, had gone missing. Last seen forking straw from one of the Arboretum's prized rose gardens earlier this morning, Orville was known to be unusually alert and fit for his age, albeit "prone to excessive chatter." Some questioned his genuine interest in all things botanical.

Others in his group—shuttled by bus from the Masonic Home, had drifted away into the Sensory Gardens and lost track of Orville this morning. The poor guy had gone un-reported until lunchtime.

A search party from Chaska PD, and the Hennepin County Sheriff's Office was currently underway. There'd been no sign of Orville.

I discovered, from the Arboretum's website, the center's primary mission: Horticultural research and education. Open to the public, special exhibits were constructed each year to highlight certain events; all original designs, cleverly created, informative, and certain to appeal to visitors of all ages.

Inside McQuinn Hall, a second greener directed me to the Tea & Fireplace Room—currently the command center in the search for Orville Gunderson.

The cop in charge, Lieutenant Sheldon Dirkson, was an old friend. We exchanged pleasantries before I leaned against a near wall, arms crossed, prepared to listen and observe.

Dirkson began questioning an elderly lady. "Your name is Mary Geneva, is that correct, Ma'am?"

"Yes," Mary replied. She wore her neatly pressed green T-shirt over a white blouse. Lace cuffs and collar seemed incongruous. Streaks of dirt had stained her tan slacks. The old lady's cheeks were carefully dusted with soft, red rouge that matched artfully painted lips. Her air of aristocracy seemed genuine.

"And you were a close friend of Mr. Gunderson?"

"Oh, yes," Mary replied with a pronounced frown. "Well, at one time, I guess." She seemed confused. A warm smile flashed briefly.

"Is that right? Well, I spoke with your friend, Seth McPhee and got the impression that you and Seth might have had a relationship of sorts. Were you involved with *both* men, Mrs. Geneva?"

"Involved? Oh, I don't know. Seth looks out for me. He is such a nice man." Her pale blue eyes glistened, wandered a bit, and settled on me. "Hello. Have we met?" She stepped closer and extended her delicate hand. "I'm Mary Geneva."

I gently took her hand and replied, "No Ma'am. We haven't. My name is Levering."

"I'm pleased to make your acquaintance, Mr. Levering. Do you know my friend, Seth?"

Dirkson scowled and pressed on. "So, Mrs. Geneva, what do you think happened to Mr. Gunderson?"

Mary straightened a loose curl. "Who? Oh . . . Orville? Yes, I think Seth must have put him someplace."

Dirkson edged closer. "Really? Why would he do that?"

"They had a tiff," she replied. "Oh Dear. Should I have said that?" With one hand over her mouth, Mary searched for affirmation of some sort.

"Where would Seth have put Orville, Mary?" Dirkson persisted.

"Hmm . . . Hmm. I don't know. Seth was upset. There was a quarrel this morning . . . or was that yesterday?" She was clearly distraught. "Seth said he'd squash Orville like a bug if he didn't, uh. . . ." Her voice drifted away. Her lovely face darkened. "I'm sorry," Mary concluded, "but I think I'd like to sit for a spell."

Dirkson led the old dame to a chair and called a huddle just outside the door. I nudged close. "Okay. She's 'off' just a bit, but Mary is flirty as hell and clearly there's an issue between Gunderson and McPhee."

He turned to his associate. "What did McPhee have to say, Richie?"

Sergeant Richie Thompson read from a small notebook: "He didn't trust Orville Gunderson. Called him 'debased; a fraud—a scabby, beady-eyed pixie.'"

Dirkson couldn't resist a smile. "Didn't care much for old Orville, did he? Okay, seems like we've got a lover's triangle working here," the cop concluded.

"Yeah, between octogenarian gardeners," Thompson added.

"My money's on McPhee as our prime suspect," Dirkson added.

"McPhee might be more of a friend though, Lieutenant. Not really a boyfriend. I think he just looks after Mary. She plays the helpless role pretty well," Thompson added.

"I don't know," Dirkson replied. "McPhee's a really big guy. What is he, six-three? Two hundred pounds? You see his hands? Big as man-hole covers. Retired farmer, he said. Tough old bird. And, he clammed up pretty fast when I pressed him about Gunderson and the old lady."

Something bothered me about all this. Mary had said there was a quarrel. *When?* I wanted to meet McPhee. "Mind if I talk to this guy, Shelly?"

Dirkson turned to me. "Go ahead, Will. If you get anything useful out of him, I'll buy you dinner."

"Where is he?"

"Sitting in the cafeteria. Follow me. He's hard to miss."

Seth McPhee was, in a word, memorable. He faced the room, looking somewhat feral as large, dark eyes tracked my walk. I noticed that his jaw was offset, broken at one time and badly set. I imagined the old guy being kicked by a mule or a cow and either declining medical help, or being unable to pay. Either way, this was a guy you didn't want to piss off.

I might have expected a man of his age to be somewhat shrunken, slightly stooped. On the contrary, he sat straight and tall. Broad-shouldered, the thin fabric of his green T-shirt stretched taut—worn over a white long-sleeved undershirt. Bits of small, withered yellow flowers clung to the sleeve edges—a few nestled in his thick, coal-black hair.

My impression was of a man who had spent most of his life laboring out-of-doors; a man comfortable with himself and quite capable of dealing with adversity.

"My name is Will Levering, Mr. McPhee. I'm a security officer with the University."

He stuck out a large hand and grasped mine firmly. "Pleased to meet you," he replied in a deep, steady voice. He looked straight into my eyes, then threw a glance at Dirkson who stood a few feet to the side.

My fingers lingered briefly as he released his grip. "You were with Mr. Gunderson earlier this morning. Correct, Mr. McPhee?"

McPhee didn't hesitate. "That's right. Call me Seth."

"Thank you, Seth. Would you say that the two of you were friends?"

"Not likely. Son-of-a-bitch wouldn't leave Mary alone. Fillin' her head with all sorts of nonsense!"

"Why would he do that, Seth?"

"Gunderson's a womanizer. Man with low morals." Seth clenched his huge fists for emphasis.

Speaking of Gunderson in the present tense was encouraging. "Tell me, Seth. Did Mary encourage Mr. Gunderson's advances?"

I watched his face change color: from a ruddy pink to dark maroon. I feared he might lean across, grab my face, and squeeze me like a grape.

Instead, he inhaled deeply and answered, "If you've met her, then you know how sweet Mary is. She drifts off every so often into a world of private make-believe. She's easily misled, and Gunderson was out to take advantage of her simpleminded ways."

"And that upset you, correct?"

"Sure did."

"Did you have words? With Mr. Gunderson?"

"You could say that. Told him this morning to stay away from Mary or I was going to pound on him then throw him in the compost heap along with all the other crud."

I stayed with him. "And. . . uh, did you?"

"What?" he asked.

"Pound on him." I imagined all sorts of nasty things a large man like Seth could do if provoked.

"Look. I'm no fool. Gunderson's gone missin' and you folks think I had something to do with it, right?"

"Well, that had occurred to us." I watched his eyes as he glanced again at Dirkson.

McPhee blew air through his nose. His crooked jaw twitched. "Do you know what a spring peeper is, Will?"

Caught off-guard, I replied, "No. I'm sorry." An image of a naked man running around late at night seemed appropriate, though.

"There's an area over on the eastern edge of the property here called the *Spring Peeper Meadow*. It's named after a homely little brown, tree frog. The male makes all kinda' high-pitched squeaky noises in the Spring. All that little peeper cares about is finding a willing lady-frog to cavort with.

Most never succeed, but they keep on peeping just the same; just peepin'
and squeekin' all day long—well into early summer."

After pausing as if he'd say no more on the subject, I asked him to go
on, and he didn't disappoint.

"Gunderson was like one of those little peepers out there in that
meadow; kinda' creepin' 'n' peepin' all around. Talkin' nonsense and bothering the ladies. Mostly, he pestered Mary. Just wouldn't shut his yap or
leave her alone."

By now, I was pretty sure Seth had done something with Orville, and
I suspected it hadn't been pleasant. *But, where did he put him?* "You think
you know where Gunderson might be, Seth?"

"You sure know how to squeeze a conversation to its rind, don't ya,
young fella'?" replied McPhee."

"Something happened to Orville, Seth. We need to find him . . .
quickly."

"I'm done talking. I'd like to see Mary if you don't mind." McPhee's
jaw cracked, and I flinched.

"Maybe later, old man," Dirkson intruded. "*After* we find Gunderson.
Should we be looking for Gunderson out in that Peeper Meadow, Seth?"

We waited for Seth to respond. Somehow, I felt the big farmer was
being clever, hoping to lead us away from Gunderson . . . or what was left
of him.

Seth merely shrugged and said nothing more.

I gestured to Dirkson, and the two of us stepped away. "Look, I'm no
horticulturist, Shelly, but it sure seems like those small dried-flowers in
Seth's hair didn't come from a bed of roses."

Dirkson gestured with both arms out—palms up. He wasn't tracking
my reasoning. Bushy eyebrows rose as one. "I'm going to send Richie and
a crew out to this Peeper Meadow, Will. I think he dumped Orville out
there someplace."

I thought Shelly was literally going off in the wrong direction. A rose
bush has to be carefully tended. My mother pruned hers every fall, then
tipped and covered them with straw. Mom, as well as these, "greeners"
would never permit weeds or any other plant to grow beneath their
beloved roses.

I opened my hand to show Dirkson a couple of the small yellow flowers earlier plucked from McPhee's sleeve. "Shelly, you have someone who can tell me where these came from?"

Shelly glanced at the flowers, a dubious look on his face. "You harvest these offa McPhee?"

"Yes. From his shirtsleeve."

"Pretty slick move, Will. Hang on." He was determined to scour the meadow. "Richie, take a search party out to the Peeper Meadow and give it a good going over. And send in that staff lady on your way."

Delores, one of the permanent staff joined us. We were introduced, and I asked, "These three love-birds were working in the rose garden, correct?"

She didn't hesitate. "Yes."

"Where exactly?"

"Seth and Mary were closely involved with the development of three roses brought to market in 2008: *Sven*, *Ole*, and *Lena*. They were both like proud parents when these cultivars were released," Delores concluded.

I choked off a chuckle. "You're kidding, right Delores?"

"She smiled warmly. About the names? Oh, no. I'm quite serious. The Minnesota Rose Society spent months selecting those names."

"Fair enough. Did Orville Gunderson share the same passion and interest in roses?" I asked.

Delores frowned, considered her reply, and peered over her reading glasses. "No, Orville didn't have a genuine interest in what we do here. He's, uh . . . how can I say this; Orville's behavior was always a bit . . . shabby. He was only interested in the ladies—not flowers. For a man his age, Orville was, uh . . . quite ah . . . randy." She flushed a bit.

"Thank you," I said. "Do you have a map of the grounds?"

She pulled a fold-out from her hip pocket and handed it to me.

"Where's the Rose Garden?" I asked.

Delores leaned in and pointed to a spot on the map. "It's just off the start of Three Mile Drive. The entrance is flanked by two giant white oak trees. You can't miss it."

I studied the map and realized that the Spring Peeper Meadow was some distance removed from the other gardens. No way McPhee could have lured Orville that far away without someone noticing. Nope, Orville was stashed someplace close to where they had been working.

I showed Delores the yellow flowers. "Where might these be planted, Delores?"

She plucked one from my palm and held it close to her face. "Looks like yellow alyssum, but I'm not sure. No, that's wrong. It's not alyssum."

Her puzzlement was bothersome. We waited.

"I know! It's melampodium. *Million Gold.* A perennial used as a ground cover. Easy to grow, hardy, and let's see, where was this used last year?" She nibbled on a nail.

I felt like I was back in 10th grade science class. "How about some place close to the Rose Gardens, Delores? Maybe the Spring Peeper Meadow? Could it be from there?" I knew better.

She didn't hesitate. "No. That's tall grass out there along with wildflowers and sedge. Besides, it's too far away."

She studied the map again and exclaimed, "The Bug!"

"Excuse me?" I asked.

She held out her palm with the small, withered flower gently rocking within. "Melampodium was used in one of our lively vignettes last year— a demonstration plot that focused on plants as bio-fuels. We called it, 'The Bloomin' Bug.'"

I knew precisely what she meant. I'd seen the area with the old tractor on my way in. There had also been a fuzzy old, weed covered Volkswagen parked behind a split rail fence.

"Thank you, Delores. Shelly, let me try something with McPhee. I think I know what he did with Gunderson." I steered Dirkson back to the cafeteria.

"We're just about finished, Seth," I assured the older man. "Just one more thing: Did Orville share your enthusiasm for Sven, Ole, and Lena?"

Seth's jaw cracked and all hell broke loose. McPhee tossed back the cafeteria table, slammed into Dirkson and bolted from the room, shouting, "Mary? Mary?"

I helped the stunned Dirkson to his feet, and we ran after the old farmer. We found him in the Tea room. His big hands rested on Mary's shoulders as he whispered in her ear until Dirkson separated the pair.

"Mr. McPhee. I'm placing you under arrest for the kidnapping of Orville Gunderson." Dirkson read McPhee his rights.

I went over to Mary. "What did Seth say just now, Mary?"

She fairly beamed from all the attention. "Why, he said to be sure and keep our little secret. . . just between the two of us. I just love secrets, don't you?"

"Yes, but only when no one is harmed in the process, Mary. Can you assure me that Orville Gunderson is not in any danger by your keeping this secret?"

Her face darkened, and her eyes filled. "Oh, no. I can't say that at all. I think Orville is . . ."

Mary Geneva never finished her thought that afternoon. She clutched her chest and fell into my arms. Dirkson radioed for an ambulance.

Once Mary was in the care of a medic, we ran from the Tea room, out the front door, and across the parking area toward the Bio-Fuel exhibits.

As we neared the Bloomin' Bug display, I slowed to let Dirkson take the lead. The vw Beetle was fenced off where it sat forlornly on a bed of moldy wood chips. Like a bristly beard, the entire surface of the old car was covered with last season's carpet of Million Gold—now completely dried, brittle, and faded. It was as if Mother Nature had voraciously claimed the old car.

A small plot of sorghum rustled in the background. Dirkson waved me to join him. Together, we clawed handfuls of plant material away from the door. Side windows were almost totally covered, so we really couldn't see what was inside.

Dirkson finally found a good grip and yanked the passenger door open. "Oh, oh," Shelly moaned. "He's in there, Will."

Inside we found the body of Orville Gunderson. The diminutive man sat behind the steering wheel. His eyes were open as was his mouth, as if about to speak. He was propped against the seat—held upright by a pitchfork. Slender, sharp tines protruded from the back of Gunderson's neck. The wooden handle extended to the floor of the smothered vw.

Dirkson backed away. "Son-of-a-bitch," he said.

"Yeah. Guess this little old peeper should've of kept his yap shut and left Mary alone," I offered.

Mary was rushed to the Riverside Hospital in Waconia that day. Once her fragile heart stabilized, Dirkson questioned her about what had happened that morning in April.

Turns out, Seth McPhee wasn't the killer after all. It was gentle Mary who had forked horny old Orville.

According to Mary, Orville had "Bumped against my behind." Startled and furious at his uninvited pass, she whirled and jabbed at him with her pitchfork. Unfortunately for Orville, he lunged leeringly just as she parried. The result was predictable.

Mary was saddened about Orville's death, but insisted, "He-He had misread my kindness as an invitation to behave rudely."

McPhee refused to admit to any wrongdoing. He continued to insist, "My friend, Mary, did nothing wrong! It was an accident."

The DA surmised that McPhee probably picked up the little man—fork and all, and hustled him over to the Bug. Once deposited inside, McPhee returned to Mary's side, and together they vowed to keep their little "secret."

The two friends were released on bail. The DA was less than enthusiastic about pursuing legal action against the old farmer.

Mary Geneva's trial has been postponed twice.

The Bloomin' Bug exhibit was dismantled and the Volkswagen donated to the Courage Center.

Johnny's Johnson

BRUCE RUBENSTEIN

ORMALLY I COULD SLEEP LATE and still find a parking place right in front of the Town Talk Diner, but there wasn't a space to be had next morning. The Paramount was playing a special 11:00 A.M. matinee: *Fashions Of 1933,* five cents for the movie, a soda and box of popcorn. The line was three blocks long, and mingled at the tail end with another line facing the other way, toward the Office of Migrant Services.

Both crowds were queuing for the same reason, to put something in their bellies. The women in the movie line were gabbing excitedly, looking forward to some entertainment I suppose, but the men looked bored, and the kids were glum. They stamped their feet to keep warm, and swiped their runny noses with their mittens. One of the indignities of the Great Depression was all the crap people had to put up with—lines, sermons, insufferable movies about what the hoi-poloi were wearing—for a bite to eat.

I found a space on Fifth Street and hurried through the lightly falling snow, stopping only to buy a special edition of the Dispatch. It had big headlines trumpeting a shooting in Minneapolis: MOTORIST GUNNED DOWN IN FRONT OF HIS HOME!

I grabbed a stool next to a friend of mine, officer Jack Moylan. Jack was a first generation fellow with a big belly, a big ruddy mug, and fists the size of Hormel hams. He acknowledged me with a nod but stuck to the task at hand, a plateful of eggs and hash browns.

I spread the paper out on the counter, and skimmed the headline story. The victim had gotten into a traffic squabble with a man in a black Hudson. That party took offense, tailed the victim to his home yelling threats, then drilled him when he stepped out of his car. The victim was in the hospital with life-threatening wounds.

It seemed a bit severe to sort out a fender-bender, unless of course the guy in the Hudson was one of the psychos who chill out in the Saintly City. They were forever resorting to extremes to remedy trifles, but usually amongst each other.

Jack mopped up the last of the yolk with a crust of toast and washed it down with a swallow of coffee. He asked me to accompany him on a chore he'd be doing for Eternal Tommy in the next few days, and indicated that it had to do with the very murder I was reading about.

I often rode with St. Paul's finest when they stuck their courage to the sticking place and set forth to do their duty. It was helpful for them to have a civilian along in ways that were incomprehensible unless you understood the layover agreement. Odd, how the past lurks in every detail of the here and now. I spent a year at St. Thomas before tiring of higher education, and I've retained a few odds and ends, among them a term used by a Jesuit philosophy teacher who referred to secular history as 'meaningless intellectual necrophilia.' Something about the eternal present being an instant that lasts forever in the mind of God.

I'm always reminded of the sheer, otherworldly goofiness of that theory when I consider the great historical events that shape our times, as well as the small ones that affect everyday life.

The little chunk of history that had the biggest impact on my life occurred in 1918, just a few blocks from where I was sitting that morning. It was there at the Green Lantern Saloon and Restaurant that Dan Hogan, a big harp gangster who owned the joint, met with John O'Connor, the St. Paul Police Chief. The two of them formalized the layover agreement, which was elegant in its simplicity. Gangsters on the lam got police protection in St. Paul if they followed three simple rules: check in with Hogan at the Green Lantern, pay the required gratuity, and commit no crimes within the city limits.

The layover gave Dan and his gang a monopoly in our town, and they held up their end by sparing us the violence that plagued other cities. That was especially true after Prohibition was repealed, and the bottomless well of ready cash that bootlegging provided dried up. For a few years bank robbery was practically the national pastime, but it was only at the tail end of that brief era that banks in St. Paul started getting hit. By then everything was falling apart, and such was the anarchy that the St. Paul Police were on the verge of going straight. But I'm getting ahead of myself.

The east coast mob took over crime in just about every city in America in the 1920s. Most of those places had been home to thugs like Dan Hogan and his gang. There was usually a brief battle between the local outfit and the outsiders, which the outsiders won. But by the time the mobsters were ready to make their move here, Hogan was dead and enforcement of the layover had fallen by default to a well-armed, well-organized gang called The Police. Worst of all from the mob's perspective, the coppers were incorruptible. They were already thoroughly corrupted by the layover, and doing quite well. Again, history had spared us. Chicago was practically next door by rail, and once in a while you'd hear that Capone's gang was trying to penetrate St. Paul in small ways, mostly dope and street prostitution, but nothing much came of it as far as I could see.

Plenty of cities had rackets like the layover during the Depression, but ours was unique in its long history and the open way it operated. The police chief and a few other coppers got rich, but everyone down to the lowliest jail guard got a little something. Ordinary citizens did ok as well. They got the security that the system brought them, plus the cheap thrill of knowing that at any given moment five or six of the ten most wanted were walking their streets.

Daring young couples would amuse themselves by frequenting certain hangouts—The Green Lantern, Wabasha Caverns, The Stahl House—where they could rub shoulders with mugs like Alvin "Creepy" Karpis, Homer Van Meter and John Dillinger. Sometimes the gals got tipsy, hoisted their shimmy skirts, and asked one of the gangsters to autograph their thighs. Karpis actually earned his nickname by the look he'd get on his face when he knelt down to sign that creamy Midwestern flesh. He always made a great show of crossing his eyes, hanging his tongue out, and licking the tip of his pen before he affixed his signature. His colleague Fred Barker, a mama's boy who frowned on such lewdness, was once heard to mutter "creepy" when witnessing Alvin en flagrante graffito, and it stuck.

A steady stream of roscoes took refuge here, which left the G-men in a state of constant frustration. The protection the police offered the likes of Dillinger, Baby Face Nelson, the entire Barker-Karpis mob, and a host of lesser known but equally lethal mugs, was so effective that the feds couldn't nab them. After awhile they didn't even try. If they managed to discover the whereabouts of a wanted criminal they simply organized a hit squad and attempted to kill him. But those guys shot back, so St. Paul was the scene of some spectacular gun fights.

The most notorious one had happened earlier that year, on an unseasonably warm spring afternoon. 1934 was the hottest summer of the dust bowl era in our neck of the woods, and in retrospect it had already begun on March 19th. The temperature topped 70 degrees. The spacious lawn surrounding the Lincoln Court apartments was bare and brown, but a few piles of snow, lightly crusted with topsoil, hung on in the shade of the north facing wall.

There were three of us in the nondescript Chevy the coppers used on such occasions, officer Jack Moylan, a lieutenant with the unlikely monicker of Swede Pandowski (both in plainclothes), and myself. We'd parked in a driveway off Lexington, where we had a view of a certain first floor window.

Pandowski had risen in the ranks despite his ethnicity, mostly because of his demeanor. He was one cool cookie, but I noticed his jaw drop as he gazed upon the proximate cause of the impending fuss.

Out in the back yard of Lincoln Court, a moll named Billie Frechette was gathering undies from a clothesline. Her dark hair was bobbed and styled in what they called a 'page boy' in those days, but only a blind man could've mistaken her for a boy. Billie was one curvaceous babe and dressed to show it, in a red halter and short red shorts. She had a heart-shaped mouth and sleepy eyes. Her rear end jiggled pleasantly as she plucked her panties off the line and gave them a shake. She turned her face so dust wouldn't get in her eyes.

"Will'ye look at the arse on that dame," said Moylan, as she headed for the back door.

"I've always said if you want to see beautiful women check out the visiting room at a prison," said Pandowski. "Not a jail, mind you. A pen.

Tomatoes love those gangsters. Why?"

"They lead exciting lives," I said.

"Uh-oh. Some excitement is about to enter hers," said Pandowski.

Two boyish looking G-men in pin-striped suits and snap-brimmed hats had just parked, and were striding purposefully toward the Lincoln Court Apartments.

"Where is that fookin' Van Meter?" was Moylan's rhetorical query, because this scene was scripted tightly, and at that moment how it would play out was up in the air.

It had all begun the day before, when a woman named Daisy Coffey called the St. Paul office of the Bureau of Investigation.

Another odd consequence of the layover was the role property managers played in law enforcement. Daisy belonged to a network of landlady/snitches who'd been encouraged to report suspicious activities among their new tenants directly to the feds. Hoover's boys had to conscript those biddies because the sources of information they relied upon in other cities were so close-mouthed here. As a result some remarkably minor transgressions came to their attention—illicit romances, drunken parties, tardiness with the rent. But every once in awhile the Gs got lucky.

Daisy had taken umbrage at the way Billie, who'd registered under the name Florence Hellman, flounced around in her scanties. She'd made a project out of spying on her. She'd been peeking in the window of number 103 the day before, and had witnessed Billie in the throes of fornication with the tenant of record, one Carl P. Hellman. The act itself must've been a federal case in Daisy's book, but what really scandalized her was an anatomical peculiarity that marked one of the participants. She'd managed to explain, in words I can scarcely imagine, that Mr. Hellman was hung like a donkey.

That rang a bell with the feds. John Dillinger had been arrested and strip-searched twice in the past year. He'd escaped both times, but not before the arresting officers took note of the same thing the landlady noticed. Word about Johnny's johnson had gone out in law enforcement circles, and the moment Daisy mentioned the crucial measurement our local BI agents (there were only two because the St. Paul office was staffed commensurate with its productivity) knew who they were dealing with. They'd suspected Dillinger was in town because he'd dropped off the map a few weeks earlier, after robbing a bank just over the Iowa line. They began having visions of glory.

They were typical G-men, clean-cut recent law school grads of the sort Hoover recruited. They'd probably been wearing lampshades at a frat party about this time last year, but they had enough sense to look for back-up. Under normal circumstances the local police would have gotten the call. Not here. In desperation they'd tried the Minneapolis coppers, who'd promised them some men, and then informed their St. Paul counterparts when the assassination was scheduled to take place.

Duty called. Moylan and Pandowski answered. They'd come to help Dillinger get away, or to be precise, they were there to supervise me while I helped him get away. They were ready to take it on the Arthur Duffy and leave me holding the bag if the feds twigged to the set up. That was the price I paid for the information I relied on to make a living.

The G-men paused at the door and consulted their watches. They were probably wondering where the Minneapolis coppers were. They'd be arriving late, per arrangement with their fellow officers in St. Paul, but they'd made it clear that once they got there their goal would be the same as the fed's, to kill John Dillinger. The burning question was, would Dillinger's henchman Homer Van Meter get here before the coppers did?

Eternal Tommy had tipped him about the ambush, after failing to reach Dillinger himself. Johnny had the phone off the hook, the moron.

The theory was that Dillinger and Van Meter could handle Hoover's boys, but once the Mill City buzz arrived the likely result was two dead gangsters. That would be bad publicity indeed for the layover. It was white knuckle time in our car.

"Five minutes and counting," I said.

"That's him," said Pandowski. He pointed down Lexington toward a man who was strolling our way. "That's Van Meter."

"Jayzus," said Moylan. "What's his hurry?"

Van Meter was whistling as he approached, so melodiously you almost expected him to break into a two-step. He was a hawk-nosed Kraut, with dark, slicked back hair, and a mean squint that belied his otherwise cheery demeanor. He was wearing an overcoat despite the balmy weather. It seemed to take him eons to reach the car.

"What's up, fellas?" he asked. "Must'a been a stick-up or somethin, all you coppers around."

"Those are the Gs," Pandowski replied, with a nod toward the Lincoln Court apartments.

"No kiddin? I'd best tell Johnny."

"They won't let you in."

"I'll figure somethin' out."

"Don't hurt those boys," said Pandowski. "Scare'em, but don't kill'em."

"Me? Kill a G-man? You must be thinkin'a somebody else, Stashew. I'm a sweetheart."

He opened his arms, and burst into song. "I'm the SWEET-HEART—of SIGMAA—KI— . . . Hold the applause now boys, don't wanna draw any unnecessary attention."

He bowed, and ambled off toward the apartment building, hands in his pockets and an aw shucks grin on his mug.

Pandowski's eyes narrowed as he watched him walk away. Van Meter was a weird combination of cornball prankster and cold-blooded killer. A former singing waiter from Ft. Wayne, he'd once told the citizens of an Indiana burg that he was a Hollywood director in town with a crew of actors, then managed to pull off a bank robbery while the police and a crowd of gawkers watched what they thought was a scene being shot for a movie. Van Meter had killed two coppers the past year, and rumor had it he'd iced several more law men between stints in the Illinois prisons. The St. Paul coppers didn't find that amusing. They would've gladly double-crossed him, but Eternal Tommy had his back. Van Meter paid a small fortune for protection. He had thousands on permanent deposit at The Green Lantern, and he made regular contributions to Eternal Tommy's slush fund.

The feds stopped him at the door of Lincoln Court. A conversation ensued. We couldn't hear, but things didn't appear to be going too badly. Nor were they going too quickly. The Mill City buzz were due any moment.

Van Meter and one of the feds abruptly headed back in our direction. Van Meter was talking loudly, to keep us apprised. His hands were still in his pockets.

"Why do I hafta show'ya my samples?" he was saying. "My car's half a block away. It's hard enough sellin' soap door to door without you guys makin' more problems. There's a Depression on, y'heard about that?"

"Just show me your wares," said the G. "Get going." They were about 20 feet away.

"Yeah, ok, I'll show'ya," said Van Meter. He whirled suddenly, arms out in front of him. A .45 had materialized in one hand, a .38 special in the other. He leveled both guns right in the startled fed's mug.

"JOHNNY," he bellowed, "IT'S THE GEES!"

Then he turned his full attention to the G-man. "RUN FOR YER LIFE, SHIT-BIRD ! MOVE IT!"

The kid took a tentative step backward. Van Meter bounced a shot off the sidewalk in front of him. We heard it whistle past his ear. He shot again. The kid turned around and ran.

The other fed dropped to one knee on the apartment house steps, took aim and fired. The bullet hit the fender of our car.

Van Meter unleashed a fusillade with both pistols in return. Chunks of brick flew off the apartment building. Holes appeared—one two three—in the pebbled glass door.

The fed was in a terrible position, with nowhere to run. He flattened himself on the sidewalk and fired a wild shot. A car going by on Lexington jumped the curb, and smacked into a tree on the boulevard. The driver leaped out, and hit the ground running.

"OH JOHNNY-BOY," yelled Van Meter, as he reloaded. "TIME TO AMSCRAY! OUT THE ACKBAY!"

Remarkably, he began whistling again as he chambered the rounds. From down the street came the sound of a woman screaming. In the distance, but fast drawing near, sirens could be heard.

The fed who'd been accompanying Van Meter had run most of a block before stopping. Then he got down on one knee, the same as the kid on the front steps. It must be a posture they teach on the BI training range. It made for a steady weapon, but not much maneuverability. Van Meter's extended arms caused his overcoat to hang wide at his sides, and the kid's first shot put a hole right through it.

Van Meter, who'd trained exiting banks, knew the value of a salvo. He blazed away with both guns.

"AGGGHHH"—the kid fell backward, screaming in pain and fear.

"Jayzus," muttered Moylan. "He hit him."

Van Meter retreated down the block. He wasted a few more shots on the fed in front, who'd abandoned all pretense of firing back and was concentrating on making himself as flat as possible.

A rag sheenie emerged from a side street, then halted his horse and wagon on Lexington when he saw what was going on.

The sirens reached a crescendo, then whined to a stop. A squad full of Minneapolis coppers screeched to a halt in the alley and jumped out of their car.

"Uh-oh. Dillinger'll be comin' out that way," said Moylan.

"Get back there, and tell those cops to come around front," Pandowski said. "Hurry!"

He meant me.

I exited the bucket on the run, knocking my hat off in the process. My heart was banging at my chest like it wanted out. I didn't blame it. I crossed the street and ran past the prostrate fed, all the while gesturing wildly toward the front, and tried to yell. My voice wouldn't work.

The cops got the picture though. They bolted toward Lexington, guns drawn, and as soon as they did, John Dillinger and Billie Frechette came out the back door, not ten feet from me.

Frechette made a B-line for a nearby garage. Dillinger followed, walking backwards slowly and cautiously, a Thompson Gun in his mitts. He was in his shirtsleeves. His big glittery eyes darted in all directions. The thin mustache he was sporting as a disguise was shiny with sweat. I dropped to the ground and started crawling.

One of the cops glanced my way, and spotted Dillinger. "OUT IN BACK—IT'S HIM!" he yelled.

He fired, and Johnny let go with a burst in their direction. I sat down in a snow pile and plastered myself against the wall.

Bullets whined past. A puff of dust exploded off Dillinger's leg, and wafted away on a zephyr. Johnny grimaced, dropped one hand to the smoking hole in his pants, then steadied that Tommy Gun and fired again. The cops hit the ground and kept shooting. Dirt flew. Bullets tattooed a car parked out in the street.

A blue Oldsmobile emerged from the garage behind Lincoln Court, and backed toward Dillinger with the passenger door wide open. He fired a final burst and got in. The Olds peeled away, turned the corner and disappeared.

I tried to stand but my legs were too shaky. I just sat there for a few moments watching the cops pick themselves up, dust themselves off, and head for their squad car to give chase.

As soon as I could walk again I joined the crowd that had gathered out front. It looked like a disaster scene in a low budget film—a car crumpled against a tree; a bunch of stunned-looking people standing around; a few kids snickering at a woman who was hiccuping quick little sobs.

The fed who'd been flat on the steps had raised himself to sitting position. He had his head in his hands.

Van Meter clip-clopped past on Lexington in the rag sheenie's wagon, wearing the rag sheenie's battered straw hat. He nodded at us affably as he went by.

I walked down the block to where Pandowski was standing over the G who'd been shot. He was comforting the kid.

"You'll be alright," he said. "It's just a flesh wound. An ambulance is on the way, and someone must have called the police."

"The Police?" The kid looked genuinely frightened. "They'll probably kill me."

Pandowski patted him on the shoulder. "Oh, I doubt it," he said.

We tried to be as unobtrusive as possible as we walked back to the car. "Now what?" I asked.

"The Town Talk," said Moylan. "I'm hungry enough to eat a nun's arse through a convent hedge."

"Why not, our work here is finished," said Pandowski.

Off we drove like thieves in the night, past the rag sheenie who was standing on the corner of Goodrich and Lexington with a smile on his face, and a wad of notes in his hand. Why Van Meter decided to pay him instead of shooting him to death for his wagon I'll never know.

Dillinger got clean away, but his luck was running out. A few months later the feds shot him dead outside a movie theater in Chicago. They say the mob fingered him because of the heat mugs like him brought on businessmen like themselves.

The coroner severed Dillinger's dick and had it sent to the Smithsonian for observation. Something about its freakish size relating to the man's criminal nature. I know that to be true because it's recorded in the annals of meaningless intellectual necrophilia. According to some off the record scuttlebutt I heard, Hoover made a plaster cast of Johnny's johnson to use for a dildo, but I can hardly believe that, can you?

As for Van Meter, he'd overstayed his welcome in St. Paul. Later that summer the buzz chased him up an alley, and shot him down like a rabid dog.

Paradise Refused

RICHARD A. THOMPSON

M**Y FATHER WAS A CHILD OF** the Great Depression, and he never quit trying to run away from it. Most of his adult life, he worked two full-time jobs, and when he wasn't working or sleeping, he was thinking about where he might pick up another one. Thinking about work was almost as honorable as doing it, whereas recreational interests or enthusiasms of any kind were the source of grave suspicion. They all smacked of pretension and delusion. Life was defined by hard, flat prairie and hard sweaty work. He didn't enjoy TV or movies, didn't approve of gambling or drinking or dancing, and he thought all books were part of some kind of white-collar conspiracy to ruin good laborers.

That only left driving. He was not an especially good driver and didn't work at becoming any better, but being behind the wheel of his pickup was the one indulgence he allowed himself. It was meditation, recreation, and validation, all in one.

He drove the same roads, over and over. The gravel or blacktop roads that led to the tiny towns and farmsteads where he grew up defined as big a universe as he ever wanted, and if he put on far more miles than he needed to cover his contract newspaper distribution route, who would ever complain? It was his daily escape.

Thus it was, that on a day in October, when the geese were on the wing and the grass, though still green, would have a slight crunch beneath the odd footfall, he was heading down the old Waltham Road, west of Highway 56.

He hummed a bit of a polka and blissfully thought about nothing. Half a mile from the Brownsdale cutoff, he encountered a man walking along the shoulder, and for reasons he couldn't quite explain, since hobos were high on the long list of people he didn't approve of, he decided to help the man out.

"Mighty cold day to be out for a walk," he said, leaning over in the cab to roll down the right-hand window. "How about I give you a lift?"

"Keeping moving keeps me warm, mostly," said the man, "but I wouldn't say no to a ride. I surely wouldn't." And he climbed in and rolled the window back up against the bitter northeast wind.

He had a weathered, hawk-like face and an equally weathered and battered hat that might have started its life as a Stetson. He was dressed in canvas and leather, in varying shades of khaki and brown, like a pheasant hunter or a farmer, and with his stooped shoulders and crooked, yellow teeth, he could have been any age except young.

"I'm Herman," he said. "Nice rig you got here. And mighty nice of you to stop for me, too."

"Where you headed?" said my father. Conversation wasn't one of his strong skills. And in any event, he didn't want this oddball character to get the idea that just because he'd given the guy a ride, he also wanted to be friends.

"The old Karl Jensen farm, by where Turtle Creek bends and heads west. You know it? There's an iron bridge there, was a WPA project once."

"If you're looking for the Jensen 'stead, you're about half a lifetime too late, bub." He liked to call people "bub" when he was feeling superior to them. "That hasn't been the Jensen place for over thirty years. They must have knocked the buildings down at least twenty years ago, and the bridge didn't stay much longer. They finally straightened out the creek and made the road run the way it ought to."

"Oh, I think you will find it there, all right," said the man. "If I decide it shall be so, Karl Jensen himself will be there, as well."

"You're goofier than a clock going backwards," said my father, another favorite put-down of his. "But I got nothing better to do at the moment than prove it to you. It's only about five miles ahead."

"You will find it there. I would bet you on it."

"Well, don't bet more than you can afford to lose, because you're about to be sadly mistaken."

Five miles later, it was my father who was mistaken, and more than a bit bewildered. The road bent sharply to the left, and next to a small grove of oak trees, a riveted iron bridge spanned a small, meandering creek now crusted over with fresh crystalline ice rime. Beyond were a barn and a cluster of smaller farm buildings and a prim Midwestern Gothic farmhouse, fresh in a new coat of whitewash.

"What in hell?" said my father, and he did a double-take.

"You see? Are you starting to get it? All it takes is a bit of faith. Drop me anywhere along here."

As the pickup came to a stop and he was reaching for the door handle, he looked over at my father and asked, "You ever know any mythology? Greek or Roman, it doesn't really matter. Different names, is all."

My father snorted. "Books and stuff, you mean? Deep thinking? My brother Delbert, he used to be big on that kind of nonsense. Personally, I don't go in for it, never did. Especially the books."

"You can get a lot of truth out of books."

"Tell it to the Marines. The last time somebody gave me a 'lot of truth,' they wanted me to go save the world from the Japs. I spent two and a half years on a damned floating gas can in the Pacific, watching Zero fighters and Hank dive bombers burn to a crisp in midair. Crazy bunch of pilots who wanted to die were trying to kill us sailors who wanted to live, all over some godforsaken islands that weren't worth the powder to blow them to kingdom come in the first place. That's what deep thinking will get you. It got Delbert a hole in the head and a hole in the ground at Iwo Jima. I got no time for it."

"The Greeks," said the old man, as if he had heard none of the foregoing, "believed that gods and goddesses sometimes interacted with humans. If a human helped one of them, even by accident, they had to grant a wish in return. Nothing was too far-fetched. Going back in time was a big favorite."

"You mean back . . ."

"Back to a time before something bad had happened."

"Like a war?"

"Just like that. Or the death of a loved one. That's what Karl Jensen wanted. Back before the death of his wife, as a matter of fact. He farms here now, with a McCormick Model H and a double-bottom plow. He raises a few dairy cows and chickens, and this time of year, he shoots a few pheasants. He likes it. Does that appeal to you?"

My father may have had a far-off stare for a moment, or a brief lack of focus, but he shook it off as if waking from a bad dream. "No," he said. "Karl Jensen is dead, but when he was alive, he was a no-good, worthless son of a bitch, even if he did have a farm and my folks didn't. He beat his wife and his horses, snored in church, cheated at whist and drank up every penny he ever made. He couldn't raise a decent crop in a greenhouse, and he couldn't pour water out of a boot with instructions written on the heel. I wouldn't give you a plug nickel for the best day he ever had."

"I see. Then what is your fondest dream?"

"Dreaming is for people like Delbert. I like things the way they are. My truck is almost new, my house is almost paid for, the roads are straight and they keep them plowed, and the past is all bullshit, but it's all past. Now get out of my sight and quit trying to mess with my head."

"Not a hard man to please," said the stranger. "Can't take 'yes' for an answer." And with that, he stepped out onto the gravel shoulder and slammed the door behind him.

At the sound of the door, my father started. Had he been sleeping, parked by the side of the road? Why else would the vehicle be stopped? Thinking no more of it, he pulled away from the shoulder and eased the machine up to fifty miles an hour. He knew he was somewhere in the vicinity of Brownsdale, but he wasn't sure just where. The roads all looked about the same these days, the land all flattened out, the small buildings mostly gone. Land that only a farmer could love, came unbidden into his mind, and he smiled, thinking that now that the land was "right," the farmers were mostly gone. On a whim, he decided to turn at the Blooming Prairie cutoff, go past where the old Hansen homestead used to be. Somewhere in the back of his mind, he dimly remembered having some kind of strange dream, but he didn't think it worth the mental energy to drag it back up. Probably a little oompa on the radio would get rid of it.

Getting senile, he thought. Is that where the old Jensen place used to be, back there? Hard to tell, now. Looks better this way, with the buildings wrecked.

*

My father would have told the story much differently, of course. He's gone now, as little remembered as the old buildings he was so ready to sneer about, and I alone am the keeper of the tale. But I didn't hear it from him. I heard it from an old man in a leather coat and a battered hat, and I know the truth of it. For although I haven't been back that way for a long, long time now, I too have driven the old Waltham Road, in the fall, when the geese are on the wing. A fine time to be alive. A trip worth making. And I know that while my father was right, in his own untutored way, to be suspicious of the gifts of the gods, there are some gifts that are worth wishing for. The gift of the storyteller is one.

Lights Out

CHRISTOPHER VALEN

MY DAD USED TO SCARE the shit out of me.

He'd jump out of a closet or a dark room and yell "Boo!" in a voice so deep I thought it came from hell. I never knew why he seemed to enjoy it, only that when he did my heart felt like a nail had been driven into my chest, and I'd piss in my pants.

"Don't be a sissy," he'd say, burping with laughter from the Jack Daniels he'd drunk. "Nobody likes a sissy."

He used words the way Jack the Ripper used a scalpel.

My mother stood up for me the first time it happened. She quit after he smacked her.

I was lucky in some respects. Hank—that's what my dad told me to call him—was in the Merchant Marines for the first twenty-two years of my life and wasn't home much. I lived in Duluth with my mother and older sister near the shores of Lake Superior. My mother had a lot of passion for the Lord, but not much for her kids. We belonged to a small Pentecostal church run by a preacher who filled our heads with horror stories of the coming apocalypse and eternal damnation. My mother gratefully helped fill the collection plate with cash. The preacher had her and the rest of the Bible-thumpers convinced that there was only one life worth living and it wasn't this one. He might've had a future as a televangelist if he hadn't run off with all the congregation's money and the Deacon's wife when I was fourteen.

I always slept in the beacon of a bedroom light. In darkness I imagined bogeymen and monsters hiding under my bed and behind closet doors. I was small for my age. Kids called me a "pussy" at school, and beat me up for sport. I pleaded with my mother not to tell the principal, but she did anyway. When the bullies found out, the beatings got worse and more frequent. She prayed for me, but apparently the Lord was busy with more important matters. I'd lie awake at night imagining elaborate scenarios in which the assholes would pay for the beatings they inflicted upon me, but, in the end, my mother did the only thing she could. She home-schooled me through eighth grade. I protested, but deep down, I was glad. You can only be a punching bag for so long.

Hank was as smooth as a reel of copper fishing line when it came to the ladies. He never spent much time at home, even when on leave. Often he'd come stumbling through the back door early in the morning, reeking of booze and sex. My mother never tired of making breakfast and excuses for him.

My sister liked sitting on my father's lap when she was little and drinking sips of whiskey from his glass. Whenever I asked him for some he'd say, "Only men and beautiful girls drink liquor, boy." I remember hearing him late at night, whispering, "Lights out, honey," as he entered my sister's bedroom.

She ran away at sixteen. I saw her once after that in a bar in Superior. She had been real pretty when she left home, but now her face was as cold and hard as a Superior winter. I knew she recognized me by the way she hesitated for a moment and opened her mouth to speak. Then her face turned red and she left quickly with two weathered men in pea coats and watch caps.

They looked as though they had just stepped off an ore boat and spoke a language I didn't understand. I never saw her again.

Despite the bullying and intimidation, I was a good student. A counselor once told me I had "resiliency." I acted like I knew what the word meant, but as soon as I got the chance, I looked it up in the dictionary.

Resilience: "The ability to recover quickly from illness, change, or misfortune; buoyancy." I liked the term buoyancy because I had been around water most of my life.

I read everything I could about nature and the outdoors. Whenever I got the chance, I'd tramp through the Superior National Forest looking for live versions of the plants and animals I'd seen in books. I went to the University of Minnesota Duluth after high school and got a degree in Recreation and Outdoor Education. During the summers I worked for the Wisconsin Park Service. One summer I volunteered as a light keeper. I enjoyed it so much that after I graduated, I went to work for the Park Service full-time.

Two years after I graduated from UMD my mother died of cancer. Still, she clung to her faith right up to the end.

"God forgives," she said to me with her dying breath. "You make sure you do, too."

We both knew whom she meant.

Hank bought a 31-foot fiberglass fishing boat with a 12-foot beam and started a charter service out of Bayfield, Wisconsin the year he got out of the Merchant Marines. He took tourists with full wallets out on Lake Superior where he showed them how to catch Lake Trout, Steelhead, and Chinook and Coho Salmon. The year before I had taken a job with the Apostle Island Park Service. My primary responsibility was maintaining the light station on Outer Island.

I liked being around light more than people, so the job seemed like a perfect fit. Outer Island had no regularly scheduled cruises, and only the most experienced or crazy boaters and kayakers dared attempt the trip because of its distance and exposed location. The island had one small campsite at the southern tip, but the Apostle Islands Cruise Service had to schedule a special trip to get campers there. In inclement weather, the exposed location of the dock made landing impossible. I brought in extra supplies since I could easily get stranded for a few days or more.

The ninety-foot lighthouse stood on a forty-foot high red clay bluff at the most remote point of the Apostle Islands, directly in the path between Duluth and the northern tip of the Keweenaw Peninsula. It had been built in 1874 to guide ships safely past the archipelago as they made runs from the Soo Locks to Duluth and Superior. Since the Outer Island Shoal lay a mile and a half to the north of the island, ships had to give the island a wide berth, or risk ripping their hulls on the rocky bottom just ten feet beneath the surface.

Besides the lighthouse, there was a fog signal building and two-story keeper's dwelling. The keeper's house was equipped with a 12-volt electric system that provided light in the evenings. I'd sit in a rocker in the living room at night, reading books and listening to the waves and the chatter on the ship to shore radio. I had a propane heater, a gas-powered refrigerator, a gas stove for cooking, and running water for washing. I brought in drinking water from the mainland.

A passageway connected the house to the tower and the cast iron staircase that spiraled up to the watch room where keepers had once kept vigil over the beacon. The watch room was encircled by an outside walkway and topped by the lantern room. The room had a lens carousel containing six replaceable acrylic panels, which made it easy to change the bulbs. All I had to do was remove the panel at the center of the upper cover.

Hank tried giving up alcohol as he aged, but the booze had hooked him like a grappling iron. He'd get out on the water with a group of rowdy anglers from the city and soon be as drunk as everyone else. So drunk, he often forgot to collect his money. When creditors eventually foreclosed on his charter business, he moved in with a good-looking woman half his age that owned a small cabin on Madeline Island. He worked odd jobs and taught her how to sail her 24-foot Pearson. Hank was always good with his hands.

Tales of Lake Superior storms and gale force winds were as common as sea gulls on the islands. I came to respect the nor'easters and the severe weather that blew in with little or no warning. Torrents of rain driven horizontally by screaming winds felt like ice picks against my face.

It was on one such night in September that I recognized the Pearson's call letters on my ship to shore. I'd been listening to the weather broadcasts when I heard the distress call on Channel 16. Hank had been up at Eagle Pointe Harbor on the Keweenaw Peninsula and was sailing alone under power for the safety of Julian Bay on Stockton Island to the south. It was a long haul, especially in a gathering storm.

I could've used the ship to shore to let him know that I was at the light station on Outer Island, that, as the waves pounded like fists against the Pearson's hull, he wasn't alone in the darkness . . . but I didn't. Instead, I sat in the rocker and wondered if Hank had ever had any regrets. I wondered if he had learned about many things in life, but believed in nothing. I wondered if he was resilient but had never known how to love. I wondered if, like me, he had always been truly afraid of the darkness inside him.

As I walked up the staircase in the light tower, I realized I'd never know the answers to my questions. But as I removed the panel on the upper cover of the carousel and began unscrewing the bulbs one by one, I knew that I had finally come to terms with the darkness. I knew that I would no longer fear it, even when the cell door slammed shut and the guard yelled, "Lights out!"

Perfect Neighbors

MARILYN VICTOR

THE END OF WINTER'S PEACE and quiet had arrived.

At one time in his life Harold had loved spring. He loved quiet spring evenings on the back porch, a warm breeze pushing through the window screens, filled with the promise of summer. He loved to watch the emerging buds on his perfectly pruned apple trees, and the birds coming to nest in the bird house he had built, a miniature of the house he had grown up in.

But that was BTR—Before The Renters. Before the next door neighbors, Louie and Ellen, had moved to an apartment in the suburbs and rented out their house. Now Harold spent warm spring evenings with the windows locked shut, looking forward to the first snowflake that would cover his carefully kept lawn in a blanket of blissful silence.

Last year he had spent a fortune fitting the house with the most energy efficient double paned windows money could buy. But it couldn't buy peace and quiet. He could still hear the weekly parties next door, the music a pulsing, eardrum throbbing beat that left him lying in bed staring at the glow-in-the-dark solar system he had painted on the ceiling.

He punched his pillow in frustration, sat up on the edge of the bed and marched to the kitchen. Grabbing up the phone, he slipped out onto his back porch and angrily punched in the number he had long ago memorized.

"Do you hear that?" he demanded of the groggy voice that answered. He held the phone out to the midnight sky, wincing at the volume of bass and music that spewed from his neighbor's back porch.

"Goddamn it, Harry! It's fucking one in the morning!"

"Exactly!" He'd be damned if he was going to be the only one who couldn't sleep. It obviously didn't bother his wife, who was still fast asleep.

He screamed into the phone for a full minute before he realized no one was listening. Fingers shaking with rage, he hit the redial. This was going to end here. Warm seasons were short enough in Minnesota; he was not going to spend another one locked inside his house with the windows closed because the renters next door felt the need to share their tasteless music with everyone within a four block radius.

"What's the matter with you!" Louie screamed. "I thought I was free of you when I moved out of that damned neighborhood. You call here again, and I'm calling my lawyer and hitting you with another restraining order!"

"Good! Then I can tell them about your lousy renters!"

"Renters? Listen you crackpot, I sold that house to them six months ago. If you got problems, call the cops!"

Harold blanched and let the phone slip from his hand. Home owners? He was stuck with them? He slumped back to the bedroom, panic constricting his chest. He couldn't go through another summer like the last one. He'd go mad. He was already grinding his teeth into pulps. Leaning next to the bedroom window, he snagged a blind slat down and glared at the party going on next door.

There he was. Jerome. As big as a fullback, pants hanging below his ass, white boxers pulled to the waist, walking around like a toddler with a full diaper. Harold had tried talking to the man. When he had politely asked Jerome to turn the volume down during the first big party, Jerome had laughed and called him an old fart. Then he held another party the next night. And the next weekend. And the weekend after that.

Harold plopped down on the edge of the bed and gave his wife a shake. "Can't you hear that?" he demanded. Millie's hearing had gotten worse since that lowlife had moved in next door. He had to repeat everything he said at least twice before he got a response.

"Huh?" She raised groggy eyes to him, her small hand dipping beneath the veil of long blonde hair and rubbed at her ear. He really had to make her see an ear specialist and made a mental note to add it to her to-do list. "Go to sleep, Harold." She rolled over, turning her back to him.

"Sleep!" He gave her another shake. "How can you sleep with all that racket going on?"

Millie made a disgusted noise in her throat and sat up, swinging her feet to the floor and toeing around for her slippers.

He kept talking as he followed her into the kitchen and watched as she poured herself a glass of water. "I am not going to spend every warm, summer night listening to that idiot next door shake my house down with his damned music."

He pounded a fist on the kitchen counter. "It isn't even music. I can't hear any music, can you? All I hear is that damned drum beat! It's making my ears throb and rattling the windows! Why doesn't he get an iPod like everyone else!"

That would have been too considerate. Old Jerome didn't have a considerate bone in his body.

Harold pulled back the kitchen curtain and stared hard at the crowd of young people partying on the neighbor's deck. "Look over there," he ordered, forcing her to turn toward the window. "Do you see a stereo anywhere? No. A radio? No. That I could understand."

Millie rubbed her ears and stuffed her hands in the pockets of her robe, staring at him as he let the curtain fall back in place in disgust and continued his tirade. "No, our lovely neighbors have to use the car stereo. Only the car is thirty feet away in the garage! What kind of sense does that make?"

"It doesn't, Harold. Now come back to bed."

"At least if there was a stereo on the deck, they'd only be upsetting us. Instead they have to upset the entire neighborhood!"

He followed her back to the bedroom. "Can't you talk to Sharlane, his girlfriend? Can't she pound some sense into him?" More than likely Jerome would pound some sense into Sharlane. He'd seen the dark glasses the woman wore even on a cloudy day and the deep blue bruises the glasses barely hid.

"Before or after I tell her she wears too much perfume?" Millie gave him a pained expression as she crawled back in bed.

"She smells like a funeral parlor. What girl wants to go around smelling like death? I was just being helpful."

"Some people would appreciate it if you'd help less," Millie said pulling the sheet over her head.

He was wasting his breath on her. She would never understand. Honesty used to be treasured when he was a boy. No one cared what anyone else thought anymore. If they did, there wouldn't be anymore dandelions around to threaten the health of his lawn and he wouldn't have to report his neighbors to the city for not shoveling snow from the public sidewalks. No one gave a damn anymore.

He paced to the closet twice before finally reaching up to the top shelf and pulling down the lock box hidden there. After keeping a close watch on all the young men that visited Jerome during the day, Harold was convinced the man was dealing drugs. Unable to convince the police of this, he had bought a gun

"Put that thing back and come to bed!" Millie's voice held an uncharacteristic irritation and he knew she had never been comfortable with having a gun in the house. Neither was he. His hands trembled, as he opened the box. He admitted to himself that having a gun scared him. It was for self-defense only, but it gave him no sense of security.

He paced the small bedroom. The party dragged on. The music became louder. No one called the police and he wondered at that. Was he the only person that was bothered by this auditory assault? He could see that it was now up to him to protect his community. He could no longer sit still and watch the neighborhood go down because of one bad seed. This would end tonight.

He quickly pulled on a pair of black trousers and despite the heat, put on his black turtleneck and a black stocking cap to cover his graying hair. His hands shook as he gripped his flashlight and waited. Millie sighed and turned over in her sleep.

It was almost three in the morning before the last of the revelers left and the night became quiet again. The only sound in the neighborhood was the distant, occasional traffic from the nearby freeway.

He slunk out the back porch and into the alley. Pressed against the alley side of his own garage, he waited. He had watched enough crime shows to know how to move around undetected. He thought he heard a door shutting softly behind him and waited again, counting to one hundred. Convinced the way was clear, he prowled across the driveway and slipped through the open utility door of the neighbor's garage. Even in the dark, the big Cadillac gleamed, its turbo-charged sound system mocking him even in the dark. Wire cutters in hand, he fumbled for the latch that would unlock the hood. A few snips and the car would be rendered useless. Then, a few clips to the wires leading the stereo system for good measure and he'd be back in bed before Millie even knew he was gone.

"What y'up to bro?"

The deep bass voice froze him where he stood. In the darkness, he could barely make out Jerome's dark shadow looming over him. He backed up a step, and felt the presence of another body behind him. He was a dead man. Through his fear he could smell death and felt strangely calm. At least some good would come from his passing. No doubt after this night played out a new city noise ordinance would be enacted and named after him.

"I asked you a question, asshole." This time he could smell the whiskey and sweat over the cloying scent of funeral bouquets.

He closed his eyes, waiting for the blow that would end his life, sorry that he couldn't have enjoyed at least one spring day of peace and quiet before he died. He hoped the angels played muffled harps. A gunshot deafened him. He stumbled backward, but was pushed forward again, cold, hard metal pressed into his hand. He tripped over something on the garage floor. Sharp pain spiked through his head. Stars burst behind his eyes and he dropped to the ground.

"Here's to us."

A crystal wine glass clinked against a bottle of Budweiser, the only sound to be heard over the relaxing music of the birds and bees that flitted through the garden.

Millie leaned forward to toss a small pair of earplugs into an ashtray followed by a lit match.

"You're going to miss them," Sharlane warned.

"I doubt that." It was bliss not having to wear the earplugs almost 24/7. For the six months Harold had been retired, it had been the only thing keeping her from strangling the man. "I've dreamed of hitting that man over the head for years."

Sharlane gave her a wide smile, the front tooth Jerome had knocked out no longer missing. "I know what you're saying. Shooting Jerome was the most satisfying moment in my life. It's almost too bad I couldn't take credit for it."

Millie shook her head. "It was almost too easy. It never occurred to Harold that he wasn't the one who pulled the trigger."

"Or the police," Sharlane reminded her.

"Just as planned." They clinked their wine glassed together again. Two birds with one bullet and a baseball bat.

Spring Cleaning

LANCE ZARIMBA

ANOTHER BLOODY LIST! What was this woman thinking? Didn't she have anything better to do? Francine picked it up and saw that it was three pages. Three Pages!

How many years had she been cleaning for this woman? Five? And it required three pages to tell her how to clean the house? She knew the routine by heart. Francine had tried to vary her tasks throughout the week, but there was always a special order that must be followed daily, and new tasks were usually added.

Francine hung her purse and jacket in the kitchen closet and walked into the utility room. She picked up her rubber gloves and collected her caddy filled with cleaning supplies. She looked at the list and sighed. "Better get started." As she walked up the huge winding staircase, she read the letter:

Francine,

I will be going to the opera this evening, and I need everything in its place. Make sure that you:

1. Run the dishwasher, but do not use the drying cycle.
2. Make sure all of the garbage is taken out. The garbage men come in the morning, very early.
3. Dust . . .

She crumpled the list and jammed it into the pocket of her required maid's uniform. No matter how hard she worked, Mrs. Riley would re-do the entire house, anyway. It was never good enough. Nothing was ever good enough for her.

The phone rang, and the answering machine picked up. "You have reached the Riley residence . . . please leave a message at the beep." The beep echoed throughout the cold halls of the Edina mansion.

"Francine? This is Rita Riley. Start from the top floor of the house and work your way down, and make sure that you clean the master bathroom first. I will be home early and need to get ready for tonight, so I'd like you out of my way."

Francine rolled her eyes.

"Francine? Can you hear me? Are you even there? Pick up the phone." Her tight voice commanded. "I bet she's not even there, the lazy . . ." Click. The line went dead. The answering machine stopped and started to flash.

She continued up the stairs. "Francine, scrub the floor. Francine, wash the walls. Francine, make my bed."

The master bathroom appeared to be freshly scrubbed. Francine doubted that Mrs. Riley would notice if she worked in here for three minutes or for three hours. The results would be the same.

Francine poured a whole gallon of bleach into the toilet. "This will make it smell nice and clean for you with your nose so high in the air." She giggled to herself.

She kicked the caddy to the side and set the scrubbing brush down on the floor. "I'll let that soak for a while, while I take the garbage out." She picked the white plastic bleach bottle up and placed it into the garbage can. She traversed the house. Cathedral ceiling to cathedral ceiling, from garbage can to garbage can. Some rooms had more than one. How much garbage could these two people have?

The rooms were checked, and she carried the few pieces of trash out. She had learned to make sure nothing was left in any garbage, not even a single strand of thread or a staple, otherwise, she'd hear about it for weeks. Francine shook her head. What a waste of time and energy.

As she lifted the lid off the garbage can, the garage door started to open. "Darn," she said under her breath.

A silver Mercedes purred into the parking spot. The car door opened, and a slender leg emerged, clad with a delicate high-heeled shoe. A full-length mink coat followed. Dusk was falling on a perfect spring day.

"Aren't you done yet?" Rita demanded. Her heels clicked across the cement floor.

"I . . ."

"I called, and you didn't pick up. I bet you just arrived."

"I don't like answering your phone . . ." she began.

"It would have been nice to know that you had heard my message." Her nasal whine pierced the air.

Francine dropped the trash into the can and closed the lid. "Well, I'd better get back to work." She turned and entered the kitchen.

Rita followed close behind. Her heels clicking sharply with each step.

Francine resisted the urge to increase her pace. She forced herself to remain calm. No matter how hard she worked, Mrs. Riley would find something wrong. She slipped on a rubber glove.

"Wait." Rita's heels clicked to a stop.

"I need to get back to work," Francine started.

"No. It's too late. I need to get ready."

"But it's only . . ."

"I don't have time for this Francine. I'll pay you for your regular shift, if that's what you're worried about."

"It's not that, I just haven't finished . . ."

"I'll finish it for you, like I always do anyway. Just go home."

Francine knew it didn't pay to argue with her. She pulled off her glove and returned to the utility room where she retrieved her purse and coat.

Rita took off her mink and threw it onto the table. The fur slipped off and landed on the floor in a pile.

Francine moved to pick it up, but Rita waved her away. "Just go."

Francine nodded and left the house. As she walked to her car, something bothered her, something she had forgotten, but that wasn't anything new. She was sure she had forgotten many things, and she knew that she'd hear about it tomorrow.

"Look at this mess. Can't she do anything right?" Rita flipped the ceiling fan on. She picked up the caddy and placed it on the sink. "How can I get ready with this mess in the bathroom?"

She slipped off her dress, turned on the fan, and started cleaning in her high heels and slip. She opened the toilet cleaner and dumped the blue crystals into the bowl. She knelt down and grabbed the brush. The water started to foam as a yellowish-green fog rose.

A funny tickle entered her throat and eyes. A peppery-pineapple scent swirled around her. A cough caught in her throat as she continued to scrub the blue foam around the white porcelain. As her coughing became more violent, a burning sensation started in her throat.

As she worked, the room seemed to grow warmer, and she was finding it more difficult to breathe. "Did that silly twit turn up the temperature?" She rubbed her neck and breathed in deeply, trying to clear her head. The pain that was in her throat moved down into her chest. She stopped scrubbing as a violent coughing spell erupted. The room was too hot, and she couldn't catch her breath. Her eyes were watering, as the room seemed to close in on her.

She struggled to her feet, but her heels slipped on the tiled floor. She fell onto her back and started coughing convulsively. Her manicured nails dug into her throat as white spikes of pain pierced her heart. Her lips turned a deep purple in color, as her tongue protruded out of her mouth, gasping for air.

As the room spun around her, her last thought was that she was going to be late for the opera.

"Francine? This is Mr. Riley. I wanted to call and tell you that you don't need to come into work today."

"Is there a problem?" Francine asked.

"Mrs. Riley passed away last night."

"I'm . . . I'm so sorry."

"It was a shock for me also. I waited for her at the opera. I thought she was just running late, so I went in and watched the first half. At intermission, I called home on her cell phone, but she didn't answer, so I became worried."

Francine held her breath.

"I came home and found her lying on the bathroom floor. Dead."

"Oh dear. Is there anything I can do?"

"You've done enough already, my dear." He paused for a few seconds. "Why don't you plan on starting up again next week?"

"Sure. But if you'd need me . . ."

"No. I'll be fine."

"Mr. Riley? Can I ask what happened?"

"You know how I warned Rita that her cleaning would kill her someday. Well, it finally did. At least she died happy, doing what she enjoyed."

"I feel responsible."

"My dear, please don't. She was pleased with your work, and I think we need to discuss a raise for you on Monday? I know Mrs. Riley would want you to have one."

"Mr. Riley, I'm speechless."

"Francine, I knew you were the perfect maid."

"But I was always forgetting something . . . why did Mrs. Riley hire me?"

"I made her hire you."

"You did? But why?"

"Francine, my wife was very particular, and she needed things done her way. So we hired you. I always knew that you would get the job done, someday." His voice seemed to be smiling.

"Thank you, Mr. Riley. You can count on me. I won't let you down."

"I know, Francine. I know."

A Million Miles of Sky

HAROLD ADAMS

B ARNEY SAT AT THE FOOT of his grandmother's bed with his arms folded tightly across his chest, and stared at a spot on the rug by the hallway door, while she talked to him from her rocking chair beside the window. His legs ached and the blisters on his heel burned, but he wore his shoes in spite of the pain. His grandmother talked and sewed at the same time, only stopping to look at him when she wished to emphasize a point.

"I don't know how to make you understand," she said, "that you have a chance to be someone. But you must take yourself in hand, not always letting your impulses sway your better judgment. Hard work and sacrifice can make a man like your grandfather important, even though he isn't much more than a handy-man, without any formal education and only an average brain. You've made a hero out of your uncle Carl because you think he's independent and acts so smart, but he's a nobody. The independence you think so much of isn't genuine at all. You gain independence from being established. You can only do as you please when you accept some responsibility, show concern for other people's opinions and become part of society. I'm not talking just about power, money, or influence, for their own sake. The thing I would hope you could come to realize, and you have the potential, is that really special respect that comes to people who work with their minds."

She shot him a piercing glance and he squirmed until she resumed sewing.

"Your grandfather has some influence in Corden because he is a hotel proprietor. Part of the town is his and he takes pride in it and tries to make the most of it. Your uncle's a clown. A crony of pool-hall bums and shiftless boozers. You have enough intelligence to be somebody. Don't throw it away."

Barney ran his fingers through his hair and looked down at his feet while she studied him.

"Do you think your uncle is happy?" she asked.

"He seems a lot happier than Grandpa."

"Well," said his grandmother, hitching her shoulders irritably, "happiness isn't everything."

"A lot of people think so." Barney shifted his gaze from the rag rug a moment, glanced at her sewing, then looked at the door.

"A lot of people are idiots." she told him.

Barney nodded, but his grandmother was attacking her sewing so vigorously she didn't notice the small agreement. Suddenly she stopped and stared at him.

"You're probably too young for any of this to have meaning, but I wish you could understand our concern for you isn't all selfish. As hard as it may be for you to believe, we've been young too. We made our mistakes and saw those of our friends and people around us. We've seen a deal of the world, my boy, and we want you to get some benefit from that. You act as if all we're interested in is spoiling your fun and getting in your way. We don't give you work to do because we want to make you unhappy, we do it because it builds character and you have to have the habits of industry while you're young, or you'll never amount to anything, no matter how clever or bright you may be."

"Sure," said Barney in a rush. "It's good for my character to sweep floors and wash windows, burn trash and haul luggage, and it makes Bertha pure to cook our meals six and a half days a week and it was wonderful for Maggie to carry the slops and run the mangle. And all that just happens to make the hotel run and the hotel is for us to make successes of us all."

She stopped sewing, but for several seconds kept her eyes on the work in her lap. She shook her head.

"You haven't understood one word I've said."

"Sure I have."

She looked up at him. "Do you actually believe it was perfectly all right for a sixteen year old boy to stay out all night?"

"I don't see anything so awful in it. It didn't hurt anybody but me. You could even say my walking all that way was hard enough work to build character."

"I'll tell you exactly why it was wrong. You had to know, if you thought for an instant, how it would upset us, and you did it out of pure defiance. You knew we'd worry—and we have worries enough without you adding to the burden. It was selfish and thoughtless, but on top of that, it was bad for you. Oh—" she hurried on as he began to protest—"I don't mean just your bodily health. I mean the way you think. I keep telling you that self-indulgence is destructive and you think that I'm trying to spoil your fun. Well, fun isn't all that counts. You can't always do just what you please in this world, and your fine uncle is the best evidence of that I can offer."

Barney sighed deeply, and his grandmother gave up.

"All right, run along. But please, try to find some nice young Congregationalist friends, and avoid band people, Catholics and heathens."

Barney wandered from his grandmother's room to the back of the hotel where Carl was putting a new fan belt on his truck.

"Hi, Slugger," said Carl, wiping his hands on a rag. "How's the other guy look?"

"All I'm sure of is, his knuckles must be sore."

"He'd be proud if he could see you. Who did it?"

"Nate."

Carl sat down on the running board and looked thoughtful. "How come?"

"I called him a son-of-a-bitch."

"That wasn't too smart."

"No," agreed Barney. He sat down on the ground near his uncle's feet. "How come you called him that?"

"He tried to make me drink more wine than I wanted, and then banged my lip with the bottle. It made me mad."

"It made you foolish. Anytime you start messing around with a bigger or stronger man, don't call him names, hit him. Preferably with something hard. Hit quick and sharp. It's good for you. Makes you all committed and you got no time to chicken out and he's got no time to get set. Adam's apple is the best place if you have to do it barehanded. Or a kick to the nuts. You hit either of those targets, not many guys'll give you trouble."

"I didn't really plan to fight."

"You damned well better plan to anytime you call a man an s.o.b."

"He hit me the first one in the belly."

Carl's eyebrows raised. "Well now, that's pretty smart for a knucklehead like Nate. I'll remember that."

Barney plucked at a weed listlessly. "I don't see how he could be Jennie's son, or Dan's brother."

"Hell, your grandparents can't see how I could have been theirs either. Maybe doctors switch things around for spite when they figure chances are poor of getting paid. You already had your chewing out?"

"Yeah." Barney moved his foot over and squashed a boxelder bug.

"You argue with her?"

"Mostly I listened."

"You're getting smart. It took the old man thirty years to learn that, and took me about twenty. If she had any sense she'd know that bawling works twice as well as any arguments she could dream up. I've had women bawl me into and out of everything, but none of them ever talked me into anything. A woman smart enough to argue is too smart to try."

"Are you going to marry Jennie?"

Carl, startled by the switch, started to scowl, then grinned. "You think I ought to?"

"Yeah." Barney kept his eyes on the ground.

"Figure I'd make a fine daddy for Nate and Dan?"

"They're too old to need a dad."

"They'd still be around. And how long you think I could be with them before I had to stomp old Nate's ass into the ground? And how do you think Jennie'd go for that? Hell, I'd probably find myself fighting all three of them."

"You wouldn't have to fight Nate. He's afraid of you."

"I been afraid of half the guys I fought. That doesn't mean shit."

"I guess you don't really love her," said Barney in a very low voice.

"And I guess you got your nose out too far again." Carl stood up and closed the truck hood. "What the hell's it to you if I marry? Why's every-body got a foot in the whole goddamn show that's nobody's business but mine?"

Barney looked at him. "You don't need to go getting mad. I just like Jennie and I know Dan worries about her and you, that's all. You got no call to yell at me."

"I'm not yelling," said Carl in a slightly reduced volume, "but—God damn!"

He wiped his hands again on the cleaning rag, stuffed it in his back pocket, pulled out his tobacco sack and rolled a cigarette. When it was lit he inhaled deeply, removed the cigarette from his mouth and studied the burning end.

"Barney, a woman is only what you can do for her. If you can't do any-thing for her, she can't do a damn thing for you. She's got to need you, or you're nothing. You got to build her up or slap her down, depending on how she is. And the hell of it is, once you get her leveled off, you done all you can and it's time to move on."

"What've you done for Jennie?"

"Just about everything. I was company lonely nights, laughs on dark days. I made her believe she was a woman again. A real one. Not just a slavey for two louts big enough to help and appreciate her –"

Barney was silent for a moment, then asked, "So what do you leave her with?"

"Everything I brought, and maybe more. If it happened with me, it can happen again. She might find a man dumb enough to earn a living and support the whole brood."

"You take everything when you leave her. You try to make it sound like you're Santa Claus, but you're nothing but a-a pirate, that came and took what he wanted and then scuttled the ship."

"Oh, Christ!" Carl started to laugh and the more he laughed the fun-nier the metaphor struck him. "Poor Jennie," he gasped, "all punctured and sunk."

"Damn you!" yelled Barney, scrambling to his feet. He swung at the jaw but Carl ducked away and Barney's fist smacked against his cheek just under the left eye, swinging his uncle half way around. Carl kept turning as Barney charged and suddenly the boy found himself against the truck with his uncle behind him. He slashed at Carl with a backhand, but only found his wrist grabbed and his arm snapped up behind his back, forcing him forward until his head and shoulder were rammed against the truck door.

"Fighting's for the dumb ones," said Carl in his ear. "When're you gonna learn that?"

Tears of shame and humiliation filled Barney's eyes. "Let me go," he choked. The metal of the truck pressed against his head and shoulder and he could feel the muscles of his pinned arm stretching under the pressure of Carl's grip.

"Say please," said Carl.

"Go to hell," whispered Barney.

For just a second Carl's grip intensified until Barney almost screamed, and then he said, "Well," and let go. Barney sank to the ground and brought his throbbing arm around until he was cradling it in his lap. Carl took a soiled handkerchief from his back pocket, touched his own cheek and examined a streak of blood.

"For a lover, you throw a pretty good punch," he said. "Course you telegraphed it about ten minutes ahead. If you'd got that in clean I'd probably have broken your arm—but I'd have to had to get off the ground to do it."

Barney knew he was trying to be generous and resented it. There was no question in his mind that Carl could have subdued him if he'd been swinging a baseball bat instead of his fist, and the unfairness of a man being so strong, fast, and wrong, seemed awful.

"Listen," said Carl, resting one foot on the running board, "you got to learn to live with things the way they are, not the way you want them. Jennie was no virgin when I came along, and I never made any promises or told any really big lies. When I told her she was special, I meant it. Wouldn't have gone to bed with her if she wasn't. You think I'm another Simpson that'd settle for Maggie?" I don't tell you I want to do something for a woman because I'm so damned big-hearted, I do it because that's where the big kick is. Hell, if I just wanted to be big-hearted, I'd pay whores and not use 'em. That'd be Santa for sure, huh? So Jennie used me and I used her—but when she wants to take it to church, it's begging for apples from an empty barrel. At the start all that mattered was the big feeling we had and the fun. Now that's not enough. She's gotta have everybody's okay and a ring through my nose and a license to wave around and a cage to keep me in. Son, the minute you start worrying about hitting the bottom of the bottle, you stop getting any kick from what's left in it. Women'll never let well enough alone. Hell, they'd freeze every creek just to keep the water from running out."

Carl sat on the running board, leaned back against the cab and crossed his legs.

"I don't see," said Barney, "why her wanting to make it permanent should make you quit caring."

Carl sighed. "Look, I haven't stopped caring. I like her fine. She's the one that's cutting the whole thing off—because I won't play it her way. You come right down to it, I'm the one who wants to keep things the way they are. And I don't worry that will she change her mind about me and quit. If she changes her mind, what the hell do I want to keep her for? What good is a woman that doesn't want you? Or a man to a woman he doesn't want? The reason married people fight so much is because they know they can't get away and it rankles them and at the same time makes them careless about what they say. A man doesn't give his best friends fits over nothing, because he knows if he does, the friend won't come back. Wives and husbands got to come back—so they can give each other hell."

After a moment, Carl leaned toward Barney and put his hand on his shoulder.

"You've got a good head, but it's full of crap. You never been in love, you never had a woman, so you really don't know what the hell it's all about. Don't think you should know how people should act. You never been really hungry, or drunk, never been shot at, or on your own a thousand miles from anybody that gives a damn. You'll learn. You'll find out because you're like me. You won't hang around here all your life, walking in crap up to your knees."

"It seems like you owe Jennie something," said Barney.

"Sure I do," nodded Carl, settling back against the truck door. "But it's nothing I can pay back. Making a man feel like a man ain't anything you can weigh out and price like spuds, you know? And you can't give it back. I made her feel like a woman, too, but I'll tell you, I don't see that makes her beholding to me. You talk about double standards, that's one the women never mention. They always make like getting laid was only a treat for the guy. Maybe it is—for some—but if that's the way for most, it's no damn wonder this world's in such a hell of a shape."

When Barney made no response, Carl leaned close again. "How's the arm?"

Barney raised and lowered it, and said he guessed it was okay.

"Good. Look, I've got to go meet a man who's giving me a gravel-hauling job. Maybe he'll fix me up with something steady enough to make me respectable. Don't give up. You never know what'll happen."

Barney stood and moved back as Carl started the truck motor. When the truck was gone, he slowly walked up to his room, stretched out on his bed, and thought about men and women until it made him so tired he slept.

Afterword

JON JORDAN

AS SOON AS I LEARNED TO READ I started hoarding books. I was reluctant to return books to the library, and I would take my mother's paperbacks and stack them in my room. As soon as I had my own money I started buying my own books. I started on a smaller scale, paperbacks by Ed McBain and Gregory Mcdonald. I was soon fascinated by series books and obsessed with owning all the books by an author. It wasn't much longer before I realized that the hardcovers look better on the shelf and I started swapping paperbacks for hardcovers. I've covered my walls with books. I have them piled all over the house.

It is safe to say I love books.

My favorite books are mysteries and crime fiction. I love the puzzle aspects of well written mysteries and I love following along as crimes are solved, or at least resolved. I love reading caper books wondering if I could get away with what they are doing. Classic noir makes me realize how good my own life is, and also allows me to watch people do things I could never imagine actually doing myself. It is escapism to be sure, but it is also a very real look at the human condition and society of the time it's written. It endures, and the best of it stays relevant long after the publishing date. And whether it changes my life or just entertains me for a few hours, I love it all. PI stories, police procedurals, cozies, historical mystery, supernatural . . . I love it all.

It is also safe to say I love the mystery genre.

In the late eighties I discovered that there are stores that combine these two things for me. Imagine! A store with nothing but books that I want to read! No cook books cluttering the shelf space that should be filled with cops and PIs. Through the years I have spent hours and hours in these stores all over the country. When we travel I check to see what local bookstores we can go to. I want to touch the books, I want to talk to the people working there and see what they read. I like watching customers discover new books and the sales people helping them do it. I love the feel of the books and the smell. I love walking slowly and reading every spine, either discovering a new book or remembering a favorite.

I love book stores.

I'd been aware of Once Upon a Crime for a while, but when we finally got to go to Minneapolis and spend some time in the store it was love at first sight. Wall to wall books, a secret room with even more. The magic moment of this visit was meeting Pat and Gary in person. Two people who feel the same way about this genre I love running a bookstore with that love foremost in their minds. They love hosting events, and they do it well. They also love selling books. I've watched. The look on their faces when talking to customers is something you can't fake. And the customers know it too. That's why they keep coming back. It's why I keep going to Minneapolis to buy books instead of ordering online. Pat and Gary think about books the way I do. We are part of the same tribe.

This anthology is a love letter from Pat and Gary to you, the fellow traveller, the fellow fan, the fellow book addict. And the Write of Spring event it is named for is their annual thank you party. And it's a great party. Loads of people with piles of books, authors smiling and talking to fans and every person who walks out of Once Upon A Crime walks out happy.

But do you know what?

It's Pat and Gary who really deserve the thank you. What they do improves our lives. They help distract us from the world around us, and they make us feel welcome. Their store is a second home (with more shelves).

So thank you Once Upon a Crime. Thank You Pat and Gary.

About the Contributors

Called a hard-boiled poet by NPR's Maureen Corrigan, **REED FARREL COLEMAN** has published fourteen novels. He is a three-time recipient of the Shamus Award for Best PI Novel of the Year and a two-time Edgar nominee. He has also won the Macavity, Barry, and Anthony Awards. In addition to his novels, Reed has published short fiction, essays, and poetry in various periodicals and anthologies. He is an adjunct professor of English at Hofstra University and he lives with his family on Long Island.

Professional artist **BARBARA MAYOR** has been a first reader, and frequent dedicatee, of Harold Adams' novels. She lives in Eden Prairie, Minnesota.

HAROLD ADAMS is the author of the award winning Carl Wilcox mystery series. He was the Guest of Honor at the first annual Write of Spring, at which the publication of *The Fourth of July Wake* was launched in 2003. He lives in Eden Prairie, Minnesota.

GERALD ANDERSON is a former professor of British and Modern European History. In addition to academic publications, he has published five novels, including *The Uffda Trial*, an historical novel set in 1926 in western Minnesota. His last four novels, *Death Before Dinner* (2007), *Murder Under the Loon* (2008), *Pecked to Death . . . or Murder Under the Prairie Chicken* (2010), and *Paul's Bloody Trousers* (2011), all feature the Norwegian-American sheriff of Otter Tail County, Palmer Knutson. Dr. Anderson currently lives in Rochester, Minnesota.

JOEL ARNOLD lives near the Twin Cities with his wife, two kids, two cats, two fish, a dog and a rat. He's the author of the mystery novel *Licking the Marmot*, as well as two horror novels, *Northwoods Deep* and *Death Rhythm*, plus various short story collections. Visit his blog Beneath the Trap Door at http://authorjoelarnold.blogspot.com.

JUDITH YATES BORGER has been rowing on the Mississippi River with the Minneapolis Rowing Club for six years. Her favorite boat has eight rowers and a cox. She prefers to row port but will take a starboard seat in a pinch. She has two published mysteries, *Where's Billie?* and *Whose Hand?*, both Skeeter Hughes Mysteries. Check out her website www.JudithYates-Borger.com.

Before he became a mystery writer and reviewer, **CARL BROOKINS** was a freelance photographer, a Public Television program director, a Cable TV administrator, and a counselor and faculty member at Metropolitan State University in Saint Paul, Minnesota. He has reviewed mystery fiction for the *Saint Paul Pioneer Press* and for *Mystery Scene Magazine*. Brookins is an avid recreational sailor. With his wife and friends he has sailed in many locations across the world. Brookins writes the sailing adventure series featuring Michael Tanner and Mary Whitney, the Sean NMI Sean, private investigator detective series, and the Jack Marston academic series. He has ten novels in print along with a number of short stories. His most recent release is *"Reunion"* in the Jack Marston series.

GARY R. BUSH is the co-editor of *Once Upon A Crime Anthology*. He writes for the children's, YA, and adult markets. His writing credits include: A children's novel, *Lost In Space, The Flight of Apollo 13* (Stone Arch Books); "If They Harm Us," in *Twin Cities Noir* (Akashic Books); "The Last Reel," in *Flesh & Blood: Guilty As Sin* (Mysterious Press); "Two Pastrami Sandwiches" and "The Price of Justice," in *MXB Magazine;* "Down Highway 61," in *Fedora II* (Wildside Press); and "Deep Doo-Doo" in *Small Crimes* (Wildside Press). He lives in Minneapolis with his wife Stacey and their Kerry Blue Terrier, Homer.

JESSIE CHANDLER is the Vice President of the Twin Cities chapter of Sisters in Crime. She's the author of the Shay O'Hanlon Caper series, which includes the titles *Bingo Barge Murder,* and the June 2012 release, *Hide and Snake Murder.* In her spare time, Chandler sells unique, artsy T-shirts and other assorted trinkets to unsuspecting conference and festival goers. She is a former police officer and resides in Minneapolis. Visit her online at www.JessieChandler.com

PAT DENNIS is the author of *Hotdish To Die For, Stand-Up and Die*, and contributing editor of *Hotdish Haiku* and *Who Died in Here?* Her short stories have been published in *Resort to Murder, The Silence of the Loons,* Anne Frasier's *Deadly Treats, Once Upon a Crime Anthology* and other publications. Her work as an entertainer includes over 1,000 performances. Visit her at www.patdennis.com.

SEAN DOOLITTLE is the award-winning author of six novels, including *Lake Country*, forthcoming in 2012. Doolittle's books have been licensed for translation in several languages and praised by such contemporaries as Dennis Lehane, Michael Connelly, Laura Lippman, George Pelecanos, Harlan Coben, and Lee Child. His short fiction has appeared *in The Year's Best Horror Stories, The Best American Mystery Stories*, and elsewhere. He lives in Council Bluffs, Iowa with his family.

JAN DUNLAP is the Minnesota author of the Birder Murders, a lighthearted mystery series featuring the adventures of high school counselor/expert birder Bob White. Jan's favorite things are the great outdoors, her five kids, and frozen custard, though not necessarily in that order. She welcomes visitors to her website at www.jandunlap.com.

CHRIS EVERHEART writes action/adventure and thriller fiction for young readers and crime fiction for adults. Winner of the Moonbeam Award for a graphic novel, Chris connects with young readers through his own struggles as a young reluctant reader. "I credit most of my personal development to my ability to read," he says. "Even though, as a kid, reading was often a struggle for me, I'm happy that—like riding a bike—once I learned I never forgot. For this collection, I enjoyed creating a story featuring a young person with a big-time problem and a dark nature that adults can relate to." A native of Minneapolis, Minnesota, Chris now lives with his wife, Pat, in the hills of East Tennessee.

BARBARA FISTER is a librarian and faculty member at Gustavus Adolphus College in St. Peter, Minnesota. She is a regular columnist for Library Journal and Inside Higher Ed and is the author of three mysteries, *On Edge* (2002), *In the Wind* (2008), and *Through the Cracks* (2010).

ANNE FRASIER is an award-winning, bestselling author of twenty books and numerous short stories that have spanned the genres of suspense, mystery, thriller, romantic suspense, and paranormal. She also writes nonfiction under Theresa Weir, most recently the 2011 memoir *The Orchard*.

BRIAN FREEMAN is an international bestselling author of psychological suspense novels. His books have been sold in 46 countries and 20 languages and have appeared as Main Selections in the Literary Guild and the Book of the Month Club. His fifth novel *The Burying Place* was a finalist for Best Novel of 2010 in the International Thriller Writer Awards. His debut thriller, *Immoral*, won the Macavity Award and was a nominee for the Edgar®, Dagger, Anthony, and Barry awards for best first novel.

ELLEN HART is the author of twenty-seven crime novels. She is a five-time winner of the Lambda Literary Award for Best Lesbian Mystery, a three-time winner of the Minnesota Book Award for Best Popular Fiction, and a three-time winner of the Golden Crown Literary Award. In 2010, Ellen received the GCLS Trailblazer Award for lifetime achievement in the field of lesbian literature. For the past fourteen years, she has taught "An Introduction to Writing the Modern Mystery" through the The Loft Literary Center.

Crime fiction author **LIBBY FISCHER HELLMANN** is writing her way around the genre. Her recent thriller, *Set the Night On Fire*, goes back to the late Sixties in Chicago. She also writes two crime series, one with PI Georgia Davis, the other with video producer and amateur sleuth Ellie Foreman. Her short story collection, *Nice Girl Does Noir*, was released in

2010. She has also written a cozy novella, *The Last Page*, and a police procedural, *Toxicity*. She has lived in Chicago over 30 years. More at www.libbyhellmann.com.

KATHLEEN HILLS is the author of mysteries featuring John McIntire, township constable in 1950s Upper Michigan. In addition to writing, she is a free-lance editor of fiction and non-fiction, primarily scientific research papers by non-native English speakers. She lives in northern Minnesota with periodic forays to the United Kingdom.

A reformed newspaper reporter and ad man, **DAVID HOUSEWRIGHT** has published 12 crime novels, including *Curse of the Jade Lily* (St. Martin's Minotaur) due out in June 2012 and numerous short stories. His work has earned the Edgar Award from the Mystery Writers of America and two Minnesota Book Awards. It has also been optioned by Hollywood and published in Italy and Japan. Housewright has also taught writing courses at the University of Minnesota and Loft Literary Center. See his Facebook page and website at www.davidhousewright.com.

CAMILLE HYYTINEN is a Wisconsin transplant and has been a Minnesotan for more than 20 years, embracing the land of 10,000 lakes as her home. With a demanding career in the fast-track computer world, she uses writing as a form of escape. When she's not busy with her family or work, you'll find her hunched over a laptop, pounding out another crime thriller.
NOVELS: *Pattern of Violence, Pattern of Vengeance*
STORIES: "Where There's Smoke . . ." (*Heat of the Moment* Anthology)
          "Sweet as Pie" (*Why Did Santa Leave a Body?* Anthology)
WEBSITE: www.chyytinen.com

E. KELLY KEADY is the author of the Peter Farrell series that begins with the critically acclaimed thriller *The Cross of St. Maro*. Keady is a trial lawyer who practices in Iowa, Minnesota, and Wisconsin and lives in Minneapolis with his wife and three children.

LINDA KOUTSKY is the book designer at Coffee House Press in Minneapolis. She also does freelance cover design for other publishers. Though there have been occasional scuffles with authors in the past, she's sure no one's been murdered. In addition to co-authoring three books on Minnesota history, Linda writes the Weekend Tourist, a bi-monthly column for two local papers that spotlights regional destinations. An avid mystery fan, this story is her first crack at fiction.

WILLIAM KENT KRUEGER writes the *New York Times* bestselling Cork O'Connor mystery series. After studying briefly at Stanford University, Kent set out to experience the real world. Over the next twenty years, he logged timber, worked construction, tried his hand at free-lance journalism, and eventually ended up researching child development at the University of Minnesota. He currently makes his living as a full-time author. He lives in St. Paul, a city he dearly loves, and does all his creative writing in a lovely little coffee shop near his home.

LORI L. LAKE is the author of two short story collections and ten novels, including four books in The Gun Series and the recently launched Public Eye Mystery Series. Her crime fiction stories have been featured in *Silence of the Loons*, *Once Upon A Crime*, and *Women of the Mean Streets*. Lori lived in Minnesota for 26 years, but recently re-located to Portland, Oregon. When she's not writing, she's at the local movie house or curled up in a chair reading.

For more information, see her website at www.lorillake.com.

JESS LOUREY is the author of the Lefty-nominated Murder-by-Month comic caper mysteries set in Battle Lake, Minnesota, and featuring amateur sleuth, Mira James. Jess has been teaching writing and sociology at the college level since 1998.

When not raising her wonderful kids, teaching, or writing, you can find her gardening, traveling, and navigating the niceties and meanities of small-town life. She is a member of Sisters in Crime, The Loft and Lake Superior Writers, and serves on the national board of Mystery Writers of America.

MICHAEL ALLAN MALLORY writes the Snake Jones Zoo Mystery series with Marilyn Victor. *Death Roll* (Five Star, 2007) introduced mystery's first zoologist sleuth and revealed what goes on behind the exhibits of a major metropolitan zoo. *Killer Instinct* (Five Star, 2011) sent zookeeper Lavender "Snake" Jones to the North Woods of Minnesota to investigate a wild wolf killing and double murder. Michael's short stories have appeared in several mystery anthologies. He lives in St. Louis Park, Minnesota, with his delightful wife. They share their home with an elderly Maine Coon cat and two young furballs.

His website is www.snakejones.com

DAVID OPPEGAARD is the author of the Bram Stoker-nominated *The Suicide Collectors* (St. Martin's Press) and *Wormwood, Nevada* (St. Martin's Press). David's work is a blend of science fiction, literary fiction, horror, and dark fantasy. He holds an M.F.A. in Writing from Hamline University and a B.A. in English from St. Olaf College. You can visit his website at www.davidoppegaard.com

SCOTT PEARSON was first published in 1987. Over the last couple of decades he has published a smattering of poetry, nonfiction, and short stories, including three *Star Trek* stories and one previous mystery story. His first novella, *Honor in the Night*, another *Trek* story from Simon & Schuster, came out in 2010. Scott makes his living as an editor for Zenith Press, a history publisher in Minneapolis, and x-comm, a regional history publisher in Duluth. He lives in St. Paul with his wife, Sandra, and daughter, Ella. Visit him online at www.yeahsure.net.

MARY MONICA PULVER sold her first short story to Alfred Hitchcock's Mystery Magazine in 1983. Her first novel, *Murder at the War*, appeared from St. Martin's Press in 1987. In 1998, writing as Monica Ferris, she began writing a new series for Berkley featuring a needleworking sleuth named Betsy Devonshire. The first was called *Crewel World*, the fifteenth, *Threadbare*. She is at work on *And Then You Dye*. To learn more, go to www.Monica-Ferris.com.

A lifelong resident of Minnesota, **PETER RENNEBOHM**, wife Shari, and Golden Retriever, Daisy, live on ten acres west of Minneapolis. They have two daughters and six grandchildren. In addition to writing, winters are spent coaching boy's hockey. Peter has had over two-dozen short stories published and won numerous awards for his work. Dogs play prominent roles in Peter's books. *Blue Springs*, his second novel was published in December 2005. Set in Minnesota and South Dakota, it's a powerful suspense novel about an eleven-year old boy and his beloved dog, Taffy. His third novel, *Buried Lies*, was released in hardcover Sept 1, 2008. A gripping puzzle-mystery set in the desert southwest, the book stays true to Peter's desire to include dogs in every book.

BRUCE RUBENSTEIN has written many true crime stories for weeklies and monthlies including *City Pages, Minneapolis/St. Paul* and *Chicago Magazine*. An anthology of his true crime stories titled *Greed, Rage and Love Gone Wrong* was published in 2003. His short fiction has appeared in *Ellery Queen's Mystery Magazine* and *Twin Cities Noir* (for which he was a Shamus Award finalist). In 1991 he received the Chicago Bar Association's Herman Kogan Media Award for a story he wrote about the conviction of four Mexican immigrants for a quadruple homicide they didn't commit. They were in the twelfth year of their life without parole sentences when the article led Governor James Thompson to pardon them.

RICHARD A. THOMPSON is a civil engineer who traded in his hard hat for a laptop and now spends his time writing mysteries and science fiction. He lives in St. Paul, Minnesota with his wife of 49 years and two neurotic cats. His debut novel, *Fiddle Game*, about a bail bondsman with a shady past, a priceless antique violin, and a band of modern urban Gypsies, was short-listed for a CWA Debut Dagger Award.

CHRISTOPHER VALEN is the pen name of Jerry Christopher Peterson. He is the author of three works of fiction featuring Colombian born, St. Paul Homicide Detective John Santana, *White Tombs* (Conquill Press, 2008), *The Black Minute* (North Star Press, 2009), and *Bad Weeds Never Die* (Conquill Press, 2011). *White Tombs* and *The Black Minute* each won the Reader Views Choice Award for Best Mystery/Thriller of the Year. *The Black Minute* also was a finalist for the 2009 Midwest Book Award for Best Mystery/Thriller. He lives in Minnesota with his Colombian-born wife, Martha.

To learn more visit his website at www.christophervalen.com.

MARILYN VICTOR is the co-author of *Death Roll* and *Killer Instinct* which feature mystery's first zookeeper sleuth, Snake Jones. She has short stories in the recent *Once Upon a Crime* and *Deadly Treats* anthologies by Nodin Press. An animal lover since she could walk, Marilyn Victor was a volunteer at the Minnesota Zoo for many years and shares her home with a revolving menagerie of homeless pets she fosters for a local animal rescue organization.

LANCE ZARIMBA lives in a haunted house that the man who invented Old Dutch potato chips built. He is an occupational therapist living in Minneapolis. His mystery, *Vacation Therapy,* and two children's books: *Oh No, Our Best Friend is a Zombie,* and *Oh No, Our Best Friend is a Vampire,* are newly released. His short stories are in *Mayhem in the Midlands,* Pat Dennis' *Who Died in Here? 25 mystery stories of crimes and bathrooms,* Jay Hartman's *The Killer Wore Cranberry,* and Anne Frasier's *Deadly Treats.* (www.lancezarimba.com or LanceZarimba@yahoo.com)

From the wilds of Milwaukee **JON JORDAN** publishes *Crimespree Magazine* along with his wife Ruth and assorted family members and ne'er-do-wells. He rarely sleeps and might be insane.

Acknowledgments

FIRST OFF, WE NEED TO THANK our dear friend and mentor, Steve Stilwell, for selling us his store. It's been nearly ten years now, and Steve continues to be generous with his support, is genuinely proud of our successes, and listens tolerantly to our whining. Next time you see him, be sure to ask if he misses it.

To Barbara Mayor, for helping us get to know Harold Adams better through cozy visits and Sunday brunches, and for finding the two Carl Wilcox stories for this collection. The last story, "A Million Miles of Sky" is actually a chapter from an unpublished novel of the same title. Perhaps this brief excerpt can help it to find a home. If you have not read Mr. Adams' work before, we hope that these two stories will encourage you to search them out.

To Jon and Ruth Jordan, publishers of Crimespree Magazine, for their unflagging support.

To Linda Koutsky for the superb book design. We gave her just a few vague suggestions, and she nailed it.

To Roger Shulze—brother, friend, confidant, and life-saver.

To Norton Stillman, who gave the okay to this project when all we had was an idea.

And to Lori L. Lake, author and web maven, who ignored our kicks and screams and took these two Luddites into (at least) the *20th* century. The most honored—and loved—of our honorary locals.

—Gary and Pat
　　Once Upon a Crime

COLOPHON

The text of *Writes of Spring* is set in Adobe Garamond,
which was modeled after a typeface by 16th-century printer,
publisher, and type designer, Claude Garamond.
Drop caps are set in the font You Murderer, designed by
Blambot Comic Fonts. The designer says, "the gruesome font
was created by dipping my finger in runny ink and 'writing'
on sheets of bristol board, perfectly simulating someone's
dying message written in blood."

And speaking of blood . . .

ALL ROYALTIES FROM THE SALE OF THIS BOOK are being donated
to the Memorial Blood Centers. Memorial Blood Centers is a Min-
nesota-based independent non-profit that saves and sustains lives by sup-
plying blood products and biomedical services. With a legacy of
community commitment, worldwide partnerships, and industry leader-
ship, this mission-driven organization is dedicated to connecting those generous donors who give blood to those in need of their life-saving gift—from
heart transplant recipients and cancer patients to accident victims in crises.
Memorial Blood Centers provides transfusion expertise and testing services
to help ensure a safe and stable blood supply that protects donors and recipients, and participates in research to advance the scientific study of infec-
tious diseases that sets the standard for the blood industry.

Memorial
BLOOD CENTERS

For more information,
visit www.MBC.org or call 1-888-GIVE-BLD (888-448-3253).